THE WIDOWS OF ....

THE WIDOWS
OF THE
MAGISTRATE

A Novel by

Keith West

GRAHAM BRASH, SINGAPORE

© Keith West, 1949

This edition first published in 1990 by
Graham Brash Pte Ltd
227 Rangoon Road
Singapore 0821

ISBN 9971-49-220-2

Cover design by Sue Harmer
Printed in Singapore by
Chong Moh Offset Printing Pte Ltd

CHARACTERS IN THE STORY

LIEN KIN WAI. Magistrate of Kow Loong City (deceased).
HIBISCUS. His widow.
LIEN MING TSU. His infant daughter.
JASMINE. Maid to Hibiscus.
LIEN (Milk name JADE ARMLET). Lien's son by Jasmine.
AH SAI. Lien's old nurse.
SSU. Driver of the Yamen Carriage.
MEI WAN. Clerk in the Yamen.
WAO HIEN TO. Late Emperor's Messenger. Now Magistrate of Kow Loong City.
SILVER LANTERN. Wife of Ssu. Maid to Hibiscus.
Her son.
TUNG HO. A rich merchant of the city.
TZE HUNG. Captain of the Yamen Guard.
MOUNTAIN STREAM. A singing girl.
HIDDEN GOLD. Another singing girl.
PEONY. Also known as Ladder of Love, the girl who had loved Lien Kin Wai in Canton, and also at Kow Loong on the night before his death.
HSIA NAN-P'O. A rich young man of the City of Sai Kwan.
LADY LOONG. His widowed mother, named Key of Jade.
MISTRESS HSIA. His aunt. Widow of Sung Tsui, late Governor of Canton.
TOWER OF PEARL. Her maid.
AH LAU. Servant at the Yamen in Kow Loong.
AH SAM. Servant at the Yamen in Kow Loong.
SU WAI. The Censor at Nan King.
GENERAL WU FANG. Whose wife embroidered dragons.
JADE STAR. The Prefect of Sai Kwan's daughter.
THE PREFECT OF SAI KWAN.
PHEASANT. Girl in the Yamen of the Prefect of Sai Kwan.
MO TING. One of the Yamen Guard (deceased).
OU LING-MA. Officer of the Yamen Guard at Sai Kwan.
KWONG HUI. Sentry at the Drum Tower at Kow Loong.
MU. An archer.
KEUNG. Servant to Tung Ho.

PROLOGUE

FIVE men sat silently round a small table in the exact centre of the great Hall of Audience in the Prefecture at Sai Kwan City. Their seats had been arranged at precisely equal intervals: it was as though they sat at the corners of a five-pointed star. Opposite each man a small, translucent porcelain cup had been inverted: at the middle of the table a wicker-bound teapot stood.

"I declare the Lodge in session," the Prefect of Sai Kwan declared, rapidly moving the five cups into a new pattern. He sat back.

The man on his left said: "Good. Now we can talk." He poured tea into all the cups but his own, and again made a rapid redisposition of them, quickly as the eye could follow. Then he filled his own cup. They all drank. "Your report?" he asked the Prefect.

"In six moons," the Prefect began, "the Society will be ready for the revolt." He was a huge man: even the efforts of his tailor had failed to hide in the flowing garments a sense of strain and bursting seams. "I have had reports from all the branches. The six months are needed to make perfect certain dispositions with which I shall not trouble you."

The man on his left, small and vital, observed: "Yes. Secrecy has been maintained?"

7

" It has," the Prefect told them. " There has been no leakage of information, save in one respect, and it is about that leakage which I wish to consult you." He drank from his cup. " There is, at the City of Rams, a certain General Wu, a Northerner, a military man whose eyes are keener than the eyes of most. He suspects. But he knows nothing."

" He has influence with the Provincial Governor? " the other asked.

The Prefect replied : " None. As you yourself should know, working in the Governor's office." He shook his great arm free from his robes. " It is futile to see danger where none can exist: General Wu's advice is already discounted by your presence."

" I shall have all his correspondence under watch," the man on the left observed. " There may have to be an unfortunate incident, and a certain name cease to have meaning. It is not the act of a wise man to under-rate the force of opponents. You are certain that you have not done so? "

The Prefect smiled.

" I have not done so," he replied. " You, Sir, in your responsible post at the Provincial Capital, will have every opportunity for checking the activities of General Wu. I shall rely on you."

" The sun has five rays," the other replied, in the accepted formula of obedience.

" And the body five senses," the Prefect answered in his turn. " I declare the Lodge closed."

They disarranged their cups and went out by five various doors.

PART ONE

PART ONE

NOW her bead curtains hung motionless against the night. Only the distant noises of a few revellers sounded in the streets, and Peony, sitting in the faint glow of her dying brazier, had her thoughts for company. Her lover, Lien Kin Wai, had left her.

So, in the hours after the night's turn, girls sit and think of the lover who is gone. The room is empty: nothing remains. His voice, his caress, seem remote: memory and imagination can conjure up mere faint images of that reality which, so short a time ago, filled consciousness with living.

Peony trimmed and lit the lamp in the corner of the room. Then she opened the shiny, black case which she had brought with her to Kow Loong from the City of Rams, and took out the copies of her lover's poems.

She had begun to read the first line of the first poem

There is no beauty in a smile

when Mountain Stream came into the room and sat on the floor beside her, without speaking.

"It was a mistake," Peony said. "I should not have come here, to the very city of which the honourable Lien Kin Wai is magistrate, and invited him to visit me. It was a mistake." She dropped the paper to the top of the charcoal in the brazier and watched it warp at the edges. "When he left me in order to return to his duties and his family, I should have tried to forget him."

Mountain Stream replied: "It is often impossible to forget. But I know what you mean. Now you have seen him again; now all the old uncertainty has returned. You were determined to break the thread of his love: you have rejoined the ends, and the knot will not pass through the eye of the needle."

Peony read, from the next poem:

> *My gardener has gone, and the beds are*
> *   irreproachable:*
> *I will beg some weeds from my neighbour.*

Then she dropped this sheet, too, on the charcoal of the brazier. The first sheet caught fire, then the second.

"I must thank you for your hospitality, and go," Peony said. "The fact that I should not have come does not alter the other fact, that I must go. He was just the same, and my heart sinks at the thought of leaving him, but I am not of those girls who can share a man."

"I have always had to share men," Mountain Stream replied. "And Hidden Gold, also, though she was the favourite of the rich merchant, Tung Ho, has not found his attention so marked of late. So she, too, will have to endure variety. But it is not wise to love a man too keenly."

Peony agreed. "No. Men twine themselves in the heart."

"You speak as if you had enjoyed experience,"

Mountain Stream said. "Our sister Golden Rod was the example for that. She loved Chiang To, who was Captain of the Guard to your lover, and when Chiang To was killed, Golden Rod hanged herself."

"That might be the best escape," Peony said. "But I do not think that I am the sort of girl who hangs herself, however sad may be the immediate world. Always my mind delights in the beauty around me, even if my heart be sad. And so I am two different girls. Therefore I shall go."

She burned the rest of Lien's poems on the brazier. Then she began to dress herself for a journey, and shut her shiny black case.

"People will probably be returning to the City of Rams, now that the sickness has passed," she told Mountain Stream. "So I shall not be greatly noticed if I do so also. I shall go when the sun rises."

Mountain Stream pressed on her money for the journey, but Peony would not take it.

. . . .

It was almost unbelievably hot, here on the dusty road just outside the City gates—hotter than it had any right to be in this, the eighth month, when the dank humidity of typhoon days is gone and men may easily labour under the sun. This sun was now behind Peony, as she trudged along the rutted road: on her right the great mass of Tai Mo Shan glowed behind the ridges below. She was taking the easier road towards the landing stages at Lai Chi Kok for, from any of the wharves in the City itself, her going would have been noticed, perhaps recorded, and Peony wished to disappear beyond the whim of a recall. At the end of her journey, if it should ever end, lay a life which should be her own, unbound by the fancies of the heart. Three times, now, she had thought that she loved, only to find this love to be some other emotion, masquerading as love. There was no such thing as love in the world, any more than love could live on these bare, stark slopes of the great range standing almost at her elbow as she followed the slow miles. . . .

But now she was no longer alone on the hot, dusty road. As she passed the path leading down from one of the hillside villages, she saw descending it the small procession which denotes a man's travelling. The reader carried on his shoulder-pole two round wicker baskets of the sort made to be carried by bearers, unlike the square, shiny cases which lesser men hold in their hands. He was sweating, and as he swung, shuffling, into the main path he wiped at his forehead with a blue cloth. The rear basket swung wide and struck Peony on the hand. Her own case fell to the ground, the catch slipped, and the contents were scattered in the dust of the path.

"Only stupid women fail to look where they step," the bearer said, and moved on.

Peony cried: "It is you who should look where you step! The Master says that *only the mean man fails in consideration for others.*"

The man in the carrying-chair ordered his bearers to set him down. He was not much more than twenty: his high cheek-bones and the long lobes of his ears spoke of breeding: his hands, hidden in the wide cuffs of his sleeves, were presumably smoothing the faces of a jade fingering-piece, for when he spoke it was mildly, without irritation, in the quiet voice of a man for whom events succeed events without catastrophe.

"To know the words of the Master is to merit a

better fate than picking your personal trinkets from the dust," he said. " I saw my bearer's clumsiness. Stand aside, girl."

He ordered the bearer to set down his load and re-place the contents of Peony's case. The bearer, obey-ing, did not dare to smile as his hands picked up gar-ments, shook them free of the dust, folded and replaced them. Peony stood watching, without further speech, for this calm young man still sitting in his chair seemed in some way to fill her with diffidence. When all had been put back, the bearer took up his shoulder-pole, the carrying-chair was lifted, and the procession moved on.

Peony said, as they left easy ear-shot: " I am in your debt."

The young man nodded without replying. The feet of the bearers left little eddies of dust suspended in the hot air above the path. Peony took up her box and made to follow.

More terrible to the lonely individual than even the uncontrollable, unpredictable menace of a crowd in being, is the potential crowd, when folk converge pur-posefully upon the one, aimed place, there to exchange their passing-pleasant characteristics for the personality of the mob itself.

Peony felt something of this as she neared Lai Chi Kok, for from every by-path men and women flowed in streams which joined and joined again as the masts of the waiting junks came into sight. She heard the expected conversation of those who passed her.

" Now that the sickness is finished in the City of Rams, there will be more room for everyone."

" Even the mother died, at last."

" They carried them away in bullock-carts. There

is many a man who was not buried in his ancestral burying-ground."

She knew that the dread disease which had ravaged the whole of the City of Rams and the country round it had ceased with the strange suddenness of an epidemic, and that these many people, impelled by the single impulse of return, an impulse set free by the arrival of the breath of news at the remotest hamlet, had set out singly but together on the road home. They came on foot, in carrying-chairs or sitting in rows on great wheelbarrows, men, women and children, rich and poor, good and evil, converging on the waiting junks.

There would be much money for the proprietors of these junks.

Then Peony stopped and looked in the black case to make sure that she had the two ounces of silver which were all that now remained to her. She had put the money in a roll of cloth in the middle of the contents.

But the roll was missing.

.   .   .   .

The blind Buddhist priest crouched down on his haunches at the corner of the paths. She thought him blind because his open eyes took no interest in his surroundings: the lined face, yellow almost as his robe, did not alter at men's passing. She remembered the lines

The priest sat in his yellow robe
While Spring balanced on the edge of a southerly
*   wind—*
You and I would think of hands soft like the wind:
When he looks at his begging-bowl does he consider
*   to-morrow's dinner?*

Of course, it was not Spring, so that the verse lost something of its application.

The priest turned his eyes to her, and she saw that they bulged, as if striving for some image distant and probably unattainable, as bulge the eyes of coupling frogs in the mating season, waiting interminably. But, again, this was not Spring, but the eighth month.

" Though I turn my eyes to you," the priest said, " I have not the privilege of sight. To me you are a breathing rustle." He held out his begging-bowl in her direction. "OM MANI PADMA HOUM," he chanted.

Peony replied: " But I have no money either. My last two ounces of silver have been stolen by a man who upset my box and took them out when he was replacing the contents."

" Two ounces! " the priest murmured. " And a polite thief."

" He was ordered to replace the contents of my box, by his master," Peony said. " But he must have taken the money. And now I have none with which to pay for my journey to the City of Rams on that junk whose masts you can see over the house yonder."

" I see no junk," the priest replied. " And if you are without money, it will be impossible for you to travel in a junk. Unless, that is, you trade the coinage which all women possess."

One of the passers-by dropped a small copper coin into the priest's bowl. He took it out and put it somewhere in his clothing.

Peony told him: " I had intended to go into one of the Blue Houses in the City of Rams. Now I have not the means of reaching them."

The priest suddenly said: " I had forgotten, because of my interest in your tale, that I do not possess desires

B

and do not understand others possessing desires. If you choose to go to the City of Rams, to the Blue Houses, you will minister to the desires of men, but not to your own desire. And since, if I understand you aright, you carry your own coinage, your loss of two ounces of silver matters not at all. Now go, for I must beg. OM MANI PADMA HOUM."

She rose to her feet, picked up her box and walked slowly towards the wharf. It seemed, under the sun, as if she were hardly moving, past the house and round the corner, interminably, to the last, widening, trodden ground which served as an approach. Behind her was life as she had known it: before her, ever larger, the junk at the wharf. Brown sails rolled high at various angles, dirty deck piled high with local and perishable merchandise, the junk bustled with activity. Men were untying the ropes which held the junk fore and aft: men and women streamed on to the junk or off the junk, the speed of their moving increasing as the time of going approached. On the high poop, on the high bow, other men stood motionless, re-acting a remembered departure. The better dressed of the passengers hurried below deck, from the sun's heat to that no less heat in the darkened places where, doubtless, they sat in half-shadow, sweating, reluctant to travel, stolidly enduring what could not be avoided.

As Peony came towards the two narrow gangways amidships, she saw again the bearers of that chair which bore the polite young man. This time the chair was going away from the junk, and the chair was empty. The other bearers, too, returned light-shouldered. Clearly the polite young man had gone aboard. She did not attempt to stop the man who had taken her silver, for it is not wise for a woman, alone, to demand justice. Instead, as if shaking from her the loss which she had suffered, she moved towards the gangway, to find that the young man had not, indeed, gone aboard, but stood now in the very jaws of the gangway, arguing with one of the boatmen. As Peony came up and seized her chance, the argument ended and they passed together, unchallenged, to the deck. She immediately moved into the mass already standing there, losing her identity in the crowd, conscious that she hated this proximity of bodies, this community of minds. The young man, instead of going below, mounted steps to the poop. The last ropes were cast off, the gangways pulled out of the water, and the sails set to aid the poles with which, even now, the junk was being thrust from the wharf, a citadel of chatter.

.   .   .   .

The sun had set below the rounded hills and the pointed hills on the west bank of the river, as the junk turned north into the common channel of the three rivers which flow south from the City of Rams. The dark had come down, as the dark should come down, like a sudden curtain before the lit activities of the un-ending day. A few lights glimmered from below, through windows, to the placid waters: on deck the steersman stood in the almost black of the poop, while a noisy game of " guessing fingers " round a lantern on the foredeck seemed the sole remaining link witn the day's movement.

Peony had begun to feel hungry. All round her stood packages of food in various stages of preparation —crated fowls, baskets of fruit, sacks of roots. And on the poop, black-cut against the deep violet sky, she saw the outline of the young man whose servant had

stolen her two ounces of silver. But for him, she could
have paid her passage-money in the ordinary way, have
avoided the fear of detection. But for him, she could
have bought food from the owner of the stores around
her, thus dismissing the dull ache which, she knew,
was only hunger. She leaned back against the long
wicker framework wherein a black pig slept noisily.
The wicker creaked and the pig breathed in his sleep
with an irregular rhythm. Then the pig rolled over a
little in his cramped position, and the container pushed
Peony sideways. She rose to her feet and climbed the
short steps to the poop, where the young man sat.

It seemed even darker here, and only the shuffling
feet of the steersman, as he shifted his stance, broke the
dark silence. The young man had opened one of his
cases and was eating *lichees* from a box within the case.

" My name is Peony," she began, " and I am the
woman from whose case your bearer took two ounces
of silver to-day, when he was putting back the spilled
contents. I have therefore no money, and hunger is
beginning to hurt."

He took out the box of *lichees* and pushed it towards
her. He did not rise.

" Sit and eat," he told her. " Yes, I recognized you
when you hurried on to this junk beside me, without
paying. I have been thinking and wondering why you
should have done so, for such conduct was not conson-
ant with the character of a girl who, earlier to-day,
aptly quoted the Master, Confucius. Let me remember.
Yes, you said : *only the mean man fails in consideration
for others*. Very apt. And now, since you have explained your puzzling conduct, I suppose it is my right
to replace the two ounces of silver which, you say, my
man stole."

"He did steal it," Peony replied, sitting down on the deck.

The young man answered: "I do not doubt it. He has always been light-fingered. Otherwise he is a useful servant. No: when I said 'you say he stole,' I was confining myself to ascertainable fact. Beyond fact lies conjecture, conjecture of varying degrees of soundness. Let us assume that he stole the money. Shall I replace it?"

She took a *lichee*. As her teeth broke into the grape-like flesh, she remembered some of the occasions on which she had eaten *lichees*. Then she said: "It depends on what you imply by *shall I*. If you ask the simple question as to what you are about to do, I cannot answer you. If you mean to ask me what I consider your right and duty, I can only make inclination marry opportunity, and say 'Yes'."

He rose to his feet, bowed, and sat down again.

"Forgive me," he said, "since I did not fully realize that I was speaking to a woman of culture and probably breeding. My name is Hsia and my given name Nan-p'o. I am twenty-one years of age, and my family city is Sai Kwan, in this province. My honourable father died four years past, and my mother, together with my aunt, Mistress Hsia the elder, live on our family estate in Sai Kwan, whither I am now going. And you?"

"I have already told you that my given name is Peony," she replied, and though my family was noble, I have done it no honour. So we shall let my family name go unnamed. I am nineteen years of age, and, since I have no money, I am on my way to enter one of the Blue Houses in the City of Rams."

"Such a course," he told her, "would be precipitate.

Since, unfortunately, I am unmarried, I cannot offer you more than the shelter of my family roof: my mother and my aunt have plans for me which include the only daughter of the Prefect of Sai Kwan, and she, when I wed her, may have views. Women have views. I have not, of course, seen this future wife of mine."

"You are kind to make such an offer," she said. "Is it not strange that we should be talking thus, led to our talk by the misdemeanour of a servant? To sit thus, in the dark. . . ."

Hsia replied: "Our family is unconventional. At least, the men are so. My aunt, also, suffers from headaches which serve her to neglect all the customary duties and habits. But my mother, who is a Loong, is very formal. She will prove our difficulty, though I shall strive to play off my aunt against her. As I said, the men Hsias are unconventional, and I find the darkness of a garden, or of a ship at night, or of a cave in the mountain, to fit well with my constant mood. Even talk such as this touches me less closely, less uncomfortably than would the same talk in sunlight." He paused, and as she did not speak, went on: "Your silence assures me that you approve my tentative plan. I shall pay your passage money. Meanwhile, eat from my store. There is plenty."

"I did not speak," she said, "but I did not wholly approve your generosity. For, if I accept, I shall be beholden to you. If I go, as I intended, to one of the Blue Houses, I shall be in no man's debt."

He laughed in the darkness. "Fate has answered your doubt for you," he said, "for you did not enquire the destination of this junk, which is bound for Sai Kwan, turning east up the lower branch of the estuary of the Pearl River. There is no chance of your choosing the Blue Houses at the City of Rams, for the junk does not go to the City of Rams, but to Sai Kwan and beyond, as I have said. So set your mind at rest, eat, and take what has been given you. A man should not try too insistently to turn Fate aside."

"I am content," she answered, taking another *lichee*.

He opened other boxes of food.

"They will probably tie up for the night soon," he said. "Whether at the river's bank or in mid-stream will depend on how the captain judges the possibility of robbers from the nearby villages. They always seem to smell the breath of danger, these captains of river-boats. After all, it is their business, just as it is mine to observe and comment. I sleep on deck with many rugs (for these nights can be chill) because I prefer clean air, and the deck-cargo exhales a less noxious air than those who crowd below. Your choice is your own."

"I have no rugs," she said, "but it seems to be a night when sleeping on deck is possible. Of course, if you have one more than you need. . . ."

.   .   .   .

The passage up-stream through the narrows called the Tiger's Mouth and then the largely poled progress along the southern branch of the estuary consumed five whole days. Hsia had paid Peony's passage money and no explanations had been asked. Three rugs had been loaned from the junk's store, and the various steersmen in their turn had been interested in the good manners of those who disregard the eccentricity of sleeping on deck. Hsia had talked a little and read a great deal from books which he carried with him: Peony had talked less, had not volunteered any information about herself except in the field of preferences for various foods, and had, with an occasional quotation, been able to remind Hsia that she was no ordinary girl.   There seemed tacit agreement that Sai Kwan was the place where conversation should begin.

.   .   .   .   .   .

Lady Loong, whose given names were Key of Jade, was very conscious of the strangeness and the strength of her position in the household of Hsia. As the sole wife of her late husband, as the mother of the only surviving Hsia in the male line, she found that the authority which her husband had been able to delegate to her during his life had become, with his death, multiplied. Here, in the old estate of the Hsias, within the walls of the city of Sai Kwan, hill-perched and stream-circled, she could exercise a power which, in its smaller sway, resembled not a little the sway of an Emperor. Money? Money had never been a consideration, for the Hsias were very rich. Servants? There had never been a shortage of these : round the central hub of Key of Jade Loong rotated the spokes of the family wheel. And she was not unmindful of the saying of Lao Tze, that the virtue of the wheel lies in the hollowness of the hub. It is the hub which makes the wheel.

She lay on a couch in her room, pondering on the slightly irritating intrusion of her sister-in-law, whom men called Mistress Hsia, as was her right, and on the circumstances which had brought Mistress Hsia to the Hsia estate in the city of Sai Kwan. As the widow of the late Sung Tsui, Governor of the City of Rams, Mistress Hsia retained a social status which made it not

quite easy to rule her: one who had been accustomed
to a profusion of *yamen* guards and servants was apt to
assume that her importance was conditioned not by
present but by past glories. Mistress Hsia had even
brought her own maid, Tower of Pearl, and the two of
them behaved as if Lady Loong did not much matter
in the scheme of things. Nevertheless, Lady Loong
knew that, in the ultimate analysis, Mistress Hsia had
no real power in the household.

When young Hsia Nan-p'o came to his mother's
room, he bore all the signs of travel. He greeted her
in the approved manner, and she asked after his health.

" I am as well as may be," he answered. " It is tiring
to lie on the deck of a ship and wait for the miles to
pass. It is tiring to have nothing to do but read. But
I happened upon a girl whom I have brought back for
you. She is a girl of culture, it seems, and can speak
with confidence, so far as a woman should show confidence, on the Classical Books. She will not tell me
what is her family name, but I do not think that her
family name greatly matters, since she has the culture
which shows that her name must be a good one. I
have left her below."

" You will remember that you are affianced to the
daughter of the Prefect of Sai Kwan? " his mother
asked. " I know the unusual nature of the processes
of your thoughts, and therefore mention what another
mother would have had no reason to mention." Then
she smiled. " We have here, also, staying with us,
your Aunt Hsia, the widow of Governor Sung Tsui.
Possibly she may need a maid. We could give the girl
to her."

Hsia Nan-p'o said: " It shall be, of course, as you
will. From long life with my late father, you speak

often with his turns of thought. You would wish to
see the girl? "

" It would be as well," Lady Loong replied.

When Peony came in, she stood silently waiting for
someone to speak to her. Lady Loong had not risen
from her couch, and her son stood behind this couch.
There was no other person in the room.

" You have been married? " Lady Loong asked,
without any of the customary preliminaries.

Peony replied: " I have. You are well? "

Lady Loong laughed.

Hsia Nan-p'o said: " My mother is unusually direct.
She brushes aside the preliminaries of meeting, as is
fitting for one who rules the household. I will reply
for her to your question by saying that we are both
well, and that one does not have to ask after your own
health, since the eyes answer, unasked."

His mother objected: " We do not know the girl's
name, and there is no need for politeness with girls
whose name one does not know. Can you work? "

Peony replied: " Any woman can work, and I am a
woman. But I should tell you, as I told your son, that
I had intended to go to the City of Rams, to one of the
Blue Houses, and am here because I did not know the
destination of the boat. I found out only after we had
cast off from the wharf."

Then there was the sound of voices outside, and
they knew that Mistress Hsia had been told.

" Aunt, I have found a girl for you," Lady Loong
said as soon as her sister-in-law entered. " You would
not be averse to taking her? "

Peony bowed to Mistress Hsia, but neither gave any
sign that they had met before. Mistress Hsia was wearing the dress of rusty pink which Peony remembered

when she had first met Mistress Hsia in the Governor's *yamen* in the City of Rams. Then Mistress Hsia spoke.

"I find that I have another of these intolerable headaches," she said. "I thought that, with the death of my husband, they would have ceased. You will excuse me if I go back to my room? The girl can come and bathe my forehead. I find that standing up is not to be borne."

They bowed to her, and Mistress Hsia went back to her own quarters with Peony. When they had entered, Mistress Hsia said: "Now, tell me what chance of Fortune has brought you under the same roof as myself. Tell me why, of all people, you should be given me by my sister-in-law. Tell me what happened to you after I left you, ill, on the way along the Pearl River when we fled from the sickness together. Tell me. We can lift the shades at the windows, for I desire to see your face while you tell me these things. My headache is not with me any longer. My headaches, as you will remember, constitute my defence against unwanted people."

Peony began to tell the tale, and Mistress Hsia listened as they ate melon-seeds together.

.   .   .   .

"I was ill for three weeks in the monastery," Peony began, "in the care of the girl Precious. When I was better, we saw the monk who can tell the future, and what he predicted was true. Precious married a man of the fields, and I, returning to the City of Rams, found that the great sickness had taken my parents and your husband and that I walked through the empty city to the accompaniment of no sound such as a city should give. After I had seen this, I went to the temple where, as the monk had told me, I was met by the

honourable Lien Kin Wai, the magistrate of Kowloong
City. I loved him, as the monk had said, and when he
went back to Kowloong on the cessation of the sickness
I found that I could not sleep. So I went to Kowloong
myself, to the house of two girls whose names had been
given me, and sent a message to him. He came, and
for a brief space all was as all had been. But with
morning he went, and the going was sadder to me than
the earlier going, so that I knew that I, who could never
share him, had made an error. I packed my few belongings and intended to go to the City of Rams. But
the boat did not sail to the City of Rams, but to this
city, and your nephew was kind to me on the way, and
so I am here."

Mistress Hsia said: "I was sorry for you. Stay here
for a space, at any rate. We shall say to the Lady
Loong, whose name means Dragon, that you have
entered my service. Thus, if her mind can be set at
rest, it shall be set at rest." She called for more melon-
seeds, and shortly these were brought in by her maid,
Tower of Pearl.

.   .   .   .

Sai Kwan was a very old city. In the dim days of
feudalism, when it had been founded by men whose
names were now forgotten, the site had been chosen
for the presence within it of the two hillocks which
would, when the walls had been built (rammed earth
between planks of thick wood) serve as the smaller,
more sacred places of the Altars of the Soil and the
Altar of the Ancestors. This Altar of the Ancestors,
always larger and more important than the Altars of
the Soil, stood at the centre of the subsequent palace
in which the family of Hsia then held sway, a palace

crenellated and defended by walls and towers of its own, but now become, in the times of comparative peace, an area of halls and courtyards wherein the Hsias might live, family on family, in contiguity and yet in partial privacy.

Over on the second hillock, the Altars of the Soil were now incorporated in the *yamen* of the Prefect of Sai Kwan, so that the ancient inheritors of the land could see, on this lesser elevation, the buildings in which the business of government went on, a competitor to their own older rights of seignory.

Round the city, the older and insufficient walls of earth now served as the cores for the great stoned fortification which kept out bandits, acted as limits in the allotment of the land taxes, and every night was the impassable barrier through which none might pass until cock-crow told of daylight safety.

In the Hsia home, Mistress Hsia had been given, as was her right, one of the outer courtyards to the north.

"It is almost impossible for us, brought up as we were in the more rational autocracy of an official household," Mistress Hsia was saying to Peony, "to realize the absolute nature of the power which an old woman can wield in an estate such as this, where tradition and immemorial custom rule without the sanctions of common sense."

Peony agreed: "Yes, it is as you say. Where there is a dowager, there is despotism."

Mistress Hsia went on: "The Lady Key-of-Jade Loong does not like you. She resents your arrival with her son in a slightly unexplained manner. You represent, through him, a challenge to her authority."

"I know," Peony replied. "But I am helpless in the matter. I have no wish to go against her wishes, just for the sake of going against her wishes. On the other hand, she shows in her words and in her actions an intolerance which may make life here difficult for me." She sighed. "It might have been better for me if I had gone to the Blue Houses, as I first intended."

"If Lady Loong has her way, you may yet go there," Mistress Hsia said. "And now I think that it is time that I had one of my headaches. Such manifestations of good birth exercise a salutary influence on women of measureless energy, such as my sister-in-law. Pull the window-covers shut and call to my maid to bring tea. Say that I suffer. Thus the whole house will soon hear of it."

Peony obeyed.

.   .   .   .

When Peony came to the Pavilion of Porcelain, named after Li Po's famous retreat in the Emperor's Palace park at Chang-an, and paused on the humped bridge over the little stream (constructed in imitation of Flying Tiger Bridge, in Li Po's retreat) she could see little, for it was the first day of the ninth month and the moon was not in the sky. The midnight was cool, but not unpleasantly so, and she waited, leaning on the balustrade.

Hsia Nan-p'o came up noiselessly behind her and had stood for a moment beside her before she was conscious of his approach. She jumped.

"You startled me," she said. "Although I had expected you, I had not expected you at that precise moment."

"I asked you to come, with a note in a surreptitious manner," he replied, "because there are things to be discussed between us."

"I am not," she reminded him, "in a position to discuss anything with you. I am here owing to your courtesy, and the courtesy of your mother, so that I have no claims and no right to object to anything which you may say."

He said: "Come inside. The night air is not as warm as it might be. Yes, I sent for you here because I do not wish my mother to know our relationship. It has been difficult to keep it from her."

"To keep what from her?" Peony asked. "Are not our relationships those of a man who has done a kindness to a woman? How then should it be needful to hide it?"

"You make nothing easy," he answered, smiling in the dark. "Nevertheless, come into the shelter of the Pavilion. I will not trouble you with the tale of its origin, or with the poems written by Li Po in honour of its prototype in the Brilliant Palace at Chang-an. No: I will say that our relationship, though it might be told to all the world, and even to my mother, need not necessarily remain so."

"I am in your debt for shelter," she said. "I know that, and admit it. But, since you cannot be aware of the events immediately before our meeting, it should be a wise thing if I told them to you. Then you will understand why our relationship cannot be altered."

"Any relationship can be altered," he returned. "But tell me what you desire to tell me. Sit down."

Peony related to him how she had spent the night before their meeting, how Lien had gone, and how she had known that it had been an error to see Lien again.

"For he is a magistrate with a wife and a second wife, and children, and honour in the Empire. It cannot be that I should have anything more to do with him, since I cannot share him with another."

"The news which completes your story will come as well from me as from another, later teller," he said. "It reached us yesterday, by a servant who had been in Kowloong City and brought the news back with him. Magistrate Lien died, in his *yamen*, on the same night as you left him. It may be that ' he left you ' is not so accurate."

He felt her stiffen against him in the darkness.

"He is dead?" she asked, her voice steady.

"He is dead," Hsia replied, and in the dark he could feel the slow shaking of her body, the silent contraction and release, the start of a shiver coming to a tense immobility, the breath held and then expelled in a shuddering sigh. There was a gulf between them.

He drew away from her, and soon her sobs became the sobs of a woman whose heart is broken, the great gusty sobs each with a shiver, and a little sound—Ahaa —that grew and died into silence.

"How?" she asked when she could speak to him.

"Men say," he told her, "that he died of the great sickness, and that there were the marks on him. It seems to have been very sudden. The morning that the ship sailed. That is all that I heard."

"I loved him," she said. "He was the man whom I loved. He could not let me give him children, and he was not troubled because of that, since he had a wife. But I—for me he was everything. I came away so as to spare him the sadness of my demands, demands which he could not grant. In our country it is not accepted for a woman so to love a man: the relation-ship is supposed to be a more formal one. But not with me! I am now one with all the women who have lost,

all the women for whom the world is empty, for whom
it does not greatly matter what happens to them. He
will be buried there? "

" I do not know that," he replied.

And now he knew that he could not talk further
with her, in the moment of her loss. He could not
even give her comfort, for no comfort was possible. It
was only left for him to go, and this he did, leaving
her crying.

. . . .

Life in Sai Kwan proceeded quietly, as life in a Prefect's city should progress. In the Hsia house, Peony
did not often leave the tree-lined courtyard where
Mistress Hsia lived with her maid Tower of Pearl in
an atmosphere of unapproachable remoteness. Contacts
with the rest of the household were few, for the Lady
Loong did not go out of her way to precipitate meetings
in which, if the past were any guide, she could expect
a cold reception and an immediate, stifling formality.
Peony and Mistress Hsia often talked of the friends
they had in common : Tower of Pearl would sit beside
them, listening : then she would go about her tasks of
replenishing the teapot.

Yet Peony knew, in all these endless afternoons, that
the young man Hsia Nan-p'o lived in the main courtyard not far from her, and that he had not shewn himself uninterested in her. She contrasted her expected
position in the Blue Houses in the City of Rams with
this quiet existence, and knew that one day, when he
thought himself safe from his mother, he would send
for her or come to see her, and that then all the old
troubles would begin, when tangled emotions dissuade
living from its straight and easy path to the byroads of

c

real or pretended sentiment and the possible intrigues of love.

For love, she knew, brought always sorrow in its train; she was reminded of the epigram of Su Tung-p'o —THE EXCELLENCE OF THINGS IS THEIR UNDOING. She had the scroll in her box now, carefully rolled.

It was twelve days after Hsia had told her of the death of Magistrate Lien. She was sitting in the Autumn Pavilion, where Tower of Pearl came towards her. Tower of Pearl belied her name, for her skin was darker than the usual, and her height well below it. She was smiling now.

" A message has come from the main courtyard, for you," she said.

Peony sighed.

" *He who rides on the tiger cannot dismount,*" she replied. " Life resembles a tiger in that respect. Peace such as this cannot go on for ever. And he said what? "

Tower of Pearl's smile grew wider.

" He said : ' At dusk, in the Autumn Pavilion, I shall come.' So there is no need for you to disturb yourself," Tower of Pearl said. " The sun is falling : dusk is not far off."

Peony said : " Help me to put the screens up. Dusk is tending, nowadays, to be a chilly hour."

When this had been done, Tower of Pearl went away. Peony lit the charcoal brazier, fetched a further supply of charcoal for it from the general store, and sat down to wait for Hsia Nan-p'o to come to tell her what might be the reason for the message. She had, however, little doubt.

.   .   .   .

" For, in this barbarous southern dialect," Hsia

was saying, "many words take on the colour of the land, achieving meanings wholly unlike their origin."

"It is as you say," Peony agreed.

He went on: "Thus the word *t'ung*, which is made up of *disease* and *common*, and means *pain* or the *cause of pain*, has come, in these southern lands to mean *love*. So *we have a common disease* means *we love*."

"It also implies," Peony told him, "that love is painful. Of that there can be no doubt in the minds of those who have experienced this emotion."

He looked at her.

"You have suffered," he said.

"It is the lot of women to suffer," she replied. "If by suffering you mean that, for me, love is tinted by the memory of those whom I have loved, you are right. The words of love, for me, are ringed round with memory: the actions and gestures of love call up, each of them, the picture of a man whose arm was bent just as yours is, whose head was thus poised. My love lives in the past, so that every burgeoning of love is but a reliving of the past. Yet it was not my husband whom I loved."

Hsia objected: "You over-stress the part which the mind can play in love. For, when all living centres down to a bright momentary spark, lasting but for a few heart-beats, the mind slumbers, giving over control to the body, whose reactions do not admit the mastery of the mind."

"My mind does not ever sleep," she said. "My body may seem to be yours, maybe, as now, but my mind recalls what has been and what can never not have been."

" There is war between us," Hsia murmured. " And in war it does not matter whether the general has conquered a city before. When the walls are down, his soldiers pour into the breach, thus, not caring whether they have sacked an earlier city."

" Or whether that city has been sacked by some prior conqueror," she said. " But you are wrong. Walls, repaired, are easier in the over-throwing."

They lay quietly for a little time. He touched her breast.

" You are asleep," he said.

She opened her eyes to smile.

" I was thinking," she told him, " of your mother, the Lady Loong. She would not be pleased to find us thus."

" My mother," Hsia replied, " is not easily pleased. For her, pleasures are the pleasures of power, whereby she rules the actions of others."

" Are your pleasures, too, the pleasures of power? " Peony asked. " For you constrain me to your will." She sighed and added : " It is not markedly unpleasant to be constrained by you."

He quoted at her :

> *Again: again.*
> *In the season of the constraining year*
> *The doves mate.*
> *Corrulently they cry,*
> *Flutter and are still.*

She replied, sleepily :

> *The tower of the attackers is fallen*
> *And the city waits, breathless, for a new assault.*

What engines will they now bring up
Against her silent battlements?

"Your skin is the skin of peaches," he said.

She answered: "But I do not love you."

He said: "Your heart beats steadily, and there are little pulses under your skin. So must the pulses of the seasons beat. You are cold?"

"No," she answered. "No. I am not cold. I shivered, because I remembered, when you spoke of the seasons, how winter must come, and I grow old. And you. Servants will bring you hot broth, and you will sip it and say that it tastes good. The cool air of Spring will beat on your bald head, one day, and you will say that the Spring breeze is pleasant. There will be no more talk, one day, of conquering cities."

"You come back to my metaphor," he told her, "like a girl to a favourite dish. And all the time you pretend not to like that dish over much."

"Your aunt has a maid, called Tower of Pearl," she said. "Do you like her?"

"Tower of Pearl? No," he replied. "But it is true that I know nothing of her."

"There are many girls," Peony said, "in your world, if you will have them. I am tired now."

"Then you shall sleep," he said. "Listen:

"The conquered city sleeps
Under the strong hand of the conqueror,
Careless of all her battlements,
Under a bright moon in a dark sky
That touches silver where it touches her."

She put an arm round his neck.

.   .   .   .

When, for the third time, Peony waited for Hsia Nan-p'o in the shelter of the Autumn Pavilion, the buds on the pear-trees seemed to be stirring. He came with the suddenness and certainty of a young man who knows what he wants, and she marvelled at the way in which men, when they see again before them the object of their desire, forget to woo, forget the tenderness which, to a woman, is more than the ultimate gift. It was as though, having once set foot on some magical mountain-top, men forswear for ever the long, anticipatory climbing towards that view-bound summit, and afterwards come to be carried thither on the backs of fantastic, imagined birds, avoiding the labour of their feet.

Yet a mountain enjoys being climbed.

Hsia, in fact, took up his conversation where he had last left it off. He even quoted the last line of the verse with which he had, then, soothed her to sleep—

. . . touches silver where it touches her.

Peony found it a little difficult to adjust herself to the unexpected speed of his approach.

"Do you not retread again, for certainty, the last few steps of the Ladder of Love?" she asked, remembering that when she had last seen her other, her unforgotten lover, Lien, she had taken that very phrase— Ladder of Love—for her love-name.

"We stand upon the shoulders of our successes," he answered, "and upon no ladder—of love or of cassia-wood. We so stand because we shall not, much longer, have the opportunity to see each other."

"I am to go?" she asked. "Whither? Your honourable mother has decided?"

Hsia cried, almost angrily: " Do not talk thus conventionally of my *honourable mother* when I bring you news of our separation. There are times when courtesy may be carried too far. This is one such time, when you lie thus with the light of the little lamp reflected twice in your eyes under your lowered lids, not sorrowing as I sorrow at the pain of this, our last meeting, but lying, self-sufficient, provocative, lovely, inscrutable, at your ease. . . ."

She asked: " Do you collect adjectives? "

He replied: " Enough for you that I collect—be it adjectives or memories. Does it mean nothing to you that to-morrow you go to the Prefect's *yamen* to join his daughter's girls? That there, in the Prefect's *yamen*, you are as far from me as the moon is in the blue sky? "

She quoted lazily:

> *In the blue sky the moon is alone*
> *I have blown out my lamp: I weep.*
> *You are far as is the moon*
> *And cannot know my love.*

When they had lain thus, silently, for a while, she went on: " It does not matter, I have found, what my present emotions may be, for there will come other emotions to take their place, and whenever I have tried to alter what is to be, it has proved worse." She sighed. " And if you tell me to run away from here, I shall but be running away from you. Here, you are near me: I can look over the space between us and say: ' he is there.' But if I go away—the blue sky is not vast enough for all those who are separated. No: I shall stay, and you will know that I have stayed, so that, even if I do not love you, I shall still be near you."

He said: "It is not like me thus to endure what is not my will. But against my mother, what is there that I can do? Nothing."

"Time is short," she said. "You should go back to your own courtyard. If they should find us together it will be worse. Your mother may send you away from here, and you will have no means of letting me know where you are. No—it is best that you should hasten on your marriage to the daughter of the Prefect, for then I shall come back to you with all her other women."

"I do not want her, nor all her women," he answered, but she shook her head and by and by they were silent again and in the fields over the courtyard walls a cicada cried, and she remembered that it was very nearly the *Season of Excited Insects*. Then (so does Spring affect hearts) she began to cry in his arms.

.   .   .   .

"From one point of view," Madame Hsia said, smoothing her two brows outwards from the centre, "I could have suggested a better girl than you, for my purpose. No—do not speak, yet. You are one of those whom Life, passing, has left a little numbed, so that you cannot justly appreciate the difficulties of my life here. Your own sorrow masked my lighter sorrows. For I have lost a husband whom I hardly loved—for I understood him too well—while you have lost lovers—two? Three?—whose faults were obscured by your lack of knowledge of them. Yours, then, is the greater loss. And so I, with my headaches, seem to you less of a tragic figure than I seem to myself. As I understood my husband too well to love him, so you understand me too well."

Peony replied: "I am sorry for that wherein I seem to have failed."

"Do not suffer regret on that account," Mistress Hsia told her. "In other ways you have done better than any other girl whom I am likely to have. I will not specify these ways, if your own intelligence does not tell them to you."

"You are kinder than I deserve," Peony said.

Mistress Hsia went on: "Consider my lot and the changes in it. My late husband was Governor of the City of Rams. Then, I created my little world of drawn blinds and headaches in order to make my world smaller and to make myself even more completely the mistress of that world. Now, mured in this courtyard, I find the converse true—that my present world is the size of an acorn, and I would make it grow. So, in following up that thought, I am led to catalogue those places, those people, where my influence is yet felt outside these walls, and I sorrow to think how few they seem. But there is one."

Tower of Pearl brought tea in, and Mistress Hsia drank before she went on: "There was the wife of this Prefect, to whose daughter you are now going. I knew her when I lived in the City of Rams, for her husband on a certain occasion was summoned before my husband, and she (for what reason I do not know) came with him on his visit. I gave her tea, and she looked at me with the hostile eyes of one whose husband has been summoned to the office of a superior. I derived pleasure from watching her, and in the end succeeded in convincing her that I, at least, was neutral. We parted amicably, and I have always remembered her as one in whose presence I was too interested to have a headache. I have written this letter, which you are to give to her daughter. It recalls our meeting, and may (since it hints at your gentle birth) make life there a little easier. For I am not ungrateful to you."

She offered Peony tea, as to an equal, and after Peony had drunk it, they parted without more being said.

.   .   .   .

The dead and now nameless men who once built the city of Sai Kwan had shewn a due appreciation of worth in making the widest, the main, street run from the Hsia house to the lesser eminence of the Prefect's *yamen*. Now, as she followed the two Hsia men along this Street of the Middle Houses, Peony compared it with the broad central street of the City of Rams, running North and South, to the detriment of what she felt was a distorted rural planning. From the Altar of the Ancestors (now the Hsia home) to the Altar of the Soil (the *yamen*) it was true that a road should run, but surely in a well-planned city the gates should determine the lie of the streets? She felt in this some small illustration of the desirous thoughts of these people, and glanced down at the small, shiny black box in her hand as if to make doubly sure that it was there, safe from the immature morals of men whose streets did not run according to the compass.

At the top of a slight rise they left behind the curious eyes of those who wondered, and saw before them the southern entrance of the *yamen*, with its gate-house over the deep cut in the *yamen* walls and a sentry standing, at the opening. It was, indeed, a city in a city, and Peony felt her heart thump unaccustomedly at thus venturing into the unknown, whence escape might not be as easy as entrance. For a moment, indeed, she wished that she had gone to the City of Rams, as she had first intended, and thought with complacency of the unequivocal life with the girls in Peacock Street, where one knew what to expect. But then the memory of her family name came to her. Should a daughter of the Chiangs, however carefully she concealed her origin, falter before feudal magnificence?

The sentry looked at the letter which the Lady Loong had sent to the Prefect, and the little procession moved on through courtyards seemingly endless but all busy, towards what must be the centre of this assembly of dwelling-places. There were great, smooth moon doorways in the squared stone walls of these court-yards, and Peony had to recall to herself that a door opens both ways before she could rid herself of the idea that these courtyard doors were like the successive mouths of a bamboo fish-trap, barring egress.

INTERLUDE AT NAN KING

TWO men walked slowly side by side upon the long paved path which ran along one face of the small pavilion standing at the centre of the great Court of Audience in the vast *yamen* of the provincial Governor of the old capital city of Nan King. At all the entrances to the court double guards had been posted.

The Censor, Su Wai, was a small, bird-like man. The embroidered crane on his robe told his high rank. Beside him Wao Hien To seemed immense, though in actual fact he was but a little over average height. He, too, had put on his ceremonial robe for the courtesies of the interview, and on this robe the embroideries shewed him to be no less high in rank than the Censor himself.

The Censor said: " We are out of the hearing of the nearest guards. Listen, therefore, but I beg of you to appear to be still discussing the abstract beauty of Su Tung-p'o's verse, as we were doing when we were near enough to them for them to hear us."

Wao replied: "The clear sun and the unusually mellow air make verse our natural subject. But I shall listen to any subject—from you."

" That my name is Su Wai, and that I am a direct descendant of the poet Su Tung-p'o is known to you," the Censor said. " What is not yet known to you is the reason for this meeting."

Wao answered: " Where pleasure is the fruit, do not prune the tree."

As they walked, the Censor carefully turned when still out of earshot of the guards.

" Secrecy is natural to diplomatists," he said. " To you, who are accustomed to more spectacular services than I, secrecy may not come as naturally, but I beg of you to adopt it. Shortly, when our discussion on poetry appears (to the watching guards) to have reached the stage where men may naturally sit over a cup of tea, we shall do so, in this little pavilion. Then I shall tell you the matter in concern of which I have ventured to give myself the delight of your company."

Wao replied: " In his AUTUMN SUN, Su Tung-p'o speaks of the aftermath of summer floods, when *at night one must move five times to avoid the damp.* It would appear that we, in this earlier month, must move to avoid the overhearing of the distrustful. That is what you implied? "

" You take my meaning," the Censor observed. " Yes—you take my meaning. See: a servant has come to the Pavilion with our tea. Let us sit down and send him away. Then, with all the courtyard under our eyes, we shall know that we are alone."

When this had been done, and they had disposed themselves comfortably so that the whole courtyard was under the eyes of one or of the other, Wao asked: " And now? "

Censor Su Wai began: *" Under a low moon shining down the Hall, bamboos throw a shadow of a thousand fathoms.* You will recognize Su Tung-p'o's poem on *The Bending Bamboos of the Valley?* Even thus, events throw shadows vastly greater than the events themselves. Now the duties of a Censor, as you know, are to *verify good government*, and in the course of our duties we find strange evidences. Putting these evidences in order, we make a picture of government. You follow me so far? "

" It is easy to follow so bright a lantern," Wao replied.

" Good," the Censor said. " Now, my picture of government in these lands *South of the River* shews that ill deeds and ill punishments gather like a storm-cloud presaging disaster. And, to prove that these observations have been made, before, by others than I, there are the deaths from unexplained illness of at least two and possibly three Censors whose duties took them in this direction. I have appointed a food-taster as a safeguard, but I foresee that I shall, with these other Censors, *travel to the West* when it seems to those of whom I shall shortly speak that I have seen too clearly what goes on in these lands."

Wao tasted the tea suspiciously.

" No," the Censor answered, " you need have no fear of the tea, for the taste, the aroma of the leaves is such that in tea the presence of any added, noxious substance is easy to detect. It is by the mingled tastes of mightier dishes that a dose of poison can be concealed." He drank his own cup and filled it up.

" Tell me," Wao replied.

" There is, *South of the River*," Su Wai said, " a society whose name—one of whose names—is the Society of the Five. Their sign of membership always includes the number five in some form. The purpose of this society is revolt against the Emperor. Do not rise and bow at that name—we are supposed to be discussing the verse of Su Tung-p'o."

Wao nodded.

"The existence of this society," he asked, "was discovered by those other two Censors whose deaths you have mentioned?"

"It was," Su Wai answered. "This is known now in the Capital, and instructions have been given to locate the officials and headquarters. But when those two died, the details of their knowledge died with them." He sighed. "Death is the final lot of all men, but it is unfortunate when it cuts short a source of information."

"You have men searching out the facts?" Wao suggested. Then he changed the tone of his voice. "*Quiet the blue dome of the sky: bright the lonely moon. Suddenly I realize this.*"

Su Wai, recognizing the quotation from Su Tung-p'o's The Great Winds, knew that Wao wished to call his attention to the next sentence—*None can measure my fear.* So he continued Wao's unfinished sentence: "*Alas! Size is relative: emotion is relative.*"

The servant had come noiselessly to replenish their tea. Until he had gone again, the two continued quotations from The Great Winds, tossing the phrases back and fore like jugglers with familiar coloured balls.

Then the Censor said: "Yes. *None can measure my fear.* Will you aid in searching out the centre and root of this infamous society?"

Wao replied, again quoting: "*After three days the wind dropped and there was peace.* Who else acts?"

"There is General Wu," the Censor said.

Wao laughed: "General Wu Fang, whose wife embroiders dragons? Good: I know him."

"If you are to act," the Censor told him, "you must seem to be discredited, to have a grievance which should make you wish to join their society. Is there no anti-social deed for which your rank and importance could be reduced?"

"I desire to marry a widow," Wao answered. "In my position, that would merit more than enough disapproval."

"We must part soon," Su Wai said. "That pretext will do. So now I degrade you to be a simple magistrate—at the City of Kow Loong, where a vacancy has occurred. Go and wed your widow, gaining men's sympathy by your fall from your high estate. Who is she?"

Wao said: "The widow is the widow of the magistrate of that very city, Kow Loong, which you have just named. Is it possible that you knew?"

The Censor smiled.

"Much is known, though much remains to be known," he said. "Come. I go to my probable dish of poison, you to your adventure. I think it would be as well if we seemed to part, here in front of these hundred distant eyes, in apparent anger. Rise."

In front of the pavilion they parted, deliberately omitting sundry of the ceremonial requirements. Wao, striding away without looking back at his host, hoped that this last and worst break of the conventions would deceive the watchers.

Back at the Central Government Inn, he was careful to seem to retain his evil temper as he made arrangements for the transport needed to convey him to the South, to Kow Loong, in none of the panoply of an Emperor's Messenger, but of a simple magistrate who has sinned against the social code by desiring to marry a widow.

PART TWO

PART TWO

THE Lady Hibiscus, widow of Lien Kin Wai, who had been Magistrate of Kow Loong City, stood under the same aspen, looking over the water to the peaks of the island opposite. She was wearing the white clothes of mourning, for it was the second month just after the Period of Excited Insects, and her husband had been dead only six months. Behind her, in the mourning shed which had been built in the *yamen* courtyard, she could hear the two servants, Ah Lau and Ah Sam, brushing out dust. From the rooms beyond came the cry of Silver Lantern's boy child, the gurgle of her own daughter, and the voice of Silver Lantern quieting the two babies. The sky was blue, and it was the hour of the Sheep.

The sky had been blue when she and her husband Lien had arrived from the north, on his first appointment: it had been blue when Lien had stood here, under this aspen, telling her the names of the islands. It had been blue on the morning when they had found him dead in his own room, six months ago. Always blue skies, under the same aspen. And when Wao Hien To, Lien's friend, and the Emperor's delegate, had come to visit her in the eleventh month and seemed to solve all her difficulties for her with a promise of return. . . .

I should be diffident in my proposal, Wao had said, *if either of us two were bound by the ancient conventions which others so highly honour. But you, as I, dare to face a fact, and if old customs do not countenance a widow's remarriage, so much the worse for old customs. Not many years have passed over you. . . .*

The old housekeeper, Ah Sai, tottered towards her from the *yamen* buildings. Hibiscus realized that she had never known exactly how many years Ah Sai's wrinkles recorded on the parchment of her face.

Ah Sai said: "The wife of the rich merchant Tung Ho desires to pay you a visit, if your sorrow does not prevent your speaking with her."

Hibiscus replied: "Conduct her to the Mourning Pavilion and send Ah Lau with tea. They have finished sweeping it out?"

"They have not swept it as it should be swept," Ah Sai answered. "But I will do what you say."

This is the question which I ask you now, under this aspen. . . .

   .   .   .   .

The wife of Tung Ho had succeeded in getting Hibiscus to sit down first.

"For," she said, "though I have seen more years than you, yet your loss is so much the greater than mine that even the strictest laws of politeness are powerless. For you have lost your husband, I my husband's son, and my loss is reparable."

Hibiscus countered: "It is true that my loss is final, but therefore it begins to hurt less. Your loss means more hazard in the future. I was sad when they told me."

"He was a fine child," Tung Ho's wife said. "Even his father said so."

Hibiscus asked: "You do not know how it happened? Or perhaps you would rather not speak of it."

The other said: "We do not know the reason. In the morning he was dead."

Then they both sat silently for a little. Ah Lau brought in the tea. Hibiscus poured her guest's cup and handed it with both hands. But they did not drink yet.

"My husband," the elder woman said, "sent by me a small quantity of silver and a few rolls of silk. He said that these were outstanding in his account with your late husband." She paused, then went on: "You will know that my husband has always undertaken the accounting of the Resin Collection and other funds on a proportion of which the Magistrate's income depends, keeping for himself only a small commission. Thus the Magistrate is spared the trouble of accountancy, and has a fixed and sufficient income at small cost."

Hibiscus replied: "Yes. And now I suppose you have come to ask, first, whether the new magistrate, when he is appointed, will consent to the same system, and, second, whether I realize that there is no more money for me, and how I propose to live. Nevertheless, I find it impossible to accept your kind present of silver and silk, for I have done nothing to entitle me to accept it."

"It is part of your late husband's right, and so is now yours," the other said. "It is not mine, nor my husband's, and I cannot take it back. I beg of you to accept it."

Hibiscus answered: "Very well. And I will act as you ask, and do my best, when the new magistrate is appointed, to persuade him to allow the honourable Tung Ho to act as his factor." She called the girl Ah Lau and told her to take the present. Then they both drank the ceremonial tea, and Hibiscus saw Tung Ho's wife depart in her carrying-chair.

 . . . .

The sunlight was muted inside the Mourning Pavilion, so that the gold characters on the red-painted ancestral tablet seemed to gather light from the corners and shine with a brightness of their own.

Ah Sai said: "Ever since he was a child he had a weak chest, so that one feared illness from that, and guarded him against chills. But to die of the great sickness. . . ."

Hibiscus replied: "I seem to wish him here now, so that he might aid me to mourn for him. I can imagine him here, kneeling beside me, telling what ceremonial acts are needed to do honour to him. Instead, I have to ask advice from others skilled in mourning." She hesitated, and then went on: "Did I do right, to have him buried here, at Kow Loong, in the piece of land which I had bought with my saved money, obeying his expressed wish rather than having his coffin taken to his family at Chang-an, there to join all his ancestors? Was I selfish so to obey him?"

The old woman answered: "I have seen enough summers, and winters too, to know that your husband —the boy whom I once tended—does not now greatly value the view from his burial-place. It is of the living that we women must think. There are young mouths to feed: how shall they be supplied? It is not con-

ceivable that you should be for ever allowed to live
here, in the *yamen* which was your husband's official
right.   One day, soon, you and I must separate those
things which belong to us from the things which belong
to the position of magistrate, for it is certain that the
Emperor cannot long delay in sending either a new
magistrate or written authority for Mei Wan, who is
now temporarily filling the post, to assume permanent
authority.   Then we must go."

When she heard this, Hibiscus knew that her husband's old nurse was hinting and was questioning.
For, although neither Hibiscus nor the Emperor's
delegate, Wao Hien To, had said anything to betray
their intentions, it must have been clear to anyone that
a new widow standing with a man under an aspen tree
and seeming happy had at least contemplated remarriage.   And Hibiscus desired to know what Ah
Sai thought of this departure from tradition—a departure which her late husband would, she was sure, have
approved, but which precedent and custom regarded
as a weakness, an undesirable bowing to the needs of
circumstance, a slight upon the dead and a lightness
of the character.   And, unhusbanded, she found it in-
creasingly difficult to suffer the constant babble with
which Ah Sai embroidered the event of every daily
meeting.   For Ah Sai would speak of dead neighbours
and friends whom Hibiscus had never met, of happen-
ings and situations plucked from the days when, at
Chang-an, the late Lien Kin Wai had been the subject
of wonder and the origin of a collection of baby-
incidents ultimately to be related with fringes to anyone not sufficiently strong-minded to close the ears.
How lovely, Hibiscus reflected, it had been to break
one's own particular silence, in the days before Lien

had died. Now pleasure came only with the infrequent silences of Ah Sai. Something would have to be done about it.

"I will consider," Hibiscus replied, "and will tell you when I have come to a decision. For the present, as I have said before, I desire to hear no more. Give me the keys of my storeroom."

When the door had closed behind her and, in the light from the high window, she allowed her eye to run over these carefully accumulated supplies for contingencies which had not arisen, she found, as she had subconsciously expected, that her mind was carried from her present troubles and uncertainties into a world of memories and unfulfilled expectancies. She saw the camphor-wood boxes containing the rolls of silk which Tung Ho's wife had just given her. The silver, she knew, would be with the other silver in the strong box in the corner. Eggs, preserved in river mud; too young to eat but ruined if they should be moved. Ginger in Kiangsu porcelain jars, blue and white in a lattice of narrow bamboo strips. Covered jars of wines in one corner: flat, dried ducks hanging from the rafters. She took down a small box and opened it. Always she liked to look at the jade which lay inside. There were only three pieces—one large, dark green mass with an unfinished carving of the characters 'Mountains in Spring' upon it—one smaller, brown-green piece with one end ground flat and polished. A seal, perhaps? And one piece of pure, translucent white, which her husband had given her, unpolished and uncut, a thing of beauty which did not commit itself to any shape, but lay snugly in the folds of a piece of old red silk, the promise of unlimited exercise of the jade-cutter's art. How like that white jade had been her husband's life! What untapped potentialities it had held!

She shut the jades back in their box, replaced it and turned round to leave the storeroom, her hand raising the latch.

Wao Hien To, standing just outside the door, watched her come out.

"You!" she cried, and felt for a moment that her knees were weak.

"I," he answered, watching her.

She saw, as she recovered from her first surprise, that Wao did not seem, now, the confident figure whom she remembered last under the aspen out in the courtyard of the *yamen*. No longer did he wear the red knee-coverings, the plumed hat of an Emperor's representative. And with the loss of this outward authority there had gone, too, some of the easy capacity, the power to over-ride difficulties, the confidence in his own rightness. He wore now the more sober robes of a magistrate : he bore across his shoulders no ivory tube for the custody of Imperial mandates. He looked a little doubtful, also, of his reception. . . . And yet he had only said : "I."

He went on : "It grieves me to see that my coming was heralded by none of the drums and gongs of ceremony, but you will have seen that I have fallen a little in the symbols of my outward importance. Without its customary plumage, I can imagine your late husband saying, the peacock is a very drab fowl." He looked at her, she felt, a little anxiously, hanging on her greeting.

She said : "The peacock is only a fraction plucked. The feathers return after a moult. But come." She clapped her hands. "You shall at least drink tea with me. You have seen Mei? He is confirmed in his office as Magistrate of this city? You will be able to tell me whither we move the household? I was looking over the stores."

Then he knew that she had not changed her mind about him. He smiled, as if a weight were lifted. "It is Mei who travels," he said. "To the Capital. They have found him a magistracy nearer civilization."

"And we?" she asked.

He said: "I trust that you have not set your mind upon a change of scenery?"

Then she understood that the Emperor had appointed Wao the Magistrate of Kow Loong.

"My dear," she said, "I am sorry—for you."

"I do not share your sorrow," he answered. "Think of all the advantages of staying here! No trains of beasts of burden pursuing interminable roads. No packing of household goods. Just a slow, a deliberate, a considered rearrangement of what is already here with the little of my own which I have brought."

She went backwards, bowing, into the larger of the rooms in the magistrate's wing. There ceremonial stools had been set, with a low blackwood table between them. The girl Ah Lau brought tea. Hibiscus sent her for salt, and proffered this to Wao as soon as he was seated. Then she poured two cups of tea, handed one to Wao with both her hands, and allowed him to persuade her to sit on the second stool.

"Ceremony is," he told her, "a solvent of unuttered words, and you shew yourself a mistress of ceremony. When a little time has passed, there are other ceremonies to be attended to, but just now let us relax formality. To begin with, let us become personal.

When I was last here I asked you to share my household with me. You still hold to your answer? "

She replied: "All the weary weeks since then, I have held to my answer. You should know that those of us who come from the hills do not change, any more than the hills change. It is kind of you to give me the opportunity to reconsider my answer, but my answer is, as it was when you asked me, 'Yes'."

He rose and bowed to her. Then they both drank their tea. Wao said: "You have more to say to me than 'yes'."

She set her cup down. "When you first met my late husband," she said, "and by your fortunate arrival saved his life, you yourself congratulated him (and me a little) in the small store we set by convention. You said that, when my husband's career had led him higher, he would be able to cultivate this lack of convention to the same high mark as you had reached. You took yourself as a standard—not saying so, but implying that, in the habits of those of your circle, the rules and regulations designed for the conduct of the thoughtless were not binding."

He, too, set down his cup and agreed: "It is as you say."

"Then," she went on, "you will not think too badly of me if I suggest that, by proposing marriage, you are paying to those conventions more heed than they deserve. I know well that what I imply would meet with condemnation from the vast majority, but that condemnation does not make a difference unless it be heeded."

Wao said: "For my part, I like simple, clear colours. As the Master said, *I hate the purple which apes good scarlet.* Let us put your reply again. First, you say ' yes ' to my offer of marriage. Then, secondly, you charge me with over-convention in making that offer. From these two I can draw only one deduction."

She replied: " You are at liberty to draw it. For, as I am never tired of reminding people, I am a hill-woman, and my sight is clearer than the sight of the town-dweller. I wedded my dead husband according to the ceremonies of my people. What other, subsequent ceremonies I endure matters little to me. I shall still be his wife. But there are more than myself to consider: there are my husband's son by the girl Jasmine, who shall carry on his name, and my own daughter. Both these need food, need clothing, need protection. If, after what I have said . . ." She stopped speaking.

"You have left your sentence unfinished," he told her.

They sat not looking at each other, as if a vase had been broken, regarding the fragments with surprised dismay. But Wao rose to his feet and walked round the room, slowly, before seating himself again. Hibiscus rose too, politely, and waited for him to sit down. Then she moved her porcelain stool a little nearer and waited.

"I find that it clears my mind," he explained. "I beg of you to sit down—my own uncertainty need not be infectious. Yes: I see your attitude now. You are being both noble and cautious. Noble, since you take the trouble to shew me how our marriage would advantage your son and daughter. Cautious, since I shall never be able in the future to complain that you gain all, I little. That is your meaning. But I do not merely gain little. I am not an accustomed lover, and in our country's habit a man seldom discusses marriage with

his future wife. Such arrangements are done by inter-
mediaries. But I, urging my unskilled horse through
the thicket of compliment, can rein upon the turf beyond that thicket and say that whatever I contribute of
stability to your household is a poor, puny recompense
for the promise at least of your constant society. As to
your other point—ceremonies do not unduly influence
me. We shall marry, or you shall assume your place in
my household without marriage, as you shall wish. I
am reminded again of your late husband, Lien Kin
Wai, and his ability to weave words into so tangible a
cloth that the woof and the warp escaped notice. I
admired that ability: I envied that ability. I now
realize that I am about to learn that ability."

She replied: "You are a man of action, and yet you
sit here talking about my husband. It does not seem
right."

He rose. "I will have my possessions brought in,"
he said. "Later you may tell me what room you would
choose."

"Let the room be the same as before," she answered.
"Shall I give orders for the mourning pavilion to be
dismantled?"

"I will do that," he said as he went out.

.   .   .   .

Hibiscus sat down again when Wao had gone. The
hour of the sheep was drawing to its close. A distant
clatter told of a vessel dropped in the kitchen. It would
soon be time for the evening meal. Somehow the room
seemed to hold, also, the ghost of her husband, Lien
Kin Wai, and she found this to be comforting. And
yet she felt that this ghost, this friendly, loved ghost
with whom she had spent so short and so memorable a

time, was moving, dissatisfied, about the room, trying
to tell her something. *My wife*, the ghost of Lien Kin
Wai seemed to say, *have you forgotten . . .* and then
the thought trailed like broken smoke. What had she
forgotten? Would he have approved of her actions, of
her words, in thus welcoming his friend, Wao Hien
To? Welcoming? She sprang to her feet and rushed
to the kitchen. The women were boiling rice.

"A bowl of broth," Hibiscus told them. "Quickly.
Take it to the honourable Wao Hien To, who is probably in his office, and apologize for its lateness." Then
she went back to the main rooms and into Lien's own
room, untouched since he had died there. She sat
down again and waited for thought.

"The wise men of the past," she could imagine Lien
Kin Wai saying, "held that the individual must never
suffer for the institution. Marriage is an institution."
And then there were no more thoughts.

.   .   .   .

In the guard house, Wao found the Captain of the
Guard, Tze Hung, inspecting equipment. Tze was a
long, lean man whose high cheek-bones retained a trace
of northern colouring. Sword-belts had been laid
out in a long line on a table along the eastern side
of the guardroom, and Tze Hung fingered each belt
delicately.

Wao watched from the door. The men on duty
stood behind their displayed belts, and Tze Hung had
his back to Wao.

Finally Wao coughed and said: "It is good to see
much thoroughness."

Tze Hung turned and bowed.

"I always inspect equipment thus," he said. "I

know no other way of seeing if my instructions have been obeyed. You would care to see more? "

Wao said, sententiously: " Do you find it best to inspect when your inspection is expected? "

The other did not answer as he dutifully followed Wao round the room.

" Your quarters are comfortable? " Wao asked, and the Captain of the Guard led him into another room where everything was meticulously ordered. One felt that ink-block and brush were confined to an exact position on the low table : not a scroll on the wall hung the slightest out of vertical. Wao's eyes roamed. In the corner, folded under the pile of rugs for the bed, he saw silk of a texture which did not seem military. A girl's jacket? And then, as his gaze came back to the furniture, he suddenly saw meaning in the arrangement, for with the bed as one side of the figure, the stools and low table, the floor coverings, had been arranged in the shape of an exact equilateral pentagon. . . .

" Your routine will follow that of the last magistrate? " Tze Hung asked.

Wao replied: " Yes, for it would not be possible to improve on it. And now I must go."

Then Ah Lau appeared in the doorway, carrying a bowl of soup. Wao took it from her as if he had expected it, and sat down on one of the porcelain stools to drink it. Tze Hung watched him.

When Wao had finished, he gave the bowl back to the girl, cast a last look round the room, bowed in return for hospitality, and walked towards his office. The Captain of the Guard looked after him with a question in his eyes.

In the office, Mei Wan, who had been Lien's clerk

and was now acting magistrate, rose to greet Wao. Together they read the official paper recalling Mei to the Capital.

Mei said: "It is well that I should be transferred, for then I shall not be compelled to attempt to follow in the steps of the late magistrate, Lien Kin Wai, whose reputation makes it hard for one as inexperienced as myself to succeed him. You, Sir, have wider experience—for you it is not so difficult. May I wish you all good fortune in your new post?"

Wao answered: "Pray accept my thanks for your good wishes, and my assurance that, despite what you say, I am very conscious of my own inadequacy. Nevertheless I shall do my best to follow in the path of one who has evidently made his mark in both your memories and your affections. I trust that I may have the privilege of inviting you to dinner with a few friends to speed you on your way?"

"I shall be delighted," Mei Wan said.

.   .   .   .

The sun had fallen to the tree-tops. Hibiscus was waiting for him.

"I have left the furniture of your room arranged as it was when my husband was alive," she said. "I have merely taken away the small cupboard which he had brought from his own home. And I am overcome with shame for myself, since I have said none of the things and done none of the things which my gratitude should have directed. Instead, I have seemed to be in a white mist like the mist of the now scattered plum-blossom, and I have spoken to you as if you were a visitor to my house."

Wao replied: "It is difficult to change the mind like a set of clothing. Reflect that you have ruled here through your husband, then in your own right. How can you expect to readjust yourself? I shall sit down, since your tangled thoughts have not allowed you to ask me to do so. Thus. Now: consider. You had no warning of my coming, no knowledge of your immediate future. You had looked over the goods of your household, wondering what would become of them and where next you would set up your house. All the while, behind this confused wonder, there was the image of myself—a dimly-seen image, half-clear, the image of a man whose future, if bound with yours, assured comfort and plenty and who, if you look critically enough, may be said to be bartering that comfort, that plenty, against your body. No!" He held up his hand. "Do not speak. I desire to say, now, all those things which I shall have neither the opportunity nor the impulse to say later, when for each of us the other may have become a habit too hard to break—a pleasant, a worthy but an inevitable habit. When we know each other better, even to formulate these thoughts may prove impossible: let us therefore admit now to each other the baseness of some at least of our motives."

Hibiscus, her eyes narrowed towards the West, said: "You assuredly seem to be setting out your worst side for inspection. And mine, also. Nevertheless, each of us is aware of these shortcomings, and now that they have, like winter clothing in summer, been brought out, aired, and inspected, we may put them safely away again. Perhaps in our future lives the winter which dictates their need will not again strike us. Who knows the future?"

Wao said: "No one can know the future. But it is for us to shape it as far as we may. I take it then that,

E

after what I have said, you still intend to accept my earlier offer, and join your fortunes with mine? It is unusual, to say the least, for a widow to remarry."

"You did not say so when, in your capacity as the Emperor's representative, you solemnized my marriage to my late husband," she returned. "You are not even the second. Do you still make that offer?"

"I make the offer," Wao said.

"And I accept," she replied. "I have been telling you so for a long time, it seems. Now you in return shall tell me why you have exchanged your red knee-covers and peacock-feather hat for the soberer garb of a magistrate."

He took from his inner pocket his eight-sided jade fingering-piece. She saw his fingers caressing the known surfaces as he answered her.

"I am," he said, "a man whose every instinct is for openness, for outspoken thoughts, for the absence of reticence. Yet I cannot even hint to you why, in reply to your question, I must abandon openness, give up outspoken thoughts, adopt restraint. I cannot even hint. All I can say is that my appointment as Magistrate of Kow Loong City has seemed to the Emperor to be a wise appointment. Now, after that thoroughly unsatisfactory reply, you should find it easy to revise your acceptance of my offer. Every consideration of wisdom should make you regard very askance an official whose futures have taken so downwards a path as this descent from an Emperor's Messenger to a magistrate."

Hibiscus replied: "If I am to ask no questions, I shall ask no questions. Your secret cannot alter my decision. Is that enough answer for you, enough third answer? And now, my lord (for that is your style) it

is late and you have travelled far. You will rest?
There will be much to do to-morrow."

He said: "I am, I see, to be managed. Well, the
experience is probably not unendurable. And I am a
little tired. This evening has seen me nearer emotion
than is my wont."

The *yamen* began again to take on the aspect of a
place where a master lived. Lights were put out. Doors
were shut. The *yamen* guard took up their duties.

And Hibiscus lay far into the night, motionless,
wondering, but knowing that she had not been wrong.

     .   .   .   .

The children were sleeping in their room.

It seemed to the Lady Hibiscus, as she stood beside
Ah Sai, her late husband's old nurse, that through the
lattice partition at the end of the reception room a scene
had come to be repeated, with only a change of some of
the characters. In place of her late husband, her new
husband dispensed courtesies: in place of those former
guests, another guest sat, attentive to his words. Of
the three girls who had, then, contributed to entertainment, two were now going through the same
motions of pouring wine, exchanging jests and adding
to the brilliance of words the roundness of reality.
For Mountain Stream and Hidden Gold were singing,
now, the same songs that, once, they had sung in this
same room: The Naughty Winter: Waiting under the
Plum-Blossom. There was wine from the same jars,
food from the same bowls. All was a return and a
reversal of time.

Mei Wan was saying: "Sir, I do not know that I
have enough expressed my pleasure and content. Or
that I have enough praised the quality of the food, the

variety of the wine, the excellence of the entertainment."

Mountain Stream put in : "We, who have mourned our dead sister, Golden Rod, find in your words some easement for our sorrow, so that the songs which we sing are not wholly like a bright mask on a sullen face."

Hidden Gold agreed : "It is not too difficult to throw off sorrow with the aid of wine such as this. I shall sing you *The Third Wife's Complaint.*

> *As the brown earth soaks up the summer rain*
> *And soon is dry again,*
> *So I, my Lord, thy smallest fallow plot,*
> *Am parched, am hot*
> *For thy communion with me.*
> *What part has she*
> *In thy benevolence, in thy profane*
> *Delights—she who has not*
> *My need of thee?* "

"This meal," Wao said, "is coloured, as it were, by the unheard but yet imagined conversation of dead men and dead women, of those who, to our knowledge, have sat in these seats and eaten from these bowls. It is as if a man, writing, were constantly finding his thoughts altered by the speech of folk in a nearby house, speech entering through his window. But what does a man so plagued do to overcome his plague? Does he not close the open window so that these voices come to him so faintly, if they come at all, that they are merely a pleasant background to his thoughts, not clear enough to be recognizable, even as words, but one with the noise of nature—the chickens, the wind—which do not disturb because they are inevitable?" He sighed.

" Let us close that window now. Sing another song, Mountain Stream."

Mountain Stream sang:

> *In a curved spray*
> *The white trumpets of the bindweed top the*
>   *broken wall:*
> *Why should those red-wood pillars fall*
> *Across*
> *The way,*
> *The way be soft with moss?*

" It is called *The Deserted House*."

Mei Wan objected: " Yet still in your song there is the cadence of sadness. Must there always be this cadence in a girl's song, so that love is always tinged with regret? "

" Wine is the cure," Wao told them. " Pour out."

" Wine is no Cure for the death of the Honourable Lien Kin Wai, the death of our sister, Golden Rod, and the departure of the honourable Mei Wan," Mountain Stream said. " He goes to the Capital, and so has cause for ultimate joy, but we women are left here, when the fumes of this wine have passed, to pursue the age-old objects of women, and to pursue them how inadequately ! "

Wao laughed: " I am here. I am not going to the Capital. Have you nothing to say of me? "

But their reply was cut short by the entry of Tze Hung, the Captain of the Guard. He bowed first to Wao, then to the others.

" For late arrival, no excuse is enough," he said. " So I do not excuse myself. Explanation of seeming discourtesy is another matter, and if you will forgive me, I can then produce this explanation."

Wao said: "It is of small consequence from the point of view of a host's dignity. It is of great consequence that we have missed your presence for the beginning of our meal, have missed your conversation, have missed your appreciation of the accomplishments of these ladies here, who are striving to dismiss from us an atmosphere of gloom. It seemed, until your arrival, that they, themselves, found this gloom infectious."

"Gloom?" Tze Hung asked. "I cannot conceive why gloom should surround you. Tell me."

Wao replied: "Before you came, I had tried to voice the feeling of the atmosphere, and in voicing it to lessen its force. I flatter myself that I almost succeeded. Then Mountain Stream, here, sang another song with which all the sadness returned. I do not think that I could bear to have it analysed again. Instead, let us speak of other matters. You, Sir, can help by telling us the doubtless amusing reason for your delay in coming. Thus, from sorrow, pleasure can spring." He laughed. "There are probably five reasons why you could not come."

Tze Hung, it seemed to Hibiscus, watching through the screen, changed face as Wao spoke. But he seemed calm enough when he replied.

"Since the universe is constructed of the five elements," he said, "metal, earth, wood, water and fire, and these five elements are the parents and the children of each other and of all in the universe, it is certain that there must have been at least five reasons for my lateness." He leaned forward, politely, to hear Wao's answer.

"And there are also the five elements, as the Buddhists say, composing each man—form, perception, consciousness, action and knowledge. But enough—

we would not press you further. Try this dish of duck.
Do you think that duck is always in season? "

Hidden Gold said: " There ducks have an advantage." They looked at her to see what she meant.
Hibiscus blushed behind the screen.

" That is not the sort of remark that I would wish
you to make," she said to Silver Lantern, who stood
beside her.

" But it is true," Silver Lantern replied. " However,
I will only think it."

It appeared that Hidden Gold's remark had lessened
the sadness of the company, for Wao became a little
boisterous, and Tze Hung lost from his face a certain
tenseness which had been present when Wao was talking in fives. Fresh wine helped. Yet, even so, the
dinner left a feeling of disappointment and failure behind it, as if the spirit of Magistrate Lien Kin Wai were
viewing them all with a querulous amusement.

.   .   .   .

Jasmine brought her boy child to the *yamen* as dusk
was falling. She was accompanied by Tze Hung, the
Captain of the Guard, and Wao realized, when he saw
this, that he had omitted to warn Tze Hung of Jasmine's coming. When she arrived at Wao's office, he
looked first at the child, and saw that it was a healthy
intelligent-looking boy. Then he thanked Tze Hung
and dismissed him.

" You have not, of course, named him? " Wao asked
her, his eyes now running over the girl who stood
before him. He saw that she was below the middle
height, that her shoulders were broad, and that the
bearing of a child had not sapped her apparent strength.
He could see at once that her family would not repay

research, and marvelled that Magistrate Lien Kin Wai, who had chosen to die and leave his wife, the Lady Hibiscus, unprovided for, should have added to his household the expense of this girl.

" It was not for me to give my son a name," she said.

Wao replied: " You should not say ' my son ', but ' my master's son ', since you are well aware that you have no rights over the boy. He is the son of Magistrate Lien Kin Wai, and will address the Lady Hibiscus as ' mother '."

She said: " I am sorry. Yet I feel that my late—master would have said the same thing more kindly."

Then Wao knew that Jasmine, too, was still under the spell of the dead man and that, to her, Wao was merely an interloper. It was therefore without much hope that he went on: " Should you prefer such an arrangement, all parties would be satisfied if you handed over the boy to his mother and considered yourself free. After all, I understand that, when your master sent you away before your child was born, he gave you a sum of money enough for your needs for a number of years."

" That is very true," she answered. " And yet I would not leave my child. My master honoured me by allowing me to be a *bearer of towel and comb*, and I desire to retain that honour, even to his memory."

There were tears in her eyes. Wao wondered at her. Then he took ink and brush, writing a rapid note to Hibiscus. He sent this by one of the *yamen* guards and went on with his official work while he awaited her coming. Jasmine stood impassively in the corner of his office, her child in her arms.

When Hibiscus came into the room, she halted in the doorway. Jasmine took the child to Hibiscus, put it

into her arms and then kotowed. Neither spoke.
Hibiscus looked at the child, then at Wao.

"Sir," she said, "it lies in your will to say what is
to happen."

Wao laughed a little oddly.

"There is a sense of strain in the room," he said.
"Who am I, a man, to interpret the thoughts of
women? And yet I must refrain from attempting to
be what I am not. A decision. The Lady Hibiscus
will dispose of the child as seems good to her. With
the other two he will make a reasonable task for her
maid, Silver Lantern. As to the girl Jasmine, she is at
the disposal of the Lady Hibiscus, and it is not my task
to say what that disposal is to be. Go now."

Hibiscus carried the baby out. Jasmine followed.

Hibiscus said: "We must consider names for him.
You may have your old room, if you wish. There are
a few things to be taken out. . . ."

Jasmine knew that Hibiscus was trying to be kind.

"You are very good," she said, slowly, as she followed Hibiscus and saw the child handed over to
Silver Lantern. She heard Silver Lantern's cries of
surprise and approval. Then she went with Hibiscus
to the room which Jasmine had occupied before she
had been sent away. The girl Ah Lau came and
carried away to Hibiscus' room the little nest of drawers
which had been Lien's. Then Jasmine sat down as
Hibiscus went out, closing the door behind her.

The driver, Ssu, had told Jasmine, on the journey,
of the manner of Lien's dying, and she sat quietly for a
while, thinking of her late master as he was. She
remembered his kindness, the weakness which he had
shewn in controlling her, the obvious but controlled
jealousy of his wife, Hibiscus, and the last night when

he had been taken from her arms to be most unconventionally present at the birth of Hibiscus' girl child, Lien Ming Tzu : she remembered how Lien had called her Little Dusky Tower when he had taken her virginity, and how it had never been the same afterwards.

She cried a little.

.   .   .   .

Some days later the merchant Tung Ho sent a sum of money which, his letter told Wao, had been collected from the Resin Office and the tribute rightly the perquisites of a magistrate. Wao checked the accounts, found that the percentage which the merchant had retained for his services was not too high, and sent for Ssu, the driver of the *yamen* carriage.

"I shall view the limits of my territory to-day," he said. "So prepare the horses for a drive. They have driven little lately."

Ssu bowed.

"I shall bring the carriage as soon as may be," he replied.

Wao waited. When he heard the noises of the horses, he put on his outdoor garments and went down the steps of the *yamen*. A crowd of curious spectators was dispersed by the blows of the *yamen* guard. They drove off.

"Is it your wish to adopt any particular order of going? " Ssu asked.

Wao said: "No. Follow your bent, and listen to me. You are a man of sense, I have understood from the late magistrate's notes about you."

" Others have said that," Ssu agreed.

Wao went on: "You are also a man of discretion, even though you keep your wife and child in the *yamen*."

" *Even?* " Ssu said. " It saves expense, and I can see that she avoids mischief."

They drove on past several streets. The people turned their heads to see the new magistrate who thus drove out without an escort of his guard.

Wao said: " If I give you a duty, a duty which is neither burdensome nor difficult, and promise you gain and advancement at its end, will you do that duty? "

" If the duty is as you describe it, yes," Ssu answered. " Tell me its nature now, for I can see that it is a secret duty, or you would not have chosen the privacy of this carriage to tell it to me."

" I wish," Wao told him, " to send a message which is not a message, and to receive an answer which is not an answer."

Ssu agreed: " Anyone can do that. Who is the man? "

Wao said: " General Wu."

" I know him," Ssu observed, flicking his off horse. " He came to dinner soon after the arrival of our late magistrate and his family from the north. Now if you wish me to have speech with him without seeming to seek it, I must have another reason for my journey to the City of Rams."

" The City of Rams is full of delightful and attrac-tive reasons," Wao said. " It would seem wise for you to express some rising dissatisfaction. . . ."

" With my wife," Ssu replied. " That would not be hard. I will see to it. When do you desire me to start? "

" Within seven days," Wao said, and Ssu turned the horses.

.   .   .   .

Bitter, bitter, is the blast of the Autumn wind.
The little Kiang-nan oranges I gave you are bitter,
  too.
Yet the cold wind shall give place to sunshine,
And, when your teeth met in the orange, you
  smiled.

They looked at the poem together.

"My handwriting lacks finesse," Wao observed.

Hibiscus replied: "But not virility. It is a neatly turned poem. The subject seems familiar."

He laughed.

"Here we sit in your room," he cried, "discussing poetry, and you say that the situation is familiar."

"Subject, not situation," she answered. "Yet the situation, too, is not wholly novel. To you it must be well-nigh hackneyed."

"No," he said. "It may seem strange in your hearing, but most of my life I have pursued more solid things than the frail bodies of women. I have many memories of battle, but few of the battle of love. I have issued many words of command, but few of endearment."

"You must understand," she replied, "that to a hill-woman such as myself it has been strange to learn to use words as the common coin of exchange. I remember that, when you yourself performed the ceremony which united me to my husband—it seems a long while ago—you complimented me. Do you remember on what you complimented me?"

"Perfectly," he said. "I complimented you on the promptitude with which you provided tea for me, your then guest."

"And now," she pointed out, "I hear the steps of

the girl Jasmine arriving outside the door, bringing tea."

When Jasmine came in with the teapot and tiny translucent cups, she did not look at either of them. She set the things down and went out without words.

" Jasmine is unsettled," Hibiscus said. " I think that she suffers from an enlarged memory."

" The disease is apparently infectious," Wao observed. " Wherever I go, whatever I do or say, I find that I am in competition with a dead man—a dead man for whom I have the greatest respect and affection, but a dead man who, alive, would have discouraged this marital conversation. He would have said, I feel, that to be dead is to abrogate the rights which one held, living. Jasmine is not alone in that."

Hibiscus said: " Jasmine's memory does not preclude the transfer of her affections. Nor, for that matter, does mine preclude their enlargement. You find the tea palatable? "

He started at the change of subject, picked up his cup and sipped it.

" It is a good tea," he observed. " I cannot deny that."

" How far," Hibiscus went on, " the affection is limited, I do not know. But I do know that the surest way to limit it is to remind me at every turn of the husband whom I have lost."

Wao smiled. " I must strive not to do that," he replied. " I will so strive. But the real purpose of my visit to your room is not one which should set you on the defensive. I came, in actual fact, to tell you that we are, both of us, surrounded by danger, and to ask you to strive, by secret awareness, to lessen that danger."

" Danger? " she asked.

"Danger," he answered. "I cannot tell you what danger, nor whence. I tell you only that there is danger, and that we can lessen that danger only if we behave to the observer as if there were no danger, as if we were two usual people behaving usually. It is an appeal rather than an explanation. Were I not aware of the danger of which I speak, I should have left you for my own room when I drank that tea. But such apparently chilly courtesy between us might make the agent of the danger suspect us of awareness. So I stay."

"You are very welcome," she said, "even though the reason for your staying is unflattering."

There was silence for a while. Each drank more tea. Then Hibiscus blew out the lamp.

.   .   .   .

For three days now, it seemed, the driver, Ssu, had been protesting his dissatisfaction with his wife, Silver Lantern. If one of the three children cried to excess, Silver Lantern could be blamed. If the noise came from her own son, Silver Lantern could be blamed the more.

"I have known households where, even with more children than three, a man might listen to a chrysanthemum," Ssu complained. "I have known women who could both cook and tend children, at the same time, with success. To put it all in one sentence, I have known women."

Silver Lantern replied, good-temperedly: "I will not answer in kind, for such is not my nature. But is it not conceivable that you, in the intervals of your leather-work, could find time to aid me? Surely. . . ."

On the fourth day Ssu ate his midday meal with

protests and went away without telling Silver Lantern where he was going.

Silver Lantern said: "Men are unaccountable. They do not consider that by thus absenting themselves, they may endanger the food of their family. My master will not employ my husband in his absence."

Old Ah Sai, smiling toothlessly, replied: "Do not expect your troubles—to do so harms the digestion. And our new master, the Honourable Wao Hien To, in every way models himself and his actions on our late master, the Honourable Lien Kin Wai, even to the extent of neglect for the full period of mourning. He spent the last night with our mistress, the Lady Hibiscus. That being so, is he likely to be less tolerant of your husband's temporary absence than our late master would have been? Your husband will surely return."

Silver Lantern was a little comforted. And, to her surprise, Wao did not ask for his carriage, nor complained of his driver's absence, and when, on the seventh day, Ssu returned, she told him of their good fortune in possessing such a master.

Ssu said: "He has his virtues. But so have I. And so, indeed, have the fine, expensive girls who live in the street of the Strutting Peacock, in the City of Rams. So you had better bring me food cooked with particular care, lest I tell you of the virtues of these girls."

She hastened to obey.

Much later in the day Ssu came to make his kotows to Wao in the office.

Then he said: "I have no explanation to offer for my behaviour." At the same time he laid silently in front of Wao a sheet of paper on which was written

Shout at me. When i have gone hide this and read
it later.

A man who was listening outside the office might
have admired the roundness of tone with which Wao
told Ssu a number of facts about himself, explained
how, had he been just, the soldiers of the *yamen* guard
should have strung Ssu up by his feet in order the better
to be a target for expert bamboos, how Ssu and his
family should have been turned out of the *yamen* into
the streets, and how thankful Ssu should be that,
following the example of the late magistrate, Wao
found himself possessed of a sense of humour which
precluded the exercise of precise justice upon the person
and family of Ssu. Wao then dismissed him, and Ssu
went back to Silver Lantern in a fittingly dejected state.

When Wao had completed the writing on which he
had been engaged when Ssu arrived, he left the office
and went to his own room. Taking a copy of the Li Ki
from his boxes, he opened it and at the same time
slipped the sheet of paper which Ssu had given him
between the leaves of the book.

On one side of the paper were writtten only the
characters which he had already read, but on the other
side he recognized the fine grass hand of General Wu.

MIDNIGHT

> *The next moon has not been born.*
> *Here a mountain stream chatters in its bed*
> *And gold is hidden under the stones of the wall.*
> *Alas! The tall northerners have come:*
> *An Empire died in the waters by the sea.*

Wao read the paper three times, and realized that it
meant that he was to meet General Wu (the "tall

northerner ") at midnight before the new moon, beside the great rock outside the western gate of the city. Here, in the last moments of the ill-fated Sung dynasty, the last emperor, with all his fleet and officers, drowned in the sea to escape the advancing Tartars. And the reference to a mountain stream and hidden gold? He remembered the manuscript which Magistrate Lien had left when he died: there were two girls named there, Mountain Stream and Hidden Gold, and these two, living in the Street of Happiness, had taken in the girl Peony when she came from the City of Rams to see, again, the lover, Lien, whom she could not forget. He clapped his hand to his head in sudden memory: the two had sung to him at Hibiscus' dinner. And the chattering in the bed; the gold hidden under the stones of the wall. This could only mean that these two girls would provide means of scaling the wall, before midnight. Why had General Wu not arranged to meet him at their house? Could it be that he did not wholly trust them? Wao decided to act as if all were enemies, to use opportunity. He put the paper back in his pocket and turned to read the Li Ki. He was still reading it when Jasmine brought him a bowl of hot soup.

"My mistress sent it to you," she said. "You must be tired after your work in the office. And yet you continue to read at home."

Wao looked up at her.

"I am reading about ritual," he told her. "For in ritual is to be found one of the main strengths of our land."

She answered: "Ritual concerns little a girl such as I am. My late master bought me from my father, and gave me to my mistress. I did for him the duty which

F

she could not do, and gave him a son. Now I serve in an empty house."

"All that you have said concerns ritual," Wao replied. "Your father sells you: you serve. All these things are matters of ritual, and are treated in this book. And yet you say that ritual concerns you little."

"I did not know that such things were ritual," she said. "That must be an interesting book, and if it tells all about ritual it should tell what will happen to me."

"Ritual tells what *should* happen," Wao said. "What *shall* happen to you is future-telling, and only uneducated people believe in that. There is nothing in this book about future-telling." He laughed. "And now, girl, go away, for I desire to finish this soup."

. . . .

On the last day of the month, when the sun had set, Wao sat in his room, waiting for midnight, when the night is still and old men die in quiet beds, unnoticed.

He sat silently, in the silent dark, dressed in the dark blue of common men, and ready to his hand, on a table beside him, he had set his great two-handled sword, that family possession which could only be drawn in defence of the family's honour, and through that of the honour of the Emperor. He had polished the blade, lovingly, and dusted the scabbard. In his pocket were two round pebbles.

How primitive, how single a thing, Wao reflected, is a sword! With its presence he was aware of all the ancient emotions which, in this year of ultimate civilization, men had thought put away, toys of the race's childhood. The watered, keen blade could solve many a problem, permitting of no second attempted solution: behind the edge of the sword followed the air of the world, disclosing secrets, tempering desire, cleaving the inscrutable. Swung in a charmed circle, the blade could clear for a man that small area of privacy in which he could live alone, himself, the possessor of certainty. Outside that circle stood the enemies of privacy, leering: only thus, with a clean cut, could their prying eyes be glazed in death.

The *yamen* was silent along the empty corridors. As he picked up the sword and belted it on, covering it with his long, blue outer coat, a sleeper stirred somewhere behind the swinging doors, and Wao stood for a moment to make sure that only in a passing dream did someone turn upon a wooden pillow. Then he fastened the straps and moved silently towards the guarded entrance and the familiar sentry. In the deeper shadow of the wall he moved on noiseless feet. The sentry stood in the entry, resting on his pike. Wao slipped into the angle just behind the sentry and made himself small against the stone wall. Then he took from his pocket one of the two pebbles which he had put there earlier, and pitched it gently back, in a high arc, so that the pebble fell against the wooden doors, standing open, through which he had just come.

The sentry stiffened: his pike moved to the vertical. He walked back towards the *yamen*, in the direction of the sound which the pebble had made. Wao stepped quietly out on the dark stones and hurried towards the Street of Happiness. There was no great wooden gate at the ward entrance, for here men came and went on their natural errands, unconfined by bolts, bars, and watchmen.

> *For who can set a bound to Love*
> *That is not scaleable by Love?*

he quoted amusedly to himself as he walked.

In the Street of Happiness a drunken man shouted obscenities: a mangy cat scurried with stolen fish into a doorway, and a homing party unsteadily mounted their horses, lanterns swinging. A girl leaned against the entrance pillars of a house, and Wao recognized her, in the dim gleam of light from within the house, as Mountain Stream, who had sung THE DESERTED HOUSE. She turned as he came level with her, leading the way into the house. In a room just off the entrance she offered to take his outer garments.

"I will not stay," he told her. "If the message was truthful, there is little time for such purposes."

She understood at once.

"My sister, Hidden Gold, is even now entertaining the sentry from that part of the city wall which rises behind us," she said. "There are steps this side, in the dark corner by the end house. I have a rope ready. Can you climb down a rope?"

"And up again," he answered. "Let us go."

Mountain Stream said: "Hidden Gold can keep the sentry here for an hour. She has promised him entertainment. I shall leave the rope hanging, until he is about to leave this house. Then I shall pull it up. The rest is your affair."

Wao nodded.

"Let us go," he answered.

.   .   .   .

As he released his one-hand grip on the end of the rope, Wao held his sword horizontally with his other hand, alighting noiselessly at the foot of the wall. He knew perfectly the path which he had to traverse to the hill whereon the great rock stood: he had dutifully inspected it, on taking office, and still could visualize the inscription—HALL OF A KING OF SUNG—chiselled deeply into the hard stone. Now, on his way to it, each stroke stood clear in his memory.

Above the steep little slope, the rock was outlined vaguely against the still dark sky. He halted beside a thin bush, waiting. And then he was conscious that, beside the rock, another figure stood, also waiting—a tall figure that could only be General Wu. There was no sound, no movement. Wao did not alter his position.

Suddenly, out of the night near him, sounded a noise with which, in his younger days, he had been familiar—the rustle of an arrow as it parted the air. The tall figure wavered, fell.

Wao dropped to his hands and knees, climbing the slope. He reached the deeper shelter of the great rock and crawled towards the place where he had last seen the figure of General Wu. His hand touched clothes.

He whispered: "It is I, Wao."

General Wu's voice replied, weakly: "There is little time for me to die properly, in a quiet mind. Listen— the Prefect of Sai Kwan . . ." Then his voice died with him, and Wao knew that he was alone.

He was possessed of a great, cold rage that his friend should thus come to his end, lying in the open. He reflected that, against this, Wu had above him, on the stone, an undoubtedly classical inscription, and that the place, however inadequate in other respects, had historical associations. He still crouched beside the body of General Wu, and suddenly there was movement in front of him. A man was coming round the rock-face.

Wao rolled over on his back beside the body, drawing his sword as he did so and laying it above his head, on the ground, the hilt still in his hand. He waited for the approach of the archer. The sky overhead darkened a little, and Wao knew that the man had reached armslength, standing beside the two of them. With a sudden movement, he swept the sword up and round, still lying on his back, with all his strength, and felt it strike, bite, and go on. The body of the archer dropped to the ground without a word. Wao rose to his feet and tiptoed round the rock in the opposite direction to that from which the archer had come. He had almost completed the circuit when he knew that he had found a second man, following his mysteriously vanished comrade. Wao had no difficulty this time, for the man had his back towards Wao, and this time the sword, swung full and powerfully, seemed hardly to feel opposition. . . .

There would be no more of them. He moved towards the body of General Wu, found and drew the General's sword, and bloodied it on the bodies of the two other dead men. He made sure that General Wu was indeed dead. The arrow had entered his chest, just above the heart. Wao wondered that he had lived long enough to tell the vital fact with his last effort. For appearance's sake he did not compose the limbs, leaving the General with the hilt of his sword lying in his unclenched hand. Then Wao cleaned his own sword as best he could on the grass beside the bodies, sheathed it and stole back by the way on which he had come.

.   .   .   .

The rope was swaying and swinging when Wao reached the base of the city wall, and as he looked it began to rise. As he seized it, he realized that the sentry must be tiring of Hidden Gold's entertainment. He pulled on the rope, to make sure that the top was tied to the timbers where he had left it, and then using hands and feet, walked and hoisted himself to the top. Mountain Stream was there.

She whispered: " He is coming now. I can hear him. What shall we do? "

Wao whispered back: " The man has left his post and merits therefore the punishment of death. Then he cannot talk. Stand here, by the rope and speak to him. I shall be near you. It does not matter what you say: he will not repeat it."

" Your coat is covered with blood," she said. " Do not touch me."

Wao took cover in shadow. The sentry came.

Mountain Stream said: " My sister gave you enough broth? "

The sentry answered: " Broth, yes . . . but is this a rope hanging over the wall? I . . ."

Wao, his hands round the man's throat, brought his head backwards and with upraised bent knee struck once at the base of the skull. Then he took the limp body in his arms and dropped it over the wall. He wound up the rope, untied it and disposed it round himself.

" You have done well," he told Mountain Stream. " Now leave me, and do not be afraid at anything which may happen in the immediately near future, for you have served your country, and shall be rewarded. Above all, speak no word of all this to any man, even if you should be brought before me in my magistrate's court. Remember—silence! "

He left her as she went again into the house and shut the door. It was not difficult to find a way back to the *yamen* without meeting questions from the curious, but under the *yamen* walls he halted, wondering how, this time, to enter unobserved. Fortune had favoured him so far—was he to fail now, at this last barrier of a sentry pacing in a narrow entry and the wooden doors at the inner end, barred on the inside? He remembered the advice which had been given him on some military campaign or other—Look first: Act second.

He took the rope from round his waist and tied the end in a running noose. Then, waiting until the sentry turned, on the small, scuffed area where every sentry turned (had he not watched it from the walls above and wondered at the uniformities of sentries?) he leaned round the corner, arranged the loop on the ground, and threw the other end over the corner of the low guard house roof on the wall above. He put the loop finally into place and had just moved out of sight as the sentry turned by the wooden doors at the end of the short passage-way and stood waiting for the seemingly interminable period between stand and stand.

At last the sentry came forward again. As he reached the loop lying on the ground, Wao bore heavily on the other end of the rope. Two tiles detached themselves and fell with a crash: the sentry's legs were caught by the rope and lifted from under him. He made one long despairing cry as he fell. His head struck the ground: he was silent. Within the *yamen* another sentry called.

Wao heard the answer from a third. He knew that they would rouse Tze Hung, the Captain of the Guard and come to investigate. There was but one chance left. He ran from the fallen man towards the wooden doors and stationed himself behind the second leaf, whose bolt ran deeply into the ground. If, as he calculated, Tze Hung used only half the door, Wao might be unobserved. It was still very dark.

And then it was all over so quickly that when he remembered it, afterwards, Wao always broke into a cold sweat as he visualized himself wedged into the angle between door and wall, the half-door opening and Tze Hung striding towards the passage mouth with another sentry in attendance, while Wao slipped through the door in the opposite direction and, unseen, crouching low, ran up the stone steps to the Magistrate's quarters and in at the door.

Even so, it had been a success gained only by a hair's breadth, for as he stopped, breathing heavily from the effort, he heard the feet of men running and knew that Tze Hung had sent the guards to search the building. Wao was standing outside Jasmine's room, and suddenly made up his mind. He opened the door softly.

Jasmine was lying on the bed, feeding her baby and looked up at him as she moved the child protectively into the shelter of her arm.

" Be silent," he told her. " Feed the child."

As she turned again, uncertainly, thrusting the nipple into the baby's mouth, he stripped off his outer clothes, bloody as they were, and thrust them over his sword on the floor against the wall. Then in his underclothes, he sat on the edge of Jasmine's bed.

" We must think of a name for it," he said. " It is not right that a boy child should for long be nameless. Perhaps you had, yourself, chosen a milk name? "

She sat up and laid the child down amidst the rugs.

"I should have risen when you came in," she answered. " But you were so sudden, and you told me to go on feeding him. Yes, I had thought of a name."

The sounds of search were nearer. " Often women name their boy children with a girl's name," he said, " in order to avoid ill-luck."

"I had thought of Jade Armlet," she told him. "That was the name of the famous Lady Yang Kuei Fei, who was loved by the Bright Emperor of the T"ang dynasty. It is true that, later, she was killed on Ma Wei Slope—Ghost Horse Hill—but she was old then, and my son will give up his milk name in a year or two, so it does not matter." Her eyes widened. "What are those noises?"

Wao went to the door and threw it open. Tze Hung, the Captain of the Guard, stood on the threshold. Jasmine sat up suddenly, and the baby began to cry full-throatedly.

"I am sorry," Tze Hung said. His eyes were suspicious. "It seems that a robber has succeeded in eluding the guards." He shouted, against the baby's high voice. "So I am having the *yamen* searched."

Wao shouted in return: "If you remove the noises your men are making, it will be possible for the remainder of us to sleep. I said 'To sleep'. Report to me in the morning the result of the search." He shut the door. Little Jade Armlet Lien was slowly pacified, but almost immediately, from the room of Hibiscus, came the protesting wail of her girl-child, angry voices and then only the child's voice.

Shortly Silver Lantern's child, also, gave tongue in the servants' quarters.

Wao observed: "One dog barks at nothing and the other dogs bark at him. Now, about names. . . ."

.   .   .   .

In the Hall of Audience, the tall red-wood pillars ran up to the invisible roof, giving the impression of the inside of a temple. But there were no great gilt gods here to listen impassively to the complaints of their worshippers. Instead, Wao Hien To, in his full robes, sat at a small table on which lay a flurry of papers; behind and on each side of him the *yamen* guards stood motionless. Beside him the Captain of the Guard stood with a scroll in his hand. In the place where prisoners were gathered before their call by the magistrate, Mountain Stream and Hidden Gold were standing, guarded.

"In opening the Court of Inquiry," Wao began, "into the deaths of the late General Wu Fang and of the *yamen* guard Mo Ting, which may be deaths connected by an unknown factor, or deaths unrelated, I desire first, in formulating my report for the Prefect, to establish the facts beyond dispute. Tze Hung, your statement."

The Captain of the Guard opened his scroll and began to read.

"At the time when the Hour of the Rat gives place to the Hour of the Ox, the sentries on the city wall above the Street of Happiness were due to change. The new sentry could not find the old sentry: instead he found a trail of bloodmarks from the battlements to the house of these two girls who are prisoners here. He informed me, and I arrested them."

Wao put a tick at the bottom of a page in his copy of the evidence. "We shall hear them," he said. "And the body of the guard?"

"When I had arrested the girls," the Captain of the Guard went on, "I caused a search to be made. The dead guard was found lying with a broken neck at the foot of the wall to which the bloodstains led. His weapon had not fallen with him, but remained on the top of the wall."

Wao said: "Good. He was taken unawares, it seems. Go on."

Tze Hung proceeded: "I followed the trail of blood from the foot of the wall into the open country. It led to the rock which is inscribed 'Hall of a King of Sung', and at the foot of the rock lay the bodies of General Wu Fang and two archers. The General had been shot near the heart: the arrow remained in the wound. Each archer had apparently been slain by the General's sword which lay beside him, near to his hand. The natures of their wounds speak for themselves. I had the bodies brought here."

"Those are all the facts?" Wao asked. When the Captain of the Guard had bowed assent, Wao went on: "They cannot be. Here we have a wall scaled without a rope. That is impossible. Where is the rope?"

Tze Hung said: "There was another happening, too, shortly after the first. Some miscreant obtained entry to the *yamen* by stunning the sentry at the gates."

"Another sentry?" Wao asked. "It would appear that the discipline and efficiency of my guards are not notable. Their training seems to have been neglected. . . ."

Into the silence which succeeded his words there penetrated the sounds of the city streets.

Finally Tze Hung said: "Any lack of efficiency and discipline must be laid at my door."

Wao observed: "The obvious is often true."

There was another silence.

Then Tze Hung said: "This second sentry was lying unconscious at the entrance gates where the passage entry emerges at the outside of the *yamen* wall. His feet were loosely bound with rope. It was, apparently, the same rope with which the other incident was concerned, for there was blood on the rope."

" The case is a curious one," Wao said, making notes. " For the blood seems to have originated near the rock called 'Hall of a King of Sung', and to have been brought towards my *yamen*. It is not clear who brought it, for there are three dead men at one end of the story and an unconscious man at the other. He was unwounded? "

The Captain of the Guard bowed assent.

While he appeared to make these notes, Wao pondered on the best means of attaining his end. For, while a man may seem, in the opinion of those who think themselves wise, to be misled by his own stupidity, this subterfuge is less convincing than that of the man who appears to be misled by his own acuteness. This second method has the added advantage of subtly flattering those who are deceived by it, rendering them the more readily confused, since they believe themselves wise.

" Before we attempt to set in order these surprising facts," Wao said, " let us arm ourselves with the statements of these girls. They will be no more than statements, for blood, rope and dead men are in a different category from the imaginings of girls. But let us hear them. You, girl," he said to Hidden Gold, " tell me what bait you advanced towards the sentry whose business it was to guard the city wall."

Hidden Gold came forward and said: " If you can call a bowl of broth a bait, that was the bait."

" He often came? " Wao asked.

" He often came," she replied, and Wao was pleased to see the Captain of the Guard nod his head, as if secretly gratified.

Wao asked: " You left your house that night? "

Hidden Gold answered: " No: did I not say that I

entertained the sentry with broth? The object of the broth was to counter the cold air : should one drink broth outside the house, the coolness of the air and the warmth of the broth would battle together, leaving no more comfort than if the man had remained inside without the broth. Who, then, would be the gainer? "

" She talks too long," growled Tze Hung, the Captain of the Guard.

" So long as justice is served, time is infinite," Wao said. " Girl, have you aught else to tell us? "

" No," Hidden Gold replied, " since I know no more."

Wao dismissed her to the care of a guard.

" Let the other girl be brought forward," he said.

Mountain Stream, he was glad to see, seemed not in any way upset by the situation : he knew her wit to be quick.

" You left your house? " he demanded.

" Even the merchant leaves his house to seek business," she answered.

Wao said : " Yet a merchant may return empty-handed."

She replied : " I fetched the sentry for Hidden Gold. It had been agreed between us."

He realized with growing confidence that Mountain Stream was only advancing information which could not be confirmed by a dead man.

" And you accompanied the sentry to the foot of the steps when he tired of your sister's entertainment? " he asked.

" To the foot of the steps," Mountain Stream replied.

" You did not ascend the steps to the top of the wall? "

" The steps are many," she said, " and unpaid."

"And so you state that you saw the sentry, and no other man?"

"No other man," Mountain Stream answered, and smiled remotely.

Wao, thankful that he had to deal with an intelligent woman, added to his notes, then signed to the guard to take Mountain Stream away.

"I will give my judgment to-morrow," he said. "This is not a case where details and the explanation of those details leap to the brain. The girls are to be kept in such custody as is necessary to prevent their leaving the city, but no more. I do not wish to upset too completely the settled habits of those who are under my care."

He rose as a sign that the audience was ended. The Captain of the Guard looked puzzled, but did not venture to say so. Mountain Stream and Hidden Gold were led back to the house in the Street of Happiness and a *yamen* guard was set at the door. When Mountain Stream spoke to this guard, he readily consented to take up a position inside the house.

.   .   .   .

Wao Hien To sat long that night in his office, preparing the report which he had to submit to the Prefect and to the Provincial Governor. The difficulty about this report was in making it seem the report of a man who was clever enough to have in his mind the facts needed to find the truth of the death of General Wu, but who was at the same time stupid enough not to be able to set these facts in a just order and so derive the key to the puzzle.

Then, again, the report must bear some suggestion of that discontent which would make the Prefect expect to find in Wao a possible collaborator. *From the poor store of my inadequate experience* might do, for it must be known that in his previous rank and dignity his experience had been neither poor nor inadequate. And yet the phrase bore all the seeming of the fashionable over-politeness. . . . He liked the phrase. Not too stupid, or the report would lack that touch of mysterious incentive needed to make the Prefect send for Wao in person : not too clever, or the Prefect would suspect that Wao saw too far into the mechanism of the tragedy . . . *I can find no theory* . . . no, that was too definite —marsh-lights should have no clean-cut edges—*I can find no coherent theory* . . . yes, that conveyed at once the inconveniently pensive and the hollowly pompous. . . .

Much later, Wao folded up his papers with a sigh of satisfaction and went along the passage towards his own room. Jasmine, opening her door a little, signed to him to enter.

"Where is your child?" he asked as soon as he had shut the door.

"Silver Lantern has him," she said. "I thought that I had fed him long enough. She is paid."

"Your mistress still feeds her daughter," he replied.

Jasmine continued : "If she had given her daughter to Silver Lantern for feeding, I should have kept mine. Three children would be too much, even for Silver Lantern. But two is possible."

He sat down.

"Why did you ask me to enter your room?" he demanded.

"I ventured to ask you," she said, "since it seemed that you did not desire to come without invitation. I waited to see, but you did not come. So I asked you."

"And why should you desire me to come to your room?" he asked.

"Why does a woman ask a man?" she countered. "I am not old and ugly . . . yet. I have no one to whom I may talk freely, for the servants have their own interests, and my mistress lives in her own thoughts. I ventured to hope that you, at least, would speak with me. It is lonely here, suckling my child and talking to him and listening to him, while outside I hear the noises of the world and know that it is not right for a woman to have no contact with that world."

He said: "You have learned to talk, I think, since you were taken from your father's house by the late Magistrate Lien."

"I have had practice," she answered, and looked at him.

They sat silently for a space.

Then Jasmine said: "When you came to me, last night, what was the cause of the blood on your clothes, and why were you bearing your sword, and why did you strive to hide from me that you were bearing your sword and that there was blood on your clothes? Did you not wish to trust me?"

While Wao looked fondly at her, he was thinking how she might be silenced. For of all the dangers, a talkative woman is the greatest danger. He put out a hand and undid the buttons of her high collar.

"My clothes are old and shabby," she said. "My late master bought some for me, and my mistress has given me others, but I do not appear as I wish to appear."

"We must consider other clothes for you," he said. "And we must consider, too, what is the accepted method of transferring a girl in your position to the

G

household of another master. Of course, it is not quite the same, but you will remember that the lady who later became the Empress Wu Hao was sent to a nunnery when the Emperor T'ai Tsung died, and taken thence a year later. And Yang Kuei Fei, also, who brought about the ruin of the Bright Emperor Ming Huang, went to a convent before she came to his household. On the other hand . . ."

He stopped speaking, his fingers busy pressing the little cloth knobs through the loops which held them, to temporary freedom.

"I am tired," he complained, yawning.

"I am not tired at all," she replied. "There has been nothing in to-day to make me so. I should not like to go to a nunnery. There are too many other women in a nunnery."

"You are still very young," he said. "Look at you! And any woman of your age should know that the life of a novice in a nunnery is a life of silence save for the chanting of *sutras* and the repetition of prayers."

"My dead master," she replied, "used to call me Little Dusky Tower, when I sat thus, looking down at him."

"*The tallest buildings start from the ground,*" he answered, pinching her.

It would never do, he reflected, to have his energies at instant demand, merely to keep Jasmine quiet. Something must be done about it. And soon.

.   .   .   .

Hibiscus asked no questions. She reflected that, since Wao had been unable to explain to her the reason for his deprivation of rank, any explanation of smaller events than that would give her a partial and no more comforting picture. What the error might be, what the crime could be, that had led to his sudden descent from the dizzy eminence of Emperor's Messenger to the humdrum position of a mere city magistrate, she was wholly unable to imagine.

This unquestioning attitude went further, so that she failed to connect a very obvious and unfeigned yawn when she took him his broth, and passed by without comment the tail of a sentence which he spoke to himself as he laboured in polishing his report—"yes, that should seem stupid enough." For Hibiscus knew that if Wao was tired, there was a good reason for it—if he wished to appear stupid, a better reason. The one might be set down to late hours, the other necessitated, for those who believed him stupid, a blindness and a willingness to credit the obvious, quite out of keeping with any critical intelligence. But then, who of those around them could justly be styled intelligent? Very few, Hibiscus decided. If any. She performed her duties, therefore, more meticulously than ever, determined that whatever Wao might be striving to do, he should not be led to failure by any shortcoming of hers.

Wao, of course, looked questioningly at Hibiscus, and she found it hard not to answer his looked question with a spoken question, but after a little Wao would nod as if in agreement, and she knew that she had acted rightly for the present.

.   .   .   .

Silver Lantern, freed for once from the burden of tending her own child and Jasmine's son, was lighthearted as the two chairs bounced along the road to the north-west, enjoyment in her triangular face.

"This is," she said, "a pleasant sample of the life which is led by rich men's wives, wives who have servants to look after their children, so that they are free to move about the world and know its pleasures." She glanced sideways at Jasmine, in the other chair, reflecting that Jasmine was a stupid girl, in spite of everything. "Look at me," she went on, "Reflect that my husband is the driver of the *yamen* carriage and that I am myself possessed of duties which spread themselves from dawn to dusk. And here I am, riding in a carrying chair along a road, as if I owned it. Do I repine because my husband, as do most husbands, has frequent and suspicious business elsewhere and comes home tired? Do I repine because of things which I cannot see? I should be foolish indeed to allow such things to depress me."

Jasmine answered: "Such infidelities as those at which you hint are the common lot of people in your position. My position is not quite the same, for I bore a man-child to my master, and that gives me rights and privileges. Further, my master was a magistrate. It is true that the honourable Wao Hien To, who has taken my late master's place, does not treat me with the same consideration as I have been accustomed to, although it seems to amount to much the same thing in the end. When a man chooses to climb into a girl's bed, he seems to forget everything but his immediate purpose. And yet I miss the gentle words which made of the night more than a division of time. I have been spoiled."

"Indeed you have been spoiled," Silver Lantern agreed. "You expect too much, and you expect it to be wrapped in the silks of culture rather than the more serviceable grass-cloth of common life. Now my husband treats me in always the same way: I am never in any doubt about his main intentions. You would do better to welcome the honourable Wao Hien To to your bed without filling your mind with a great deal of foolish romance. For romance lives only between the pages of printed books and on the lips of story-tellers in the market-place, and does not ascend the *k'ang* of any but girls of rank and riches." She laughed. "I am always tempted to compare my husband with one of those water-buffaloes which you can see, patiently ploughing, in the rice-fields, under the rein of a boy of not more than ten summers. You have heard the old saying?

> *Silently he splashes amidst the pools*
> *Silently he stands at the end of the furrow.*
> *But, when he sights his mate, his nostrils itch*
> *And ten ropes prove useless to hold him."*

Jasmine agreed: "They have that in common. Where are we going?"

Silver Lantern pointed to the buildings ahead of them, just off the road.

"That is the Convent of Jade Serenity," she said. "It is the wish of our present master that you should stay there for a little while. It is not for us to question his wisdom."

Jasmine cried: "But I do not want to go to the Convent! I hardly thought, when he spoke to me of it a night ago, that he intended it for anything but a jest. How can a girl like myself, who has borne a man-child, be expected to live in a convent, where the women are like dried *lichees*, rough and unpromising in the mouth? How can I . . ."

Silver Lantern interrupted: "You must not raise your voice as you are doing, unless you expect our bearers to be more acquainted with the wishes of your heart than is customary in a magistrate's household. I do not know why our master desires you to enter this convent: I have no further instruction than to take you there and see that you are handed over to the care of the abbess. There is money to be handed over to her for the service of the gods, and after that my duties are over. If you do not yourself know the reason, it is not likely to be other than the obvious reason. Have you been too pressing in your demands?"

"I have asked nothing which is not my right," Jasmine said, more quietly. "Why could he not have said that he did not desire to come to me? Many a woman has sat, lonely, in her own room, waiting for the man who did not come. Could he not have told me that he was tired of me? I should not have troubled him, if I had known. But to send me to a convent...."

"It is an experience for which you will be the wiser," Silver Lantern rejoined. "When it is over, you will come to his bed fresh and exciting. It is like a man giving up his visits to the wine-shop for the sake of greater delight when he returns. And indeed you are fortunate, for it is our master's privilege to do as he wills with us, and he might have sold you into another family. Instead, you will have time to reflect on your short-comings, to devise new pleasures for him. What other purpose could he have?"

But Jasmine was not listening to Silver Lantern. Instead, she was drawing a parallel between herself and the immortal Yang Kuei-fei, that almost legendary beauty who had nearly brought the T'ang dynasty to disaster. Had not Yang Kuei-fei been first in the favour of Prince Shou, the eighteenth son of the Bright Emperor, and had she not from there been taken into the harem of the Bright Emperor himself, to gain his love and become the most powerful lady in the land? Had not she spent a little time in a convent, before the Emperor took her? And was not Jasmine going, it seemed, to a convent? Men were strange, in wanting their women to come to them from the seeming sanctity of a holy place.

The Emperor had first seen the Lady Yang when she had been bathing in the Hwa-Ching Lake. Jasmine pictured herself being lifted by attendants from the tepid water, to see the Emperor himself watching her. Was tepid water provocative? There was no pool in the *yamen* at Kow Loong, there were no attendants to lift her from the water and only half hide her from the Bright Emperor's admiring eyes. But the honourable Wao Hien To had once been great in the present Emperor's service, and might again be great. Power, and domination, and the soft hands of attendants. . . . All would come, in time. Here, now, she was following precedent, in thus entering her convent. The Convent of Jade Serenity. As if she desired serenity!

They had reached the great South gate of the Convent. In the first courtyard she saw the pool: leaving their chairs they crossed the slender bridge on foot. Of course, no one bathed in that pool. Still, it was a good omen. She looked round her at the rooms, guest-chambers, library, lining this first courtyard. Here the women lived. The nun at the entrance-gate: would be a sort of sentry.

" There are three more courts," Silver Lantern was saying, " first the Hall of the Four Great Kings, where the guardians of the four directions stand, then the Precious Hall of the Great Hero, where the Three Precious Ones stand and watch the quietness of the walled serenity, then the Hall of Assembly, where teaching is done. . . ."

Then the abbess came forward to receive them, and Jasmine listened.

"What my name was," the Abbess told her, "is nothing. My name is now Jade Thought. I do my best to deserve this name, for I spend much time thinking about the gods."

"My father's name was Pang I Hok, and mine Jasmine. I was taken into the household of the late Magistrate Lien Kin Wai, and have borne him a son. Now it seems that to have a son to a magistrate is not enough."

The Abbess, in her brown habit, sat motionless. The habit concealed her body. Her eyes were wide and empty, as are the eyes of all who look for too long upon the gods.

"I do not know," she replied, "whether you come of your own will or of the will of another. Money has been sent with you, for the service of the gods, and that gives you a right to our courtesy and to shelter and food under our roof. If you will, you may begin to study in order to become one of us. If you will, you may have one of the guest-rooms and spend your time by yourself. Your man-child is not with you?"

"He is looked after by another," Jasmine said. "For that, I am glad. If you will allow it, my things can be taken to a guest-room, and I will tell you, later, what I desire for my future."

"Your future," the Abbess observed, "may not ultimately be your own affair. But for the moment it shall be as you say."

.   .   .   .

Silver Lantern had set down and helped in arranging Jasmine's few possessions. Then she had gone, and Jasmine was left alone.

The room possessed little but a bed. Light entered from narrow windows, high in the walls. These walls, plastered, had once been red. There was a lamp. Jasmine lit the lamp, for it was nearing evening, and sat down on the edge of the bed. She rose, took two of her own rugs and spread them on the bed before sitting down again.

Somewhere in the buildings voices were chanting a *sutra*. She did not find anything strange in the singing of a Buddhist Sutra in a nunnery which was devoted to the strange gods invented with prolific skill by the followers of Lao Tze; for she knew, or at least guessed, that the accretions of Taoism had led that creed far from its founder's intentions, if indeed he had intended there to be such a creed at all. She realized, as the thought pressed through her mind, how much she had learned, had gained, since Lien had first taken her into his household, a rather stupid girl of fifteen, skilled in no art save that of the broom.

> *The Buddha is kind,*
> *He is ever considerate.*

She felt no desire to join in thus chanting sentiments in which Lien had not believed. Nor, she thought, did her mistress Hibiscus, nor Wao Hien To, who had assumed the magistracy, believe in such sentiments.

> *The world's folly is pain:*
> *The Buddha weeps for it.*

She fell to remembering when Lien had first slept with her: she transferred the memory to Wao, remembered Wao. Men were all the same. What matter was it, should they call a girl Little Dusky Tower, should their hands caress, their voices be the voices of love?

A girl served their purpose, and then was put aside.

> *All the world's sorrow is as nothing:*
> *In Nirvana sorrow is forgotten.*

Did Nirvana, that Heaven where desire is dead, ever come to girls like herself? Desire—wanting things— was too certain, too vital a part of just being alive. Could the empty eyes of the Abbess conceal no desire? Was the Abbess a woman who did not think at all like a woman?

And this bed, which was not hers. . . .

She rose to her feet and went out of the guest-room. At the main entrance a nun sat, waiting. Jasmine turned towards the clear chanting of the interminable *sutra*

> *For each desire we die once:*
> *For many desires we die often.*

Jasmine went into the hall. There was the smell of incense and of many women in a small space. She took up her position at the back of the other worshippers and began to join in the chant.

She found that she knew many of the words.

.   .   .   .

"And why," the Abbess asked, "should the *sutras* of Amida Buddha not be sung here? There are many gods, and we worship all. It is better to worship many gods than to worship none."

Jasmine said: "I know nothing of the gods. My father was a poor man, and we had money only for the kitchen god, on his festival. Even that money had to be taken from the housekeeping money. It is right, as you say, to worship at least one god, but few have the time or money to serve more."

" The women here," the Abbess answered, " are not rich women. They have not the ability to buy rich presents for the gods, to pay others for the serving of these gods. No—these women serve the gods directly. And whether this service be to Amida Buddha, who grants them surcease of desire, or to Kwan Yin, who sometimes gives to them the desired fruit of their desire, matters nothing. They worship—that is all."

" I wanted many things," Jasmine told her, " when I left my father's house to go to the *yamen*. Some of those things were given to me, and some I took for myself, but always their attaining left me with a yet further desire. Then that, too, was fulfilled, to give place to another. I have borne my late master a man-child, and I thought that by so doing I should be honoured amongst women. How was I to know that, when his wife Hibiscus had given him a girl, he would send me away? He did not even know whether my child would be a boy or a girl. Yet he sent me away. And then, while I was away and heard nothing of him, he killed himself. At least, I think that he killed himself. The doctor did not say that he had killed himself, but spoke of the sickness, which killed many in the City of Rams. But I do not believe the doctor. If my master had not killed himself . . ."

" You are concerned with the things of earth," the Abbess said. " You think of the things of earth, of children, of husbands, clothes and food. Now you are amongst us, who think of eternal things, who strive by prayer and by our peculiar life to hedge out from our being these things of earth of which I have spoken. You struggle against yourself, at one moment giving up your desires, at the next clinging to them. Wait.

See whether, in our company, you will lose the desire for desire, or whether, by the opposition of your unschooled nature, your desire will grow and become intolerable. I can do nothing to help you. OM MANI PADMA HOUM."

. . . .

It was ten days, ten days of uncertainty and waiting, before messengers came from the Prefect of Sai Kwan. Tze Hung brought in, with all due ceremony, an officer of the Prefect's *yamen* guard, and Wao, watching Tze Hung sideways, could only account for his lack of interest in the contents of the unrolled scroll by imagining that the purport had already reached him.

The written scroll, after acknowledging Wao's report on the death of General Wu and complimenting the author on its clarity, good judgment and excellent style, suggested that the puzzle could best be resolved by personal consultation between the Prefect and the magistrate who had examined the witnesses. The letter concluded in a maze of erudite allusions to various classical precedents for murder.

Wao did his best to seem puzzled at all this, and even went so far as to ask explanation from Tze Hung on a point of scholarship which he felt was likely to be within Tze Hung's compass. Then he announced his intention of replying on the morrow, commended the Prefect's officer to the care and courteous attention of Tze Hung, and gave a creditable performance in the role of a puzzled magistrate as he paced his office floor with a careful scowl upon his face and an obvious irritation at the interruption caused by simple and reasonable questions on the part of those whose proper business it was to ask those questions.

That night Hibiscus, when she brought him his

broth asked: " Has all gone as well as you expected? "

Wao nodded.

" If I do not say to you why and in what respects I am pleased, I beg of you to believe that there is a reason for my unusual reticence," he answered. " In the business of the Emperor discretion comes before all else. By the way, the girl Jasmine will need some new clothes to comfort her in her present enforced seclusion. Can I trust you to see that she has these clothes? "

Hibiscus reassured him on the point.

In the morning an invitation was brought to Wao from Tung Ho, the rich merchant in Harbour Street, to drink tea for a few idle moments before the sun reached its height.

I am despatching this poor note and a couple of rolls of silk by the hand of my boy Keung, Wao read. *Pray forgive any lack of courtesy in his demeanour, for I have trained him badly. I venture to ask if you would include your Captain of the Guard, Tze Hung, in the invitation, and the officer who, I understand, has come from the Prefect of Sai Kwan. I have a sample of wine from Chefoo for your enjoyment.*

Wao ran his eye over the boy Keung—a weedy youth with a loose mouth. He indicated by a gesture that Keung should lay down the two rolls of silk.

" If you will convey your master's invitation to the Captain of my Guard, and to the guest from Sai Kwan who is in his charge," he said, " I shall be in your debt. Any of my servants will direct you."

Keung did his best to remember to bow. Wao was amused to see that, from his bearing, the contents of the note were not unknown to Keung, and further that it could not, from the boy's manner, come as a surprise to either of the other two. The deduction was an obvious one, and Wao smiled gently with satisfaction as he realized how clearly, to a man used to reading the motives of others, the merchant and the two officers were bound in a common purpose. Wao felt quite convinced that to those three he might add the Prefect of the city of Sai Kwan. He called for his official, visiting robes and summoned the driver, Ssu.

"In the space of time which you will need to harness the horses," he told Ssu, "I shall be ready to pay a ceremonial visit to the merchant Tung Ho, in Harbour Street. Allow those round you, as you prepare the horses, to hear of my intention. And have this silk taken to the Lady Hibiscus."

Ssu bowed and went about his duties. The boy Keung had not returned to Wao's office after taking his message, but Wao felt it to be diplomatic not to call attention to this discourtesy. After all, where a man mixes with an unaccustomed class, he should shew no surprise at the strange behaviour of the members of that class. He fell to remembering what his predecessor, Magistrate Lien Kin Wai, had written of Tung Ho in that long diary which he had left behind him—that Tung Ho was a man whose *high, narrow countenance* and *determined chin* yet allowed him to be kindly-hearted. And, yes . . . Hibiscus had told him how his baby son had died and how the child's mother sorrowed at her loss. Not cultured—ambitious—proud of his wealth's power. . . .

Ssu told Wao that the others had set out independently for Tung Ho's house in Harbour Street, and indeed he found them there when the carriage set him down and Tung Ho came, bowing, to welcome him. Wao was very particular to observe all the prescribed courtesies for two men greeting, ignoring wholly their difference in rank, for he felt that the advantage lay with him if it came to a competition in stereotyped manners, and advantage is advantage, however gained.

The strange officer from Sai Kwan, small and sharp, with a face very like that of a monkey, had seemingly been well educated (for a military man), for he, at least, did not lack formality in his greetings.

"I am a man of the city of Sai Kwan," he began, " whose family name is Ou and his given names Ling-ma. . . ."

As he went through the formula, Wao was irresistibly reminded of one of the historical plays which were becoming fashionable. It was amusing to think of himself and of these other three as actors, playing a part upon a real stage. His own part—a seeming stupidity which would make easier their approach to him on behalf of the Society of Five—was not too easy, and at every turn he was compelled to remind himself not to shew, by a too natural acuteness, that he was aware of their intention. The bait, he reflected, must not seem more intelligent than the fish. But which was the bait, which the fish? Each side was concerned in the deception of the other. . . .

When they had seated themselves at the round table where a fine set of tea-cups spoke of wealth while thin, wafer cakes told equally of a good cook, Tze Hung said: "It is not often that I, in this isolated spot, have the pleasure of meeting others from distant places."

Tung Ho gave a merchant's smile as he filled a cup.

"I am further honoured in that your pleasure is brought to fruit at my poor house," he said.

Ou Ling-ma observed, deprecatingly: "You must not think that my own city of Sai Kwan, though it enjoys the dignity of a Prefecture, has much more to offer than this city of Kow Loong. Each has gates and walls and a Drum Tower and a supply of Blue Houses. . . ."

"Ours are very poor," Wao said, understanding that the conversation was to be steered to the testimony of the girls Mountain Stream and Hidden Gold. "There are only a couple of girls with any pretensions to education, and though I have, on occasion, used them in my *yamen* for the entertainment of my guests, that is as far as I would go." He sighed. "Rumour credits the city of Sai Kwan with far more numerous girls of far greater attainments. It is even said that your excellent Prefect has a party of girls trained for his own delight and that of his fortunate guests. But I imagine that the rumour is due to the desire of each of us to possess fairer and more intelligent women than our neighbours, and has no basis in reality."

Tze Hung looked at Ou Ling-ma as if for permission, and then said: "Rumour, in this instance, does not wholly lie."

Ou Ling-ma took it up: "There is no fascination in apparent evil. I think myself that the secret, the clue to this fascination lies in those in the past who have practised evil, for each of them had qualities wherein they transcended their fellows."

"The tyrant Chou Hsin," Wao said, "is a case in point. Or, rather, the woman who urged him to his tyranny, to his evil, for her sake. The woman Ta Chi. What a name! Essential Dawn! What woman now has such a name? And therefore, linked with corruption lies perfection—her corruption, her perfection."

"When the rebel Wu Wang took her," Ou said, "none of his men would kill her. At last his aged adviser, Tai Kung, shielded his eyes and slew her."

"She must have been very lovely," the merchant Tung Ho observed, feeling it his time to speak.

They looked at him as if he should not know anything of beauty, or of corruption, for a merchant is not qualified to speak of things of the spirit.

Then Wao went on: "For her, Chou Hsin made a feast of venison hanging on trees round a wine lake, with naked youths and girls pursuing."

"Then why the venison and the wine?" the merchant enquired.

"These things are too high for you," Tze Hung told him. "Chou Hsin, the last of the Emperors of the Shang Dynasty, lost his empire for this woman. You—for what would you lose an empire?"

Then they were all silent.

Wao asked: "And one may find these things at the *yamen* of the Prefect of Sai Kwan?"

"Some of them," Ou Ling-ma replied.

Wao rose to his feet.

"I must do myself the disservice of leaving you," he said. "This excellent tea would dictate otherwise, but I am called to my *yamen* and to my office by the memory that I must pen my report to the Prefect."

"You will allow me the privilege of carrying it?" Ou asked.

"My mind is not certain," Wao replied. "It may be that I shall decide to return to Sai Kwan with you, if you will do me the courtesy of shewing me the road. I have not decided, yet, but during the night, when thoughts spring unbidden, I shall decide."

"I shall ask your decision early," Ou Ling-ma said.

Then they parted, ceremoniously, thinking of the girl Essential Dawn, who had destroyed an empire,

H

two thousand four hundred years before. And Wao
did not think at all of the journey which he purposed,
but only of the loveliness of a face which had stayed
the hand even of the executioner.

.   .   .   .

It was midnight, and Hibiscus had been waiting for
him. He lit three more candles.

"You will forgive me for thus shedding light into
the corners of the room," Wao said. "For reasons
which would merely distress you if I were to detail
them to you, I regard dark corners with distaste."

"In corners," Hibiscus replied, "there may lurk
either danger or the thought of danger, and either
should be remote from your mind when you do me
the honour of coming to my room."

He laughed ruefully: "So you understand what I
have not said. That is as well, for I think that it would
add to my sadness if I thought that you were wholly
unaware of my feelings. And yet I cannot tell you
what this danger is or how it has arisen. For you, as
for many women, duty dictates the suppression of
curiosity."

He laid his silken undergarments on a long chest
against the wall.

Hibiscus said: "Even as silk wards off the cold, so a
wife's confidence can ward off the distress of danger.
With me, you may feel that we are one, and that
danger is remote here, where a strong bar across the
doorway excludes the greater world. Here, with me,
you need feel no anxiety: here, with me, you need not
seek to confine warmth within silken garments. And
so, with your mind at rest, we need not waste these
candles." She blew out the three which he had lit.
"Besides, one lamp, where I have set it, will not too

obviously betray my blushes. You would not, surely, have me play the innocent girl at this stage of our companionship and, if I chanced to blush, you might feel less confidence in my ability to comfort and support you. Is the danger immediate—the danger of steel and a sudden stroke—or the more remote yet none the less real danger of men's words and their consequences?"

"I must not say," he answered, coming towards her. "I must not say. But it is permissible to tell you that the danger does not stop with myself—it aims, also, at you. While I am away, it is possible that there may be trouble here, in the city of Kow Loong. I must leave you to make what plans seem good to you, for I cannot foretell what shape the danger may assume or what steps you should take to counter it. Were matters different, I should take you with me to the city of Sai Kwan, whither I go to-morrow, but it is needful to give the impression of unsuspecting confidence, so that you must stay here, living your usual life and turning to the outer world that face of high certainty which is your normal veil."

"Danger," she told him, as she moved over to make room, "is no stranger to me. I am, as I often had occasion to remind my dead husband, a hill-woman, and to such people danger is more natural and more acceptable than to the weaker, protected women of the towns. True, we may lack some of the refinements of spirit which men sometimes seek, but . . ."

"You lack nothing," Wao said, "as you are apparently ready to demonstrate. Set your mind at ease on that score."

"When you ride to-morrow to Sai Kwan, thus," she said, "remember that you need not fear for me, or for your household. Keep to a steady trot, and watch your companions. Ah—I see I need not tell you."

"Your dead husband was fortunate in you," he said. "I do not think that he realized how fortunate he was. To-morrow, as now, I shall ride with my mind free from anxiety, free from foreboding. You know the poem *Men Ride the Same Road?* "

> *Men ride the same road with different purposes:*
> *Their knees jostle while their thoughts diverge.*
> *Visiting Flying Swallow this Spring morning,*
> *You seek promotion, I—delight.*

"Yes, I remember it now," she said. "You cannot seek any further promotion, now, so that I presume you seek delight."

"We both seek delight," he answered. "In that our thoughts do not diverge. But, for me, there is no need of Flying Swallow for the attaining of delight."

.   .   .   .

Early on the next morning, before he dealt with such cases as were pending in the Hall of Audience, Wao sent a message to Ou Ling-ma, saying that he had decided, himself, to go to Sai Kwan shortly after noon, and that he would appreciate Ou Ling-ma's company for the journey. Then Wao gave orders to Ssu, the driver, to have the carriage made ready, and to lead a good horse as well so that Wao might feel a saddle between his knees if the mood took him. He completed the cases in the Hall of Audience, evolving several nice judgments and one punishment peculiarly adapted to deter the criminal. Then he ate his morning rice and arranged for a change of garments to be put in a small case.

Hibiscus said: "So you are going? Take care."

He answered: "A man going into danger is on the alert. You have the harder task—to seem to trust and yet to suspect. I shall rely on you, since I must rely on you. We shall, I hope, cross the Lo Fu ferry before dark, and stay to-night at the Government inn there. The next evening should find us at Sai Kwan. After that, who can foretell?"

"*You seek promotion—I delight,*" she quoted. "But if you fail to gain your promotion, I, too, lose my delight. Still, I know that you will do what is best. Keep warm at night."

They parted without further speaking, and Wao took his seat in the carriage. He drove himself. Ou Ling-ma rode beside the carriage, and Ssu, on the spare horse, followed them at such a distance as to make conversation private.

The road to the north led along high ridges for the first twenty miles, until they should come to the Sam Chun River and the Lo Fu ferry, where the carriage would have to be persuaded on to the deck of a boat at the flimsy wharf. All other streams on the way were fordable, when they should drop down from the ridges towards the lower ground.

Ou Ling-ma sang to himself a song of the wars against the Hu barbarians, to whose slanting glance the poet Tu Fu compares the eye of a painted falcon. He himself was not unlike a small falcon with the face of a monkey, predatory, fierce.

He sang:

> *The soldier stands alone upon the fortress wall,*
> *Bound to his life by not desiring death:*
> *Below, about, five rivers circle,*
> *And he remembers the fish in the stream*
> *At home, where the garden ended.*

Alas, that peace at home means war abroad:
Alas, that lives should purchase other lives.
For always to each good there is another evil—
The fisherman congratulates himself on his catch,
But the fish is not contented.

"You are fortunate in the quality of your voice," Wao said, "and the matter of your song interests me also. What were these five rivers which reminded your soldier of the stream at the bottom of his garden at home?"

Ou replied at once: "The Wu, the Wei, the Han, the Chou and the Li. Did you not know?"

"You have them by heart, as in a ritual one has lines by heart," Wao said. "And indeed the words of your song are, in some ways, not unlike the words of a ritual. *The fish is not contented*, for instance, or *to each good there is another evil*. One might almost imagine these lines chanted by men who had something in common."

Ou answered: "All men who sing the same song have in common at least a knowledge of the words of that song. How otherwise could they sing?"

Wao quoted from the Master, Confucius: "*Singing, at the foot of the rain-altars. . . .* I think that I shall stretch my legs upon my horse. You will forgive me if I call the driver?"

When Wao had mounted and ridden off with Ou, while the carriage dropped to the rear, they rode for some while without speaking further. Then, at a narrow place, their knees met.

"*Men ride the same road*," Ou murmured at the end of his apology. "One has indeed need of Flying Swallow here, for in the air there is more space for manœuvring." And Wao felt almost certain that in Ou's voice there was laughter and a question. He decided that, last night, he and Hibiscus could not have been speaking in such privacy as they had imagined, and was glad that he had said nothing, then, which might have had reference to the Society of Five. He had been quite general, he thought, in all that he had said to his wife.

"Thoughts jostle, also," he replied equivocally, and Ou thought about this for some time before, in his reply, he took the safe course of a quotation from Li Po, which could have had no possible bearing on any-thing. . . .

   .   .   .   .

They came to the Lo Fu ferry at dusk, when the ferryman was about to go home for the night to his hovel on the far bank. When Ou Ling-ma shouted for him, he came grumbling.

"It is almost too late for crossing," he cried as he got into the boat.

Wao observed to Ou Ling-ma: "'Almost' lacks the precision of 'quite'. I am reminded of an incident at this actual ferry, in the days of the Empress Wu, of the Han dynasty."

Ou replied: "I have not had time to study the histories as I should have wished."

Wao said: "After the Emperor's ambassador had been assassinated, you will remember, by the ministers of the King of Nan Yueh, as this neighbourhood was then called, and the Emperor had ordered the conquest of Nan Yueh, so that the provinces of Kwangtung, Kwangsi, and Tongking came into the Empire, those men who first came, under the Emperor's power, to settle here, were men of action and courage, men of instant decision. And their women, too, put fear behind them. Such were the lovers Wei Sung and Breath under the Wistaria."

" I shall be delighted to hear," Ou said. The ferryman had persuaded his boat alongside the little wharf. Wao saw him make fast. The long rope running upstream to a stake in the corner of the south bank sagged into the water. Ssu manœuvred the carriage on to the boat, the ferryman cast off and with his long sweep kept the boat's head towards the north bank. The long rope from the bows was now taut. " It is a terrifying thought," Ou went on, " that if the ferryman lost his sweep, the boat would swing idly in midstream."

" The application of what you have observed will appear also in my story," Wao replied. " Well, these two, Wei Sung (who was the son of the new Prefect at Sai Kwan) and his lover, Breath under the Wistaria, determined to run away from the eye of the Prefect of Sai Kwan and live in the City of Kow Loong, from which we have just come. But you will be aware of the opposition which facts often exhibit towards the ideals and wishes of men, for after the two of them, in one of the Prefect's carriages, had evaded the sound of pursuit, as far as the ferry, they heard, just as they stepped aboard, the calling of men over the rise yonder, and knew that before long they would be intercepted."

" A lamentable situation," Ou dutifully supplied. " May one enquire the outcome? "

" In order to understand the outcome," Wao observed, " you must remember that the time of which I speak was the period of the Han dynasty, not long after the Warring States. In those days men possessed courage, as I have said, over the mean. Well, Wei Sung saw his hopes vanishing and his very life in peril. He acted

at once. No sooner had he stepped ashore on the south
bank than he bound the ferryman's hands behind him,
after taking his outer garments, and ordered his lover,
Breath under the Wistaria, to take the ferryman out of
sight into a wood near by. He gave her his knife as an
instrument of persuasion, and she obeyed him at once.
He slipped into the ragged outer garments of the now
absent ferryman and took his place upon the boat.
Soon, almost before the girl and the ferryman were
out of sight, the Prefect himself arrived on this, the
north bank, with three soldiers of his guard. They
called for the ferry, and Wei Sung worked it over the
stream towards them, not too fast. They hastened
aboard, with their horses and bade him cast off. The
Prefect, a fortunately aloof man, ordered his guards to
make enquiries as to any passengers lately passed over
the ferry, and Wei Sung mumbled enough for the
guard to recognize that their quarry had preceded them.
At the south wharf he stepped ashore on the pretence
of making fast, taking his sweep with him, and pushed
the ferryboat back into the stream. As you yourself
have pointed out, a boat thus released reaches midstream and remains there."

"The Prefect, although he was the man's father,"
Ou asked, "did not recognize him?"

"No," Wao replied. "The Prefect was, as I have
said, an aloof man, conducting his conversation through
subordinates, and the subordinates had not had any
intimate knowledge of or acquaintance with the son.
No—it was as I have said."

The ferryman had brought the ferry to the wharf.
They mounted their horses, Ssu followed with the
carriage, and the two men continued talking.

"And then?" Ou demanded. "The tale is but half

ended. We are left with the Prefect and his men
swinging idly in midstream and the other actors somewhere on the south bank. I should be grateful if you
would allay my uncertainty about their fate."

"First, the Prefect, then," Wao said. "Strangely
enough, neither he nor any of his three men could
swim. And, while it is easy to persuade a horse down
a slope into water, it is quite a different matter to convince a horse of the safety of a leap from the deck of a
ferry into a flowing stream. They did succeed in pushing one horse over, but in the water the rider fell off
and was pulled back on board, while the animal, sen-
sibly enough, reached the north bank and set off without a second thought for his stables at Sai Kwan."

"Horses are wise animals," Ou said, patting his
own. "And then?"

Wao went on: "Wei Sung soon caught up with the
girl and the ferryman. He took them to a remote
village, one of those perched amidst the precarious hills
through which we have just passed, a village having, as
you well know, practically no connection with the outside world. Here he lived in a small house (for he was
not without funds) and a couple of servants. The
ferryman, blindfolded, was taken back almost to the
river bank, and then released. He found the boat and
its passengers still in midstream, and after some uncertainty as to the wisdom of his action, pulled it into
the bank by hauling on the single rope to the bows.
Fortunately the Prefect was a man with a sense of
humour, despite his aloofness, and when the ferryman
shewed him where the spare sweep was hidden in the
bottom of the boat, the Prefect roared his amusement.
He rewarded the ferryman for his wisdom and, when
they had recrossed the stream, the Prefect and his men

rode back to Sai Kwan—except for the man who had fallen off in midstream, who was very reasonably made to walk. Thus his clothes were dried by the exercise, and he had plenty of time to reflect on the unwisdom of an unstable seat even under damping circumstances.

"At Sai Kwan the Prefect published an order that his son and the girl should meet with no further opposition to their marriage, and news of this reached the village where the son was living, some six weeks after the episode. Wei Sung returned to Sai Kwan, and his father, true to his word, sent go-betweens to the girl's family. The marriage took place two months later, just in time to make certain that the bride suffered no serious inconvenience through bouncing in the marriage-chair as she was carried to her husband's house. They say that she exhibited a most maidenly modesty when she first came, formally, face to face with the husband with whom she had lived for six weeks, and all the relations were extremely pleased with her."

"A charming story," Ou Ling-ma admitted. "Here we are at the Government Inn. I trust that they have good food available, for I feel hunger."

"That should have been arranged," Wao replied, "since they must have known that you were returning to the city of Sai Kwan."

Then the two men parted, and Ssu made arrangements for sleeping in the care of the horses. Later, the innkeeper served a meal which shewed, indeed, that he had expected to have to serve it, and Wao felt very comfortably satisfied when he was shewn to his room and made preparations for sleeping.

.   .   .   .

Wao stirred under his rugs in the intense dark of midnight and was instantly awake, listening to the soft sounds made by the man searching his belongings. In the stealthy quiet, Wao's ears reported accurately the whisper of each fold of cloth, the rustle of silk. He could hear his letter from the Prefect being unrolled, and rolled up again. Then the sound of a door opening and shutting. Clearly the letter had been taken away for reading. Sure enough, after a little the door opened and the letter was replaced.

There was no purpose in action. If danger had threatened, the threat would have been made real at some other, more convenient time and opportunity. This could only be a reconnaissance, an attempt to discover whether Wao suspected the activities of the Five, their bearing on the death of General Wu, or whether he was really the rather dull, formal, unimaginative official of his pretence. And since the luggage which he had brought with him contained no evidence one way or the other, Wao was confident that, in the light of the morrow, the problem would be, for the estimable Ou Ling-ma, as wholly unsolved as it had been yesterday.

He composed himself to sleep again, and in the room the rustle of search proceeded, unheard.

.   .   .   .   .   .

The morning opened bright and clear when, after an early meal, Wao and Ou Ling-ma started on the last stage to Sai Kwan. It was, for Wao Hien To a day of freedom, for clearly he was intended to reach the Prefect's *yamen* in safety. Why, otherwise, the uneconomic course of allowing him to reach Lo Fu unharmed? The road ran between lower hills now, stream-intersected, with cultivation on the slopes and the pitiful devices for irrigation of terrace after terrace by the power of a man's muscles alone. The life-blood of the rice was tilted, splashed and carried up the slope, to flow sluggishly back to the lower levels. Then the whole process had to be repeated. On this rested the lives of the men and women who could be seen working in these paddy-fields—their monotonous, uneventful lives, with no intrigues to give an appetite for those lives, no sudden, imminent sword-danger to threaten and excite. Wao decided that he could never make a successful cultivator of the land, fighting only the elements, in a physically safe civilization whose roots seemed secure under tier after tier of officialdom. And, even had these countrymen known that there was a conspiracy afoot to shake those roots, a conspiracy to overthrow the dynasty and supplant it—by what? He did not know—the greatness of such events would have seemed to these men so far beyond their caring or their compass that they would stolidly go on with the eternal sequence of seed, planting out, growth, ripening and harvest, convinced that the identity of empires mattered little to men whose sole concern was with the rice-plant and the cycle of the seasons.

Ou Ling-ma, though he looked puzzled at a side-glance, talked animatedly as he rode beside the carriage in which Wao had again taken his place. Ssu was a lighter man, and the horse might, conceivably, need to be fresh, untired by the bearing of Wao's greater weight and dignity.

"A good horse knows the status of the rider," Wao said. "As, in the old days, the Master, Confucius, would come to Court apparently weighed down with the responsibilities of office, so that his sleeves touched the ground, so a horse, if his rider be important, will sweat more freely than a horse carrying a lesser man."

Ou replied: "You have said two things at which, if a man wished to cavil, he might cavil."

Wao said: "Tell me."

"The first was in comparing the Master, Confucius, to a horse," Ou answered. "That does not shew a proper respect."

After they had ridden on for a little longer, Wao made his reply.

"By comparing a horse to the Master," he said, "I compliment the horse. What is your second error?"

"It is," Ou replied, "that even granting the horse's ability to discern the rank of the man upon his saddle, the horse cannot know more than the immediate worth of his rider, so that he should sweat as freely for a groom who has stolen my clothes, as for me myself wearing them."

"To suggest a state of society," Wao answered, "in which your groom could steal your clothes, is to strike at society's roots. For even to imagine it makes it possible, and under the Emperor it could not be possible. Therefore your suggestion savours of political indelicacy. I do not approve of indelicacy."

They rode for an hour without speaking further.

Then Ou said: "I appreciate your meaning, when you speak of political indelicacy. I must apologize for my behaviour, since I am in a sense your host. Let us forget it."

Wao replied: "Willingly. And, since you have yourself suggested that on you in part devolve the duties of host, will you not discharge those duties by retaliating with a story? The stretches from river-bed to river-bed tend, at length, to monotony, and there is no solvent of monotony as efficacious as a well-told tale."

"You are assuming," Ou told him, "that I shall be

able to tell a tale well. It will be hard to achieve the standard of your own ferry story, but I will try. I shall choose, if you are agreeable, the story of General Ssu-ma Ting and the poet, Wang Hsi. You have heard it?"

"Not to my knowledge," Wao answered. "Not to my knowledge."

Ou began: "Wang Hsi, like most of the poets in the period following the T'ang dynasty, wrote much of nature. He had a keen eye and ear for detail. You remember his *Day of Little Rain*?

> *The rain falls at first gently, then steadily.*
> *The light changes to a translucency.*
> *Dusty earth turns to brown, then to dark brown,*
> *As the sound of dropping breaks the silence.*
> *Familiar, trodden soil, crumbling underfoot,*
> *Now takes on the terrible threat of growth,*
> *As if forests were stirring to their birth,*
> *Promising drowning in a green sea.*
> *The sides of houses, below the eaves,*
> *Darken as streaks of rain spread:*
> *The first trickle runs through the bamboo pipe*
> *Into the great water-jar below it.*
> *A broken cloud moves over the grey heaven*
> *And the rain stops suddenly.*
> *The rain-bird, too late for my comfort,*
> *Rings his clear note across the trees.*

I have always thought it a singularly exact piece of portraiture."

Wao agreed: "It rings with the rain-bird's note."

Ou continued: "At that time, as you will know, there was much fighting in the country, between generals with their own armies and other generals with other armies. It so happened that Wang Hsi, who had been the holder of a Prefecture, had so endeared himself to the men of the garrison that they elected to fight under his leadership rather than that of any general however skilled in war. General Ssu-ma Ting, on the other hand, led an independent band. These two bodies of men were encamped on opposite sides of a river valley, and it was clear to any man who cared to look, that a battle was inevitable. In fact, since both General Ssu-ma Ting and Wang Hsi were inclined to courtesies more than is usual, they had sent emissaries to each other and agreed on the morning of a certain day for the battle."

"An eminently cultured arrangement," Wao observed. "Those days were, indeed, refined." He sighed. "And yet, how wise are we in attaching a name to a virtue? Nevertheless, I pray that you will continue your tale."

Ou said: "Shortly after midnight it started to rain. General Ssu-ma Ting did all the things and issued all the commands suitable for the occasion: bows were carefully encased, the war-chariots had a thin covering of sand on the floor to give wet feet a grip: sword-hilts were bound in straw. So well, so thoroughly, did the General take these wet-weather precautions that at dawn, when the long line of battle drew up on the ridge above the river valley, his men had suffered almost no loss of fighting power. The captains were confident: the drivers of the chariots encouraged their animals while they wove them small, conical hats of straw: the archers cast calculating eyes at the sky, estimating the chances of a break in the downpour. But Wang Hsi . . ."

"Wang Hsi was a poet," Wao mused, aloud.

Ou continued: "Wang Hsi was, as you have recalled, a poet. He had spent the night sitting in his

tent wrapped in extra clothing, for he expected a cold.
He had found, by experience, that the exchange of his
own warm quarters at home for the draughts and dis-
comforts of an outdoor life invariably brought on a
cold. And, surely enough, at about midnight, just as
the rain began, Wang Hsi sneezed. He wished himself good fortune and began to plan a poem about rain.
It was, indeed, that poem which I have just recited to
you. So that, just after dawn came with the arranged
hour for battle, he found himself with a completed
poem, a freely running nose, and an army not in the
least fitted for combat. When he realized this, it was
already too late to take any useful action. He spent a
moment or two reflecting that a poem might, if the
poem were good enough, be more than a compensation
for a lost battle, and gave the order to form battle-
line."

"You would not claim courage for him?" Wao
asked.

"The word *courage* has no meaning, where poets are
in question," Ou told him. "Well, Wang Hsi's men
moved forward, disconsolately, to a lost battle. They
were even too depressed to remember their families at
home. They came to the edge of the ridge on their
side of the river, to find that General Ssu-ma Ting's
troops, punctual and precise, had already crossed the
river and were advancing up towards the wet, dispirited
troops of Wang Hsi. Now the latter, being a poet and
therefore sensitive to social atmospheres, knew, even at
that distance, how rage must be in the mind of General
Ssu-ma Ting at the delay in keeping an appointment.
Desirous, therefore, of explaining how a poem had
diverted his attention, Wang Hsi waved the paper in
the direction of General Ssu-ma Ting, whom he could

I

dimly discern through the falling water. The troops nearest to Wang Hsi, seeing this gesture, followed by another in which he wiped his streaming nose, took it to be the signal for the advance. The drums beat— the soaking troops, anxious to express their feelings, rushed forward towards the enemy who was even now struggling up the ridge on the wet and slippery nearer slopes. It was a massacre. The bowmen of Wang Hsi used their wet strings to strangle their opponents: the slithering chariots, moving down-hill, had all the advantages of position and no possibility of manly hesitation: the foot-soldiers, sliding down on their heels, bore down their enemies by sheer momentum, and it was not long before Wang Hsi, on the river bank, received the surrender of General Ssu-ma Ting, and the few of his force who had survived the on-slaught. After the surrender they went through the poem together, and General Ssu-ma Ting, who had received some classical education in his youth, sug-gested 'steadily' in the first line, instead of 'heavily', which Wang Hsi had at first written. The emendation was made (though the ink ran a little) and the sun came out. That is the story."

"I am edified by your tale," Wao said. "It has both point and moral, and the possession of both is rare."

They rode on together in great content, for greatly different reasons. Ou Ling-ma rejoiced because he felt that his story stood higher than that of Wao. Further, its merit had been openly acknowledged.

But Wao Hien To, as they rode even farther past the point where the road had forked to the City of Rams, realized with profound relief and pleasure that, if a man is telling a story as well as Ou Ling-ma had been, he has no attention left for such details as a sealed

letter pushed over into the road from the back of the
carriage by Wao's foot while he listened with obvious
ear; or Ssu's stopping to pick up the letter while pre-
tending to examine his horse's hoof; or the furtive way
in which Ssu had dropped further to the rear as they
came towards the fork and had then taken his way
towards the City of Rams with the letter which Wao
had written to the Governor. This letter reported the
state of the conspiracy and asked for the support of
such bodies of trustworthy men from the Governor's
forces as should make resistance seem futile except in
the eyes of those who had nothing further to lose. . . .

At last, when Wao felt that it could not further be
waited for, the question was put.

"We seem to have outdistanced your servant," Ou
observed. "Shall we call a short halt for him to come
level?"

> "*When they brought him a sword, he weighed it in*
> *his hands:*
> *When they brought him a horse, he stood and*
> *looked at it.*"

Wao quoted, and reined in.

Ou replied: "The Marquess of Chou, was it not?
You honour your servant."

"Parallels do not necessarily constitute honour,"
Wao said. "Maybe his horse picked up a stone. Let
us wait, as you suggest." Then he laughed. "If you
are too orthodox to hear with pleasure the aphorism of
the Master, Lao Tze, to the effect that *he who does
nothing will not be disappointed*, perhaps the cor-
responding observation of Confucius, that *the seasons
revolve but God does not intervene*, will be nearer your
heart. Let us rest." He threw the reins over a bush,

and the horse started to graze. Ou tied his reins more carefully, and soon both men were sitting by the side of the road on a convenient bank.

"I fear," Wao said, "that I have been over-indulgent with my driver. Confucius told us that servants take advantage of kindness, and our modern experience confirms his view."

Ou replied: "Yes. I have found it so myself. I do not wish to waste time, for we shall arrive at Sai Kwan towards nightfall if we move on now, whereas much waiting or a going back to find the explanation of your driver's absence would bring us to the last few *li* of road in the dark."

"Provided that you *know the road*," Wao quoted, "all will be well. There can be no unforeseen dangers from robbers in the neighbourhood of the Prefect's very *yamen*. So we can wait, at least for as long as it takes a man to eat a large bowl of rice."

"Do not remind me of my empty stomach," Ou returned. "Exercise invariably hungers me."

As they talked together, Wao began to feel more certain that his scheme had worked, that Ssu, riding at his discreet distance, had seen the letter which Wao had written early in the morning at the ferry inn, had stopped, picked it up and then, slowing, taken the road for the City of Rams. Wao had not been completely certain until his room had been searched: that, and an undertone of amused tolerance in Ou's attitude, had now confirmed the feeling that he was being carefully escorted to Sai Kwan merely in order to discover whether he had, in fact, an inconvenient inkling of the plot wherein the Society of the Five was now immersed. He realized how little he knew of the plot beyond its bare existence, and how much he must find out, by instinctive and intuitive methods, before the arrival of the Government forces three days from now. . . .

Ou was saying: "Your driver must have met with some misfortune. Would it not be wise to return?"

Wao used Ou's own argument: "But if we return as you yourself have pointed out we shall certainly reach Sai Kwan only at an inconveniently late hour. . . . It would be better, I feel, to leave a message with the officer in the next village . . ." He left the sentence in the air. "But it is wholly for you to decide."

Ou Ling-ma was clearly more perturbed at the disappearance of Ssu than the mere loss of a servant could excuse. He still hesitated.

"I am uncertain," he said. "It would be inconvenient for you to lose the services of your man, even temporarily."

"The Prefect, I am sure," Wao replied with as great heartiness as he could achieve, "will have many servants. Surely he can lend me one, for a few hours, until this wooden-head appears? I can hardly . . ."

Ou made up his mind.

"With your consent, we shall proceed," he said. "Too late an hour for our passage through the narrow paths would be worse than the temporary loss of your servant. If you will be so good . . ."

They untethered their horses and took up the road. As Wao heard the wheels taking him momentarily farther from the fork to the City of Rams, he sighed with relief. Ssu and the letter should, by now, be well out of reach of any intercepting messenger who might be sent from Sai Kwan. . . . His relief was such that he sang under his breath Tung-p'o's Song of the Cranes.

.   .   .   .   .   .

After darkness has fallen, any city takes on a magic seeming. Approaching as he did towards the South Gate of Sai Kwan City, Wao had little attention to spare from the task of keeping the wheels of his carriage in safe tracks, but even so he was half aware of the great walls as a rising blackness against the already black sky, of the Gate House with its three tiers of winged roofs, standing above the walls, of the remote sound of voices and life which flowed over the walls towards him as he drove slowly after Ou Ling-ma along the last of the narrow causeway between occasional rice-fields and the stunted dwellings of those who lived outside the protection of the city because they had nothing worth protecting. An occasional light glimmered in these mean hovels: sometimes these lights were reflected in the open water-channels bordering the causeway. His imagination, or such of it as he could release from his task, was compelled to supply a picture of the packed life inside the city: only in imagination's mirror could he see the narrow streets, tilted roof after tilted roof, houses leaning together as if to speak in the darkness, the streets erring a little from the straight ideal, as the whim of their builders had set them, and glittering above this turmoil of roofs the two hills whereon, he had heard, the mansions of the Hsia family and the *yamen* of the Prefect stood, foci of all the city's activities. So could the sight have been had he been standing on the wall's top instead of intricately threading a worn causeway towards the great, closed gates of the city; so could the sight have seemed had not everything been enfolded in the velvet cloth of the darkness.

They halted on the wide flagged area in front of the gates. Wao noticed with surprise that there was but one great gate in use, for the smaller entrances beside it, designed for men unencumbered by carriages, had been built in, solidly, with the same huge blocks as faced the wall itself.

Ou Ling-ma called to the sentry above the entrance, and soon Wao heard the sound of the sentry's voice telling the Captain of the Guard that travellers waited outside. A few men came from the nearer hovels beside the causeway, drawn by the attraction of incident, gathered to gape.

"Gates are not opened after sunset," Ou explained. "There will have been special orders for our admittance."

"It is ever a source of danger to admit unknown men in the dark," Wao agreed, deliberately sententious. "It is better to exclude a friend than to admit a foe."

Ou glanced sharply at him, but Wao seemed to be possessed of a childish interest in the mechanism of the gates, which now swung slightly apart, outwards, in the centre. The Captain of the Prefect's Guard passed out, with two men, to the paved emptiness where the little group of two seemed isolated figures of porcelain beside the animals and the motionless carriage.

The Captain of the Guard introduced himself in the accustomed manner, and after Wao had replied with suitable or rather more than suitable courtesies, Ou Ling-ma explained: "Our friend's servant fell behind at some time or other when we were busied with agreeable conversation, and we waited some while for him to reappear. It would seem that he must have suffered some accident. I left word at the posts for him to be speeded on his way."

Wao observed: "Sir, I should take it to be a very welcome courtesy if, on his arrival, you would have him bring the horse under the gates and stable it with care and attention, for the animal is a red horse, one of the descendants of those horses which Pan Yu brought from Balt many years ago, and such horses are delicate. They have great hearts and sweat blood. But they need constant care and forethought. When the Master, at the burning down of the stables at Lu, *did not enquire about the horses*, it was not about such horses as mine that he did not enquire." Then he laughed. "Of course, such means as you adopt to impress my servant with the offence of late arrival constitutes another matter. All that I have the temerity to ask is that the horse shall not suffer for my servant's fault."

Both the Captain of the Guard and Ou Ling-ma did their best to set his mind at ease. One half of the gate was opened and the carriage driven in. Wao followed to the stables and saw that the grooms were careful of the comfort of the horse. Then, with Ou and two men from the guard they walked up the main street to the Prefect's *yamen*.

Now, so soon after nightfall, Wao would have expected the streets to be full of men going about those first pleasures which, with the sun falling, succeed the day's labour. Men with lanterns should have been about their purposes, women without lanterns about theirs. The shops and stalls should still have held late customers sitting in argument over a price under the flicker of dim oil lamps: eating-shops should have been noisy with those who distrusted the cooking of their wives or wished to keep those wives in ignorance of their present company.

But it might have been midnight, for the stalls had been taken back into the shops and the front doors barred. The smeary surface of the street stretched untenanted from house to opposite house: only a starving cat prowled.

"They were ordered to be in their houses by sundown," Ou explained, sensing Wao's wonder. "On at least one day in each month this is done. The Prefect feels that such discipline is desirable, and so, expecting your arrival, he issued the order for to-night. It makes government easier if, occasionally, orders are given which have no rational explanation so that the people learn to obey, without thinking, these orders which, at other times, may have a reason and an origin which makes obedience really necessary. You follow?"

Wao said: "I see the happening, and I hear your reasons. As yet, the two are not married in my mind. They will be. At present I am tired, and the hollow behind my stomach calls loudly, imperatively, for food. Once that need is satisfied, my mind may resume its function. Do not, I pray, press me to think."

The other laughed: "It will soon be over. Inside the *yamen* doubtless cooks curse our tardiness, but what is that to us? You will, I hope, find the Prefect's entertainment a full compensation for your present discomfort. Between ourselves, I feel the same myself. Let us wear a brave front."

At the *yamen*, under the gate-house, all was lights and movement. They were received, ushered, welcomed, conducted. The Prefect, himself, standing at the door of his own living-quarters, came half-way forward to meet them. Wao retired, bowed, advanced. The Prefect retired a little less far, bowed and advanced. Ou Ling-ma introduced them.

"You come to my poor house," the Prefect said, "at a fortunate time. Only this morning one of my cooks returned from the City of Rams, where he had been sent in order to learn to cook roast pigeon in the manner peculiar to the Pin Kun eating-shop in that city. So I trust that you will not be too weary to appreciate the dish."

Wao included Ou Ling-ma in his gesture. "No man, I feel," he replied, "should be too tired for roast pigeon. But I fear that our tardy coming will have upset your cook."

He had never seen a man as large as the Prefect. To be both tall and fat is a blessing given to few, and Wao spent a moment to reflect on the unequal distribution of fortune.

"My cook has been starting pigeons for the last hour," the Prefect said. "Thus one bird, at least, will merit your approval, I trust. Come—we talk while your stomach thunders." He led the way to the door of the reception-hall and stood aside for Wao. They jostled for last place and finally, with difficulty, managed to enter together.

A small, round table had been set with three Kiangsu porcelain stools at what seemed to be the centre of a great cavern of darkness. A single lamp stood on a tripod behind each stool. Far away, behind a carved lattice, there was the noise of cooks : at the diametrically opposite pole, behind a similar lattice, dimly lit by a few paper lanterns, Wao could just make out the quick movements of women, hear the whispered word. Somewhere above the little table, lost in the mysteries of the invisible roof-timbers, a whispering echo dwelt. It was as though the three men, now seated round the table, were surrounded by a warm but dimly translucent curtain of black cushions, in obscurity.

The Prefect, his voice matching his size, made only one concession to formality. He raised the tiny wine-

cup which had been filled to brimming, and said:
"Drink up, so that you may, without further dallying,
start on the meal which you have so well earned. We
can talk afterwards: first eat."

"First feed the people, then educate them," Wao
quoted, and the Prefect nodded agreement at this
application of the Master's wisdom.

Ou Ling-ma said nothing. They began the meal.

. . . .

It was four courses later, and chopsticks had been
exchanged for flat-bottomed porcelain spoons in honour
of the roast pigeon. Wao was astonished to discover
that the meat, indeed, could be taken in a small ladle,
and that without the pigeons shewing signs of overlong
hanging. He belched politely.

"It is a wonder to me," he observed, "that these
usually recalcitrant birds have so yielded themselves to
this mastery of your cook. I do not wonder at your
prescience in sending him to learn the method at the
Pin Kun eating-house."

The Prefect smiled. "The cook's skill is only half
the tale," he said. "Like yourself, I was formerly
under the illusion that solely on the nature of the
sauces, the frequency of the basting, the timing of the
roast and the intensity of the fire, rested the quality of
the result. But I was in error."

"I wait instruction," Wao replied. "Even if the
whole process be not explained and set down on permanent paper, it would be interesting to learn this
further clue. I imagine that, by giving it to me, you
do not wholly betray this secret. What is the explanation?"

"A simple explanation," the Prefect admitted.
"But one which I should not have been prepared to

hear without surprise. Eat your last spoonful, and I will tell you." He watched, with considerate care, until Wao was ready. Then he finished: " The pigeons must be capons."

"Capons!" Wao cried. "But who ever heard . . ."

"It is a delicate operation, a skilled operation," the Prefect told him. "But, in view of this surprising discovery, my cook had the intelligence to buy (at an exorbitant price) and bring back with him a whole crate of pigeons thus converted into a suitable condition for roasting. Is it not essentially amusing that the thing should be so simple? I laughed when I was told of it."

Wao agreed: "It has the elements of humour, even to me. Perhaps you find it even greater humour than I do."

The Prefect looked sharply at him and raised his wine-cup.

"Drink up!" he said.

Ou Ling-ma drank with them. "This is the fifth course," he observed, apparently for no reason. But both he and the Prefect watched Wao and awaited his answer.

Wao said: "If you count the wine, it is the sixth. But I have been too tired with my journey to be certain how many courses I have enjoyed. Now my fatigue seems to be passing, and even as I speak I begin to find in the idea of a caponed pigeon for the fifth course (for I must defer to your judgment) more humour than I did upon hearing of this device for ensuring the remarkable tenderness of the birds. By the way, I beg of you to compliment the cook for me on the excellent results of his journey to the Pin Kun."

The other two looked puzzled for an instant. Then the Prefect continued.

"In view of your journey," he said, "I had not arranged any great entertainment for you to-night. You will, I trust, favour us with your company for a few days? To-morrow, perhaps, we might enjoy together our poor local re-enacting of one of the ancient ceremonies. To-night—just a few songs."

"I shall be enchanted to hear them," Wao replied. "They will, with their subtle cadences, make sleep the sweeter."

Ou Ling-ma rose to his feet on the Prefect's nod.

"He arranges these things," the Prefect told Wao.

"He has shewn himself a proficient horseman," Wao rejoined. "If he has also abilities where music is concerned, he is indeed gifted."

"You shall see," the Prefect answered. The pigeons were taken away, to be succeeded by bamboo-shoots, dried mushrooms and Kiangsu rice.

.   .   .   .

"When I first heard of your coming," the Prefect said, "I had the idea of inviting a young acquaintance to meet you—one Hsia Nan-p'o. He lives in the Hsia *yamen* over yonder. His father has *gone to the West*, so that his mother rules. There is also in the same *yamen* an aunt, Mistress Hsia, whose husband was the honourable Sung Tsui, the late Governor of the City of Rams."

"I should have been delighted to meet the young man," Wao replied, and waited.

The Prefect continued: "But then I thought that you would be tired after your journey hither, and decided to defer the pleasure of his company until to-morrow at least. Then I purpose as entertainment my own poor stylized reproduction of the early ceremonies of the *hills and rivers*, when the young people from the villages met for the Spring matings, boys and girls seeing for the first time those from other villages than their own, going through the primitive ceremonial of choice, singing songs in alternate lines, giving each other tokens. The prospect interests you?"

Wao replied: "It does. Such a prospect should interest any man with a claim to culture, however poor. I heard, when I was last in the City of Rams, before the late sickness, that Governor Sung Tsui himself was well informed about ancient ceremonies, and it will be instructive to discover whether his nephew, of whom you have just spoken, retains any of the knowledge of his late uncle."

The Prefect nodded appreciation of the point.

"To-night, however," he said, "there will be five dancers singing songs, perhaps, or performing dances which have no such long and (to us) disreputable history. These five shall have instructions to soothe, rather than to stimulate. I shall, of course, place a couple of them at your disposal, later, when you retire. You shall make your own choice."

Wao knew that he was expected to take this as ordinary courtesy. He returned to their earlier subject.

"This young man Hsia," he asked, "is cultured?"

But, being measurably human, he did not hear the answer, if answer there were, nor did he see whether by gesture or attitude the Prefect had heard him. For, as Wao now leaned forward on his porcelain stool, turning away from the table on which the food still steamed, he could watch the five girls who had now come through the lattice at the women's end of the hall and now stood, motionless and in line, before them. Each girl wore a skirt of the palest green silk, sweeping the floor. On this silk the cloud-watermarks gave the impression of a deeper green. A loose orange-brown jacket hung rather low, in easy folds. Above, a yoke of the same orange-brown silk, edged with green and white (like the lower edge of the jacket), concealed the shoulders. The sleeves were uncuffed, wide. The five girls took up their positions, four at the corners of a square with one girl in the middle.

Wao, his mind full of indecision, leaned forward in order to seem polite. Could he broach the matter of the Society of the Five now, or would that perhaps precipitate matters so that he himself, together with what knowledge he might have acquired, would be eliminated before the arrival of the Governor's troops? If he delayed, he might not, in the intervening two days, find out enough to break up the conspiracy.

There seemed something vaguely reminiscent about the girl in the centre.

The first girl sang GATHERING DILICHOS without accompaniment. Wao praised her performance and the Prefect acknowledged the praise.

The second girl sang WILLOW BRANCHES, and Wao called to the Prefect's memory how the poet Po Chu-i had referred to the same song when he climbed a mountain with a young dancing-girl.

The third girl performed a posturing dance, and Wao dutifully spoke of the Lady Kang Sun, who had excelled at this dance, and how the poet Tu Fu carried in his heart's record the memory of one of her pupil's dancing. The Prefect with equal politeness decried her performance by comparison with the immortal Li Si.

The fourth girl sang a song of tea-gathering, which Wao had not heard before, suiting her actions to her words.

Wao said: " She sings well, but why does she say *che* when she means *cha*? "

" She was born in Ta Li, amidst the Min Chia," the Prefect said, "and in Ta Li and the surrounding country the Yunnanese accent makes a little for impurity of speech. But her body is beautiful."

Wao agreed: " It is. But *cha* means *tea* and *che* means *clear water*. She might as well pronounce *mei*, which you have just applied to her body, as *mi*. For a she-monkey clearly differs from *beautiful* as vividly as does *cha* from *che*. Nevertheless, you were right in your description. An amusing child, too, I should imagine."

Had he met the fifth girl before? He urged his memory in vain.

He urged his memory in vain until the fifth girl, alone, sang a song which Wao knew that he had read, not heard sung.

> *Sadly had the great general*
> *To leave his lady:*
> *Through the gate he rode*
> *Over the fields to the Army.*

When he had heard the song through, Wao knew at last that it was a poem written by Tu Fu, which he had seen in the diary of his late predecessor, Magistrate Lien Kin Wai, and now he remembered the girl. She had stood slightly to one side as he and Lien were passing from the tent, on the hill beside the White Cloud Monastery at the City of Rams, when Lien had deputized for the Governor, during the sickness, and Wao had come to see that Lien was conducting his business satisfactorily. Wao had tossed his head back to her, saying: " Your cook? " and Lien had answered something or another. What was the girl's name? A flower. Yes—Peony. And she had sung that poem so that he might recognize her.

Ou Ling-ma had returned. They split melon-seeds.

"You are thoughtful," the Prefect observed.

"My heart is sad to think of beauty which I have hitherto not enjoyed," Wao replied. "I regret the wasted years."

Ou laughed.

"You have the *guest's choice* of a couple," he said. "So stifle your regrets." Then he waved a hand to the girls, now still and silent. "Is it your wish, Sir, to see them more closely?"

The Prefect asked: "You would not wish my recommendation, made on the strength of some acquaintance?"

Wao said, experimentally: "The body has five senses, so who am I to judge by only one—the sense of sight? And yet . . ."

"There are five elements," Ou replied, "and without all five the Empire would not be as we know it."

"*Know* includes all your five senses," Wao returned. "Yes, bring the girls closer." As he deliberated on the wisest course for choosing Peony and one other, without appearing to shew any great preference, he observed the eyes of these girls—eyes at once reticent and desiring, eyes defensive but experienced, eyes competing but yet content. "I think, after all," he went on, "that I should like to study the accent of Yunnan. You, girl, stand aside."

The fourth girl moved out of his immediate view.

"Her name is Pheasant," the Prefect said, "and I have already told you of her most striking characteristic."

K

"As to the rest," Wao said, "I can judge between them only by what I know of them. And I know only that which I have just seen and heard. So we have a dancer, a song of dolichos, another of willows, and one about soldiering. I have always admired the military mind."

"Her name is Peony," the Prefect said, "and she is pert."

The other girls were sent away. Pheasant and Peony poured wine for the three of them, and shortly Wao yawned. Ou and the Prefect rose to their feet.

"Your journey was tiring," the Prefect said.

"Rest is a recreation," Ou observed.

Wao replied: "Yes," to both of them and was taken to his room. The two girls hurried in advance, and when Ou opened the door, Pheasant and Peony were sitting side by side on a low divan, watching him. Wao waited until the sounds of his host's footsteps and those of Ou Ling-ma had died away. The two girls had risen and were standing waiting for his instructions. He saw that the box of personal clothing which he had brought with him had already been unpacked and most of the contents set out in readiness. There would be no object, therefore, in looking to see whether the separate hairs which he had rolled up with the documents at the Ferry Inn, after the previous search, were still in position. He had no doubt, now, that his actions and everything about him were being subjected to constant and searching scrutiny.

He seated himself on the edge of the great *k'ang* which occupied most of one end of the room. A foot or so above the *k'ang* there was a grille in the wall: imagination supplied the listening ear.

"You, Pheasant," he said to Peony, "will remove

my boots. You, Peony, will fetch warm water, for I am dusty and tired after my journey."

" She is Peony," Pheasant said.

" You will do as I said," Wao replied. " The names do not matter." He rose to his feet and sat down again on a porcelain stool in the middle of the room.

When Pheasant had gone from the room, Peony busied herself with his boots.

" I had the honour of being noticed by you when I was with Magistrate Lien Kin Wai at the White Cloud Temple," she said in a low voice.

" I remember," he replied. " Pull! And you desired to recall yourself to my memory by singing the song about *the General's girl*. Why did you do so? "

She overbalanced as the boot came off, but recovered herself.

" I thought that you were on the Emperor's business," she answered. " And there are things happening here which it is the Emperor's business to know. So I sang the song by which, I hoped, you would remember me, for I saw Magistrate Lien shewing you his poems, that time at the White Cloud Temple. Alas, I was happy then. Did he die without pain? "

Wao replied : " The doctor said so. No : I read the poems in his diary, and knew that none but you, beside myself, could know them. The other boot. This girl Pheasant—she is to be trusted? "

Peony shook her head. " No," she said. " But I shall manage that. Behave as if you did not know me. Take her first, of us two, and make her drunk. I have a medicine."

He signified assent. The sounds of Pheasant's return came to them. He spoke sharply to Peony, in a harder voice.

"If I had known your clumsiness," he cried, "I would have chosen another girl."

Pheasant came in with warm water in jars, and cloths. She seemed pleased.

"Let me," she said, elbowing Peony out of the way. The second boot came off. Wao smiled at Pheasant.

"You may continue," he said. "This other girl has fingers which slip. The water is warm? Then you may wash me. Tell this other girl what you need her to do, for she seems incapable of acting intelligently for herself."

Peony retired a little from them. Pheasant went about the business of removing the dust of travel, smoothing tired muscles. After a while Wao went over and lay down on the *k'ang*. "There is a muscle here, in my back," he said, indicating its position with a forefinger. "I think that I have strained it. No— here. Work upwards towards the heart. No—you are still *missing the gold*. If I shew you on your own body, maybe you will find it easier." He unbuttoned her coat and turned her round. "There. You feel it? Good. Then do mine."

She let the coat drop from her arms and busied herself massaging Wao's back. After a little Wao rolled over.

"The Prefect was right in what he told me," he said. Then he called Peony. "You, girl, fetch wine now. Then, when you have poured our cups out, you have my permission to leave us."

Pheasant's eyes were bright in the low light of the little lamps, as her fingers kneaded his leg muscles.

"You are almost as strong and tall as the Prefect," she said.

Wao replied: "You cannot always judge strength by

tallness, and certainly seldom do tallness and strength run precisely together." Then he laughed, as Peony came with wine in little cups. She knelt to give one to Wao with both her hands. Then she gave another to Pheasant.

"You, too, may drink," Wao nodded. "And then you may go for a space. I will call."

They drank. Pheasant poured a second cup for Wao and allowed herself to be persuaded to drink another herself. Peony disappeared through a door at the far end of the room.

"What did you mean about the Prefect being right, just now?" she asked.

He answered: "Had you my eyes, you would not need to ask the question." He made room for her beside him. "Did he not say that you were beautiful? You are the Prefect's favourite?"

"He has been very kind to me and done me much honour in sending me here to you," she replied, moving towards him. She sang softly:

> *The untimely leaves which Autumn did not shed*
> *Are fallen now, upon your marriage bed*
> *And so the young tree stands*
> *Nude, shivering—*
> *Folds ineffectual hands*
> *Before the Spring.*

Wao said sharply: "*On Dead Leaves Blown Through Your Window at the Ching Ming Festival.* By one of the T'ang poets—I forget which. You said ' shivering' like a girl from Yunnan. That is not how poetry should be spoken."

"I was born in Ta Li," she answered, "and so I

speak, sometimes, with a little of the speech of Yunnan.
I am sorry if I have displeased you." She sighed. "I
was trying to please you."

"It is better not to speak, then," he said, still a little
roughly, for he felt sorry for Pheasant, as he looked
into her wide eyes and through the dilated pupils,
wondering when Peony's drug would take effect and
those eyes close in an irresistible sleep. It did not seem
to be a quick drug. . . .

She said, suddenly: "It is hard for me to remain
silent. I did not know that there were men like you,
to whom the writing on the wine-jar means more than
the taste of the wine. Why should your feeling for me
rest on the one sense of sound? If I blow out the
light, so, another sense is useless. With which one sense
would you rather love me?"

Wao took her in his arms in the darkness.

"With the earliest, primitive senses," he said. "So
must our ancestors have felt when first, to their enquiring hands, silk came for fingering. So must they
have dreamed when the scent of some discovered
flower struck newly. So must they have known when,
for the first time, a cook succeeded in blending the
sweetness of honey with the tang of vinegar. Or the
fiery inspiration of this wine with the softness of your
sharing lips. Alas, now I have mingled the senses
again and appreciate all of you."

"Your hands are velvet," she murmured. "I have
not felt like this before. You are no longer angry with
me because I say 'velvet' as a girl from Ta Li must say
it? For velvet is the same, however you name it."

"Dawn is far from us," he said. "All round us the
yamen seems to be breathing in the steady sleep of an
exhausted man. Only distantly can I hear the call of

the sleepy watchman, out there in some courtyard, under the sky."

" Dawn is too close for me," she replied. " Too close, for even if the Prefect allows me to come to you to-morrow, that will be but two nights taken from eternity."

" You should not be too serious," he told her. " You are of no importance in the great scheme of the Empire : I am of no importance. When we are dead, other men and other girls will lie thus in the warm darkness, say-ing to each other that there is no moment quite like that moment. In a hundred years tombs will have received us, and the rounded glory of your breasts will be an emptiness in a wooden box."

" There is to-night," she said. " You are not angry any more ? "

" I am not angry," he answered. " My fear is that I stretch too far the terms of the Prefect's hospitality."

She did not seem to be in a position to reply to this.

A little later, Pheasant said : " I . . . I . . . Oh . . . I," and went limp in his arms.

Surprised at the suddenness of it, he arranged the girl on the top of a pile of rugs just below the grille in the wall, so that her flesh sealed its opening and he could no longer hear the faint, attentive breathing behind it. He put another rug, a trifle regretfully, over Pheasant, and called Peony softly.

She came at once.

" Your medicine is effective," he told her in a whisper. " But it took its effect later than I had anticipated. An embarrassing drug, for a man does not expect to find a girl's body become like water in his arms in a moment, like that." He flicked his fingers. " She did not even yawn."

Peony said: "It is a Taoist drug, discovered in the search for the Elixir of Life. It is like the blow of a hammer—at one moment all is as you would expect, while a moment later she is as you see. And they say, though I have not myself experienced the virtue of this drug, that it takes effect only at the instant when the Ying mates with the Yang, so that the attention is elsewhere. But that is probably an old woman's tale."

"It was more than very near to the truth," Wao said. "Now, come and sit here on the *k'ang* with me. As you see, I have stopped up the listening grille by rolling her body against it, so we may talk safely, even here, if we whisper." He laughed, softly. "The situation has novelty."

She smiled as she sat down beside him. "Seeing us now," she said, "a man would not think that we were talking of anything serious. Perhaps it is better that it should appear so. But I feel a little embarrassed."

"Embarrassment is the fear of being correctly misunderstood," he said. "However, I will set your mind at rest, thus. Now, tell me what is in your mind and should shortly be in mine."

She began: "I was sent here by the Lady Loong, the mother of the honourable Hsia Nan-p'o, whom I met on the river-boat and who brought me here. I am, if you wish to tie a label on me, a gift to the daughter of the Prefect. She and the honourable Hsia Nan-p'o are affianced, so that one day I should return to the Hsia mansion in the train of the Prefect's daughter, and so re-enter his household."

"The honourable Hsia Nan-p'o, to whose name you give so persistent a handle, has decided *to borrow a weed from his neighbour*," he quoted from one of Lien's poems. "I deduce that the weed is not unwilling. Continue. Tell me of what happens here, and why you desire me to know of it."

Peony went on: "To begin with, all was as might have been foreseen in the household of a great man such as the Prefect. His daughter is pleasant, although she has been spoiled into expecting everything to be done for her. But she is kind. And then, one day, there came into the women's rooms a man who was a eunuch. Now eunuchs live in the Emperor's palace, and this is not the Emperor's palace."

"It is like finding a capon in a hen's egg," Wao said.

"Yes." She went on: "It is true that he bore only a message from the Prefect to his daughter, and the message was not important, but my mind was filled with misgivings. I myself was born to a family of an old and honoured name: I have read the Books, and I know that when a Prefect has eunuchs in his household, his ambitions rise above the ambitions of ordinary men. Or of ordinary Prefects. During some time after this nothing happened to confirm my fears, and I had, indeed, almost forgotten them. Then, one day, there was a ceremony."

"Tell me of this ceremony," Wao ordered. "For from ceremonies one may judge the nature of the minds of men."

"The ceremony," she said, "was called The Meeting of the Five. The Prefect's own family were not present, but all the rest of us stood, silently, while the eunuchs (for there were five of these) chose twenty of us. . . ."

"Twenty!" Wao exclaimed.

"Twenty," she said. "There are many more girls than you have seen. Those twenty, of whom I was one, were given great peacock fans, like those which,

we read in the old histories, the Emperors at Chang-an
need in order to be hidden from the eyes of the irrever-
ent, during audience.   And, indeed, when the Prefect
entered, he was attired as an Emperor is attired.   He
seated himself on a throne which had been covered
with rich rugs, and the girls carrying the fans moved
to the sides so that the Prefect was visible to the men
in front of him.   There were four of these men.   One
of them was that Ou Ling-ma who was with you and
the Prefect when we entertained you at your meal.
Another one, and I think two, came from the City of
Rams, for their faces were familiar to me and I knew
that I had seen them through the lattice of my father's
hall.   But I could not remember when I had first seen
them, or what names they bore."

"We shall know, later," Wao said.   "You have a
good memory, and it is pleasing to discover that your
father held office under the Emperor.   No—do not
start—I shall not enquire further just now.   Tell me
how this Meeting of the Five continued.   Your tale is
so remarkable that I have almost forgotten my dissatisfied condition.   Proceed."

She looked at him a little fearfully as she went on:
"These four men performed the *kotow* to the Prefect,
and it was the number of their *kotows* which filled me
with misgiving.   I counted them.   Had they been five
kotows, it would have seemed only a part of the ceremony, harmless, natural.   But I counted them, and
these men bowed their foreheads to the ground before
the Prefect not five times, but nine times, and there is
only one within the Four Seas to whom men bow the
head nine times."

"It is the right of the Emperor and of no other,"
Wao agreed.   "And then?"

"Then the audience ended—except that each of the men who had been given the audience said a sentence in which the number five was named. Then the Prefect joined the other men at a table in the middle of the room, and we took the fans away and that was all." She looked up anxiously. "Have I told you what is clear to your mind?" she asked.

"You need tell me no more," Wao replied. "Set your mind at rest. All shall be resolved in a short time. I may not tell you how it will be resolved, but resolved it shall be. And now. . . . Did you, also, take some of your drug?"

She was startled at the sudden change of subject.

"No," she answered. "I did not need to drink any of the drug, for I desired to speak with you. Oh—I have understood. You would not! I . . . ."

He said: "Your mind is full of past sorrows and future fears. It would be a kindness to set it at rest, as Pheasant's mind is at rest. Why? Do you belong to any man? Do you not desire to honour the Prefect's intention, when he allowed me, his guest, to choose you two girls?"

She blushed.

"I would beg of you," she said, "not to exercise the right which, as a guest, is yours. I have no right, my-self, to ask this kindness, but I do ask it. Has not my story been payment enough? Must I always pay?"

"Since we have time left to us," he said, "tell me the story of that sadness which shines in your eyes. Tell me of the events which led you to the bed of Lien Kin Wai, at the Temple in White Cloud Mountain. Tell me what love of his memory yet remains, that you should refuse yourself to me. Tell me."

She said: "No. But you will know how to deal

with this society and its aims? You will be able to act so that the Emperor suffers nothing from these men? I wondered . . ."

"You are skilled in speech," he told her. "You know how to change the subject when the subject is embarrassing. Set your mind at rest: I have no such intention as you fear. When will the girl Pheasant awake?"

"I think she begins to stir," Peony told him. "If you will excuse me, I will leave you. It would be better for her to find you alone with her when she awakes. Then she will not suspect that she has slept, and so you will be free from danger." She rose to her feet. "I thank you, Sir, for your kindness to me."

"I was the friend of the honourable Lien Kin Wai," Wao answered. "That is the reason. Now go, for I would prefer Pheasant to awake in a set of circumstances so identical with those under which your drug took effect, that she will not know that such a thing has happened. And your presence, for such a purpose and for such an end is needless. Go now."

Peony *kotowed* to him before she went out at the door at the other end of the room. Wao rolled Pheasant from her pile of rugs, inspected with amusement the pattern printed by the grille, and took such steps as were necessary to set Pheasant's waking mind at ease.

When, indeed, the girl woke from her sleep, she did so with such suddenness that Wao himself was bewildered. And, as if to convince both of them that no gap of time had passed, her first words were those with which, some hours before, she had greeted oblivion: "I . . . I . . . Oh . . . I."

He reassured her in his best manner.

.   .   .   .

When Peony came with the dawn, she set down the bowls of hot soup which she had brought, and went back for warm water and towels. Pheasant was wide awake, and raised her finger for silence.

"He is asleep," Pheasant said in a whisper. "Do not wake him. Take the soup away. And be silent."

Peony was reminded of all the wild mothers which, in cave or tree, in open country or tangled thicket, crouch in protection over their young. For the surprising thing was that Pheasant, her head raised as she lifted herself on her elbows amidst the rugs, seemed to radiate a maternal fierceness quite at variance with reality. . . .

Wao said sleepily: "Let her bring the soup. And the wet towels. For if I wipe—or you wipe—the sleep from my eyes—— Do not crouch there over me, girl, as if you were guarding me."

Pheasant said: "I am sorry," and took the towels from Peony.

When Peony had gone and they had drunk the soup, Wao said: "Well?"

.   .   .   .

The boy Keung bewailed his lot. It was not that he objected to the dangerous post of taster to his master, the rich merchant Tung Ho. Not at all, for poisoning was not, Keung felt, a thing to be feared. Sensitive, he knew that Tung Ho's absent-minded use of him, the thoughtless thrusting into the boy's mouth of the first morsel from each dish, proved Tung Ho's confidence in Keung's uselessness. Besides, there had been occasions when Tung Ho, deliberately, had not allowed Keung to sample his food, and if that happened, Keung was sure that Tung Ho anticipated no attempt upon his life. In fact, Keung had lately had other, and less welcome, duties thrust upon him. Messages and the like.

Take this unpleasant journey by carrying-chair from the City of Kow Loong to the Convent of Jade Serenity, in order to find and, if possible, talk with Jasmine. Keung felt the duty far outside his scope. Besides (and this made him resent his commission the more keenly, Jasmine and Tung Ho's favourite girl, Hidden Gold, had once, at a picnic, conspired to take off his clothes and mock at him as he sat, lone and forlorn, in a shallow pool of sea-water. " Is it a man? " they had mocked—or something like that, and Keung remembered only too well how this affront to him had made him blush to an unpleasing colour. Of course, he did not like girls under any circumstances. Was that his fault? he asked himself. Girls were upsetting things, and now he had to find this girl Jasmine and ask her as indirectly as possible about the events of some days past, when General Wu had been killed outside the city.

What did his master hope to gain from this questioning?

The nun at the convent gate seemed to sense his misgivings, for she asked : " What business have you here? Though it does not look as if they would refuse to admit you."

Keung replied, without descending from his chair : " My master, the rich merchant Tung Ho, has sent by me a present of fruit and bags of rice, and I have instructions to deliver this gift to the Abbess herself, so you may as well let me pass."

The nun did not reply as she moved aside and fingered her beads. The chair-bearers and the men carrying rice and fruit made ribald remarks as they crossed the bridge over the pool, so that Keung had difficulty in retaining the attitude of a man who has heard nothing. At the entrance to the cell of the Abbess another nun stopped them. Keung told her to hasten.

When the Abbess came to them, even the bearers were silent, and Keung found this gratifying.

" I have brought presents from my master, Tung Ho —presents of fruit and bags of rice," he said as he stepped from his chair. " My master particularly instructed me not to hand these presents to anyone but yourself."

" Put them down," she told him. " And what service does your master desire in return for these gifts? "

" My master's honourable wife," Keung said glibly, "is purposing to travel to the north, to the City of Rams, by very easy stages, since she is a delicate lady, and my master has instructed me to discover whether you would be willing to receive her."

" Any traveller is welcome," the Abbess replied. "Everyone knows that. So there must be some other reason. What is it? "

Keung looked at her eyes and looked away quickly.

" My master had heard that you have, staying here, a woman by the name of Jasmine, from the Magistrate's family. He told me to speak with this woman and discover from her whether the rooms are suitable for his wife," he said.

The Abbess returned: " If you wish to have speech with the woman, why did you not ask for her in the first instance? Must men of the city always believe that we are fools, to be put off with a soft word and an invented tale? But our order bids us be humble, and think the best. I will send to ask the woman Jasmine

if she wishes to speak with you, and if so, you may
enter. You must leave these men to wait for you."

Other nuns took the presents to the store-rooms. By
and by word came that Jasmine would talk with Keung,
and shortly he found himself standing at the entrance to
her room.

When she came out, she said: "I should not have
said that I would see you, had I not been curious. Why
have you come?" She led the way in. They sat down.

"My master," Keung said, "hearing that you were
here, desired to offer you a place in his own household.
He said that, in his opinion, the judgment of magistrates is not infallible, and that it was wrong for a
young woman like you to be here. He sent you this
bag of silver as proof of the worthiness of his intentions."

A nun came in with a teapot and two cups. Then
she went away again without speaking.

"It is a dreary place," Keung observed. "I wonder
that you came."

Jasmine said: "It was not of my own will. But your
master should have asked the magistrate. It is not for
me to decide. Why did he not ask the magistrate?"

Keung answered: "He would have done so, had
the honourable Wao Hien To not left his city and gone
to visit the Prefect of Sai Kwan. My master thought
that, if you were agreeable to the idea, he could ask the
magistrate on his return to the city. Did you not know
that he had gone?"

Jasmine said: "He does not tell me everything. You
should have asked his wife, the Lady Hibiscus, whether
I was not wanted."

"And if my master had done so," Keung replied,
"do you imagine that the Lady Hibiscus would have

decided one way or the other in the absence of the honourable Wao? That would have been beyond her power."

Jasmine made as if to drink. Then she said: " You remember when I last had the honour of meeting you? It was by the sea."

" You treated me as no girl should treat a man," he cried. " I do not think that the idea was wholly the idea of your friend Hidden Gold, as you would probably have me believe."

" You were amusing," she told him. " I remember that, even if I do not remember much else of the afternoon. Was it before, or after, our meeting at the dinner to General Wu? "

Keung, who had been wondering how to introduce the subject, said: " After. Did you hear of the sad, the inexplicable death of the General? It caused the honourable Wao Hien To much thought and trouble. I believe it is because of the death of General Wu that the honourable Wao Hien To has gone to see the Prefect." He sighed. " But people such as you and myself seldom hear the truth of these matters."

" They do not greatly concern us," Jasmine answered. " I knew that there was trouble, and an enquiry."

" Is he kind to you? " Keung ventured.

" That is the sort of thing to which one does not reply," she said. " It is no affair of yours. But he trusts me."

They both drank tea.

He said: " It is good to know that you think that he trusts you. So he has told you more than was revealed at the enquiry? He must trust you greatly, if that is so. But I find it hard to credit. Why should I believe that he trusts you, as you say? "

L

Jasmine said: " But he *does* trust me. I have proof of it."

" Proof," Keung returned, " must be shared to be believed. What does he do, then, to make you say that you have proof of his trust? What happened on the night when General Wu was killed? "

" I cannot tell you what happened on that night," Jasmine replied, " for I do not know what happened. But as for proof of his trust in me—was it not proof of trust when he came to my room when the guards were searching the *yamen*, to ensure that I was not frightened, instead of going to the room of the Lady Hibiscus? "

" That, certainly, goes to shew that he considered you," Keung answered, " though not that he trusted you. If he had wished to conceal his movements, or what he had been doing before he came to your room, that would have been a different matter. Did he wish to conceal anything? "

" What could he have wished to conceal? " Jasmine countered.

Keung said: " How should I know? How did the honourable Wao Hien To behave when he came to you? Much may be learned from a man's behaviour. Did he treat you ceremoniously? Did he remove his outer garments and put himself at his ease? Did he seem to have been running? Was he short of breath? Was he armed? "

" If I told you the answers to all these things, you would be as wise as I am," Jasmine told him. " So you cannot expect me to tell you. If your master really intends to take me into his house, it would be a different matter. But I should need proof of his intentions, other than your word."

Keung rose to his feet.

"I will bring you proof, further than the bag of silver which I have already brought," he said. "Walk well."

. . . .

Back at the house of Tung Ho, Keung said: "She knows much, but she will not speak unless you promise to take her into your household. But, from her very reticence, I can say that her master came to her room in a great hurry when Tze Hung's men were searching the *yamen*, and that he had something to hide. What, she would not say."

"It is enough," Tung Ho said. "Wao must have seen the death of General Wu, and must, also, have slain the men who slew General Wu. Whether the General told him, before he died, of his suspicions, it is impossible to say. But I must warn the Prefect that Wao's seeming innocence hides knowledge, and that he is probably only waiting an opportunity to turn that knowledge to the advantage of the Emperor's men and to the disadvantage of the Prefect. I will write a letter to the Prefect, and you shall take it to Sai Kwan. Leave me."

. . . .

It was evening. Dusk had descended on the convent courtyard, softening angles everywhere. After the dusk, darkness.

Jasmine lay on the k'ang in her room, her hands clasped behind her head, incuriously conscious of the little world of yellow light thrown by the floating wick in the lamp. The wick needed trimming: she detached the lamp flower and watched the knob of glowing soot die to greyness, then to invisibility. It was supposed to be good luck if a girl could detach the whole flower, unbroken. . . .

From the Hall of Assembly came the indefinite chatter of women's voices in a Taoist prayer.

It was strange, she reflected, how a convent such as this could mingle the doctrines of the Buddha and of the Master, Lao Tze, to give a satisfying whole, whence women might derive comfort. Always the lot of women seemed to be sorrow followed by a small, inadequate compensation for that sorrow. They had to make up the weight of natural compensation with the counterpoise of religion, of these wailings and prayers. Her own life had been like that. There had been the healthy drudgery of home life, her father's harsh words, her mother's hard, earthly common sense. Then Lien Kin Wai had bought her, and sometimes life had seemed too lovely to be possible. Then Lien had sent her away to have her baby—or perhaps not to have her baby, but merely to be absent when the Lady Hibiscus had her baby—and when Lien died she had been sent for, again, to return to the *yamen.* Wao, who had sent for her, had been kind, often. And then she had been sent away, again, to this convent, this house of women. . . .

The bell in the Assembly Hall was rung, once.

Why had Wao sent her away? Was it in fear that she would tell about the night when, bloody, he had come and loved her while the guards searched the *yamen?* Could he be afraid that she would reveal to someone else about the bloodstained clothes, the sword hidden under those clothes on the floor when the guard came? There was the coming and going when the body of General Wu was brought in. . . . That was what the boy Keung had been hinting at, during their talk that afternoon. Had she said too much? Had Keung desired to discover what had happened on that night? Keung had been a servant to the rich merchant, Tung Ho, and men told curious tales of the power of money. . . . Did Tung Ho really mean to offer her a place in his house, and would her master agree? But she should have gone to Tung Ho without coming to a convent.

What had there been, to conceal, that night? Had Wao, himself, killed General Wu and then, in her room, pretended never to have quitted the *yamen*? Then he would not wish it known, especially to a powerful man like Tung Ho, who might make all kinds of difficulties. . . .

The bell was rung again, twice, as the voices momently ceased.

The problem was beyond her. She must ask advice. However unpleasant, she must ask advice of Silver Lantern, at least, and possibly of the Lady Hibiscus herself. Besides, she could see if Silver Lantern was treating her son with that care which he needed. . . . She rose from the *k'ang* and took her bag of silver. The rest could wait until later. But silver was always silver.

   .   .   .   .

" Why has the girl come back to the *yamen*? " Hibiscus demanded.

Silver Lantern changed from one foot to the other.

" She has brought some tale," she said, " full of nonsense about the boy Keung, who is Tung Ho's boy, as you know, of how he came to see her at the convent, and how he tried to discover from her what she knew of the death of General Wu."

" I do not wish to see her," Hibiscus replied. " What could she know of the death of General Wu? Even less than I know myself. Tell her to return to the convent."

Silver Lantern said : " She first enquired as to your

health, then as to that of your daughter. Only then did she ask to see her own child. She was very well-mannered."

"Let her come," Hibiscus replied. "Courtesy dictates courtesy, even between women."

When Jasmine was brought in she *kotowed* to Hibiscus.

Hibiscus asked: "What is this tale about the boy Keung?"

After Jasmine had told Hibiscus of Keung's attempt to find out the truth of the death of General Wu, and of the offer to take her into Tung Ho's household, she said: "May I go? There is no longer any need for me to live in the nunnery. I do not know why I was sent there in the first place."

Hibiscus sent her to fetch tea. While the girl was thus occupied, Hibiscus pondered the position. She realized that she herself understood it even less than the girl Jasmine understood it. And since Wao had himself refused to explain, for what he must have considered adequate reasons, so it must follow that Wao desired his plan to be carried out. Jasmine must be sent back to the convent and told not to talk. A letter to the Abbess would prevent any of Tung Ho's men seeing her again. All must await the return of Wao from Sai Kwan.

Hibiscus decided on this course without much confidence. It was a pity, she reflected, that men seldom told women of their plans, when those plans mattered. How, then, could the women be expected adequately to deal with the unexpected, to mould the original scheme to fit new facts? All that could be done, in order to avoid blame, was to keep to the original intention, so far as that was clear.

On Jasmine's return with the tea, they drank together quite formally, and Hibiscus instructed the girl to return to the convent.

"When he comes, I will ask him," was all that Hibiscus would say.

Jasmine went back.

. . . .

Mistress Hsia, widow of the late Sung Tsui, Governor of the City of Rams, sat in her room in the gloom of utter depression. The bamboo blinds had been unrolled, and nowhere did the sun lighten the corners of this room. On a small table beside her a padded teapot stood. Her maid, Tower of Pearl, anxiously watched her mistress as she drank the pale straw infusion.

"I marvel at the whims of Fate," Mistress Hsia told the girl. "I marvel, because I am powerless to do otherwise. Here am I, who have for years pretended to have headaches as a defence against an unwelcome world, now suffering in actuality from a headache. I, who have pretended that sunlight hurts my eyes, am now suffering that very hurt, where little sun is. In front of my eyes seem two circles of broken, written characters, surrounding a small patch of clearness, as if I were looking through small holes in a wood partition. Outside these circles I can see nothing. More tea, girl."

Tower of Pearl said, as she refilled the cup: "The trouble will pass, as all trouble passes—unless it changes to something worse. At least, I have found it so. One can but wait."

Mistress Hsia cried, almost in anger: "I have no wish to wait. Men, and servants, both must wait for the decisions of women, but I am not accustomed to

wait. Ah! Now there is a new pain, from the top of
my head downwards, backwards and to the right. And
all is blackness now, below my eyes. Only the upper
world exists any longer: the lower world has gone, as
I shall go, to the darkness of the Three Springs. Never
has this happened to me, and I begin to know the sense
of fear."

The girl shivered, for living with Mistress Hsia had
made her share, in a measure, the mind of Mistress
Hsia. They looked at each other.

"If only," Mistress Hsia cried, "you could do something other than pour tea, girl, it would not be so hard
to bear. But you continue to pour tea as if tea were,
indeed, a cure for all ills. Why can you not read to
me from the old books, as that girl Peony used to read?
Why can you not with your fingers smooth my forehead into stillness and take into your own hands the
pain which now pierces my head? Why. . . ."

Tower of Pearl answered: "I cannot do any of these
things. Shall I go to the *yamen* and ask Peony to come
to do them for you?"

"The Prefect's daughter would not let her come,"
Mistress Hsia said. "That is as certain as the pain in
my head. There is but one way—to rely on courtesy,
and pay a visit to the Prefect's daughter, to ask her if
she would let the girl Peony smooth my forehead with
her skilful hands. Call the bearers of my chair—we
shall go to the *yamen*. Have the chair brought into
the hall, and darken the hall first. Put soft cushions
in the chair, and tell me when it is in readiness."

The high sun had fallen half its way down the sky
as the closed carrying-chair followed by that of Tower
of Pearl with two bearers passed from the darkened

hall to the courtyard and so, through the great Hsia
gates, to the street. The four bearers picked their way
more carefully than was their wont, for word of Mistress Hsia's affliction had reached them. The wide,
straight road dipped from the Hsia mansion, through
the populous town, to rise again to the entrance tower
of the Governor's *yamen*.

Sitting with closed eyes in the screened carrying-
chair, Mistress Hsia saw, in her mind's eye, this fall
and rise of the path which her bearers' feet must take,
saw it as a symbol of life itself, from the high, lovely
peak of youth, through the depression of middle age's
frustration, to the summit, again, when age gave judg·
ment and appetite declined. Then, she mused, a
woman can enjoy the passing days, unburdened either
by the insistent call of the passions or the growing
failure to satisfy them. The steady, shuffling rhythm
of the bearers' feet marked off the passing days on this
imagined life's passage, as she knew thus, in darkened
simile, what she had been, what she was and what
she must yet be. She threw her thoughts from her,
separating the oiled cloth blinds of the chair to
look out through a narrow space at the busy world of
man.

For as the procession passed, the leading servants
would clear a way with voice and gesture, and then the
streets were suddenly frozen into stillness as the chair
went by, for it was seldom that the people of Sai Kwan
had the pleasure of seeing a Hsia chair pass their doors.
Deep in dark shops tradesmen stood, curious, until the
red uniform of the house of Hsia had gone : at street-
side stalls bargaining ceased, to give place to staring :
the itinerant brass-smith set down his burden to see the
chair swing by : a public letter-writer set down the

character *wan* for stupid when he had intended to write
wan, to marry : small, dirty children stayed their games
in wonder at unfamiliarity and a lean cur sidled out of
the pathway, fearing the unknown.

Mistress Hsia suddenly realized as she gazed through
the crack in the blinds, that her headache had gone
(except for a distant throbbing inside her forehead)
and that her eyes once more reported the world round
her in its accustomed lines and colours. She rolled up
the front blind, only to have it slip from her fingers and
unroll again. She struck sharply on the shafts of the
chair and was set down.

When the bearers had rolled up the blinds and
secured them, they picked up the chair again and moved
off towards the *yamen*. Mistress Hsia wondered why
this return of her faculties should have taken place at
the lowest point of the dip, as if in confirmation of the
picture which she had formed, not long past, of her
life's unrolling. Behind her Tower of Pearl bounced
gently upwards, wondering if the lifting of the blinds
betokened a return to her mistress's usual calm. But
then, Tower of Pearl reflected, why were they going to
the *yamen*, when the ostensible need for Peony's skilled
fingers seemed to have passed? She abandoned specu-
lation, enjoying the moving scene, for it was not often
that Mistress Hsia ventured into the world from the
quiet austerity of her own rooms. . . .

. . . .

Her parents had optimistically named the Prefect's
daughter Jade Star, and all her eighteen years had
seemingly been coloured by the effort to justify their
choice. She had intended to greet Mistress Hsia with
just that shade of condescension which their differing
ages left possible : when the guests were at last shewn

up to the guest-room in the women's apartments, they found Jade Star carefully posed at the doorway with two maids behind her and two more carrying the materials for tea, as if they had been freshly brought in. Mistress Hsia, even as she greeted the girl, noticed how formal the reception was.

Mistress Hsia said: "I had started my visit to you with a selfish motive: now I find that motive lacking, and face you with no other desire than that of again making the acquaintance of the girl whom, if my memory serves me well, I last saw at my husband's *yamen* in the City of Rams, when your father came to visit us on matters of state. You were very young then, and I remember that your two little pigtails had been unequally tied."

Jade Star murmured: "You disarm me, with these revelations of the dim past. Nevertheless I, too, have a memory, and I recall the sweetmeats which you ordered your maids to give me in order not to distract the attention of my elders." She found herself drawn, inevitably, towards this woman who traded the memory of a child against the formality of a Prefect's daughter. "I regret that I never had the opportunity of meeting you again, though I have long awaited your pleasure. After all, we are not far apart, now that you have returned to your family's home on the other hill."

Chairs were brought. Tower of Pearl was taken away for a servant's gossip.

When the two were alone, Mistress Hsia went on: "This afternoon, not long after I had eaten my midday meal, I was afflicted with such a headache as left to me only my instinctive movements. I remembered how, with earlier headaches, I had enjoyed relief at the hands of the girl Peony, whom my sister-in-law, the

Lady Loong, sent to you as a present some months ago."

"I am sorry to hear of your trouble," Jade Star answered. "Such pains indeed make the world a strange, an unfamiliar place. Yes, it is true that a girl named Peony was sent to me by the Lady Loong. But I do not think . . ."

Mistress Hsia raised a hand. "Do not disturb yourself," she said. "As the chair-men carried me hither, the headache and all the other troubles vanished, leaving me unharmed. I am thankful. But, as I had started to call on you to ask for the loan of the fingers of the girl Peony, so now, with my need passed, I felt that the expedition should not be wasted, and so I came, as I had first intended, to drink tea with you."

Jade Star made the gesture of one who knows that her kindness will not be called for. "I shall send for the girl," she said. "It may be that, if she smoothes your forehead, the pain which you have suffered will be driven even further from you." She stretched out a hand for the little gong beside her.

"I pray you not to disturb the rhythm of your household on my account," Mistress Hsia objected. "It is wholly unnecessary for you to summon her. No—let us drink and talk, and then I shall return home with my mind full of other things than my own troubles. And yet, the girl was of gentle birth—the daughter of the late Magistrate Chiang, of the City of Rams. Her conversation was amusing and, at times, instructive. I have spent some pleasant hours with her."

Jade Star struck the gong. To the maid who came, she said : "Tell the girl Peony to come here. My visitor desires speech with her."

By and by Peony came and stood just inside the doorway, looking from one to the other.

Jade Star said to her: "Mistress Hsia does us the honour of paying us a visit. She tells me that you have, in the past, eased pains in her head by the art of your fingers, and as she has lately suffered in that way, it is my wish that you should do for her such service as you were accustomed to do before you were sent to me."

Peony bowed low to Mistress Hsia and came to stand behind her, smoothing gently with her fingers and thumbs the skin of Mistress Hsia's forehead, of her cheek, of her neck. Jade Star watched with interest.

"Mistress Hsia tells me," she said as Peony worked, "that your father was a magistrate. Had you given us the same information, it would have been our right to have treated you more politely, in accordance with your birth."

Peony answered: "Those days are very dead, and I have forgotten them. I did not wish to claim for myself any different treatment, merely because of the past. And as I do not desire to claim privilege, so I deny the responsibility which rides with privilege. I am happier as I am, and I beg of you to rule from your memory any such knowledge as you now possess of me."

Mistress Hsia observed: "You were ever talking in the brave words of the classics, girl."

"She does not have the opportunity for such talk," Jade Star said.

Peony worked behind Mistress Hsia's ears, to her throat.

"Your fingers still know their old magic," Mistress Hsia told her, "even if your manner of life has changed. That, I am sure, is enough. The pain has fled—such of it as remained."

Jade Star said: " She has been entertaining one of my father's guests—the Magistrate of Kow Loong, one Wao Hien To. We strive to keep up the old standards of hospitality, and my father gave him two girls to look after him."

Mistress Hsia cried: " But I think I know this honourable Wao Hien To. He and my lamented husband had affairs of state in common. Now you tell me he is only a magistrate of an insignificant city. What has happened to him to give displeasure to the Emperor? "

" There is a tale," Jade Star said, " that he desired to marry a widow—the widow of the late magistrate of Kow Loong City, one Lien Kin Wai. Naturally the Emperor would look with disfavour on one who wishes to wed a woman who has already possessed one husband. The Emperor would consider how many unmarried girls would gladly have made him a wife. My father says so. But this Wao Hien To does not sound to me the sort of man to have affairs with your late husband—I thought him a little slow, even stupid."

" He was never stupid," Mistress Hsia said. " He was an Emperor's Messenger, and Emperor's Messengers are never stupid. I wonder what has happened to change him, for I certainly remember him as a man of wisdom and of wit." She laughed. " You and I would be speaking of two different men." She turned to Peony. " You, girl, who were given the privilege of entertaining him last night, did you find him stupid? "

Peony replied, carefully: " To have *the privilege of towel and comb*, even for a single night, is not to be able to judge the worth of a guest. One speaks in the accepted phrases. There is little opportunity, little opening, for the free flow of wit and wisdom."

Mistress Hsia smiled at her. "You are guarded, girl," she said. "I imagine that experience has given you the ability to postpone judgment or, having judged, to conceal your verdict under politenesses. For we are no nearer, this lady and I, to knowing which of us you consider to be in the right, and whether the honourable Wao Hien To is indeed, *slow and even stupid*, or *a man of wit and wisdom*."

"I do not commit myself," Peony answered, "since, as I have said, such sharing as I have known with our guest has not been the sharing of minds."

Then they stopped talking about Wao Hien To, for the door opened and the Prefect ushered in Wao. When the women had made much ado of fetching porcelain stools and the two men were comfortably seated, the Prefect waved a hand towards his guest.

"You, Mistress Hsia," he said, "and you, my daughter, will understand and I hope excuse the informality of this visit. For the widow of a Provincial Governor cannot fail to have learned broadness of mind, and to a dutiful daughter her father's actions should not be in question. Had it been otherwise, I should have hesitated to bring my guest to see the women's rooms and to talk with the women."

Wao said: "In the past I have had the pleasure of meeting Mistress Hsia—in happier days for both of us."

Jade Star laughed at them all.

"This is most unaccustomed," she cried. "In my apartments there is seldom this restrained interchange of complimentary small-talk. I find it strange."

The Prefect observed: "I have allowed my daughter too much of her own way. The fault is mine. Greet your guest with due courtesy, my daughter, and forget for a while your own affairs. Come!"

Jade Star did not shew an ill grace as she knelt before Wao and made the prescribed obeisance. He felt that her heart was sound, that what her manner had suggested at first had been the *gaucherie* of one striving to appear to be a personality in a household where there was already a stronger personality. He knew that if her father had been merely an ordinary father, Jade Star would have proved herself an ordinary girl with ordinary virtues. So he pressed her to rise from her knees, protesting that the honour was too great for him.

Mistress Hsia said : " It is amusing to see this interchange of compliments. When I last met you, Sir, your attitude was the attitude of a man who held valueless these outward signs of custom."

" I have learned," Wao replied, " that there is wisdom in conforming to the rules of conduct. So now I conform. In fact I have been discommoded by my host's easy manners : I am not used to such intrusions into the women's apartments. I am both honoured and uneasy."

The Prefect rose to his feet, rolled the porcelain stool next to that of his daughter and sat down again.

" The change of heart which you have suggested for our guest," he said, " reminds me of a poem which I read the other day. It is not a wise act to anticipate comment, but I cannot avoid the comparison between our guest's former lack of respect for ceremonies and his present conversion on the one hand, and on the other the poet's description, in three lines, of a natural scene and then, through his formal, literary fourth line, the implication not only of a kind of longing for the refuge of formality, but also an unspoken regret that he had not, in the first three lines, made use of those literary allusions which, in the Sung poets, could compress a philosophy in a phrase, establishing a relation between the writer and an erudite reader which makes the poem intelligible, as a poem, only to a hearer who has been brought up with phrases for toys and epigrams for playthings."

Mistress Hsia replied: "Your prologue, like a good sauce, makes my mouth water. Is it too much to hope for the main dish?"

Wao, trying to make a remark in character, said: "The good cook thus sauces the appetite: the go-between extols the bride to the bridegroom's parents: the salesman shouts his wares. You are, Sir, in the best tradition."

The Prefect continued: "It is a poem which I found in some old documents the other day. Possibly the work of one of my predecessors. There is no author's name attached to the poem. It is called *Evening in the Sixth Month*.

> *True, there are birds behind the rigid moon,*
> *But not here, in my garden, where green plums*
>   *hang motionless:*
> *Even the roar of insects is become a twilight*
>   *whisper.*
> *I wait in vain to see a wild goose, homing.*

"You will observe the suggestive first three lines—suggesting the scene, the time of day, even the weather. Then, in the fourth, we have that typically Sung reference to wild geese, which everyone knows are the symbol of the homesick, and the messengers of lovers. You may understand the first three lines without being literary, but the last . . ."

Peony asked: "Would you have the kindness to repeat it? I believe that the adjective 'rigid', applied

M

to the moon, occurs in an old Han poet. Yei Mei, I think."

The Prefect repeated the poem. Then he said: "It would seem that you have been well brought up, girl, thus to seize upon a familiar word."

"We have just heard," his daughter told him, "that she comes of a well-born family, holding office under the Emperor."

Peony said: "I did not desire that to be known. It is easier to live with one's fellows if the question of pedigrees is left unraised." Then she turned to Mistress Hsia. "Is the pain in your head less now?"

Mistress Hsia suddenly remembered herself: "Girl," she said, "you are at your old magic. You must know, Sir, that she was with me before my sister-in-law, the Lady Loong, sent her to your daughter, and often, when I have suffered from my ever-present headaches, she has charmed them away, as she has now done with the peculiarly violent headache with which I began my journey to your hospitable daughter. Indeed, she is accomplished."

Wao echoed, feeling that he should speak: "She is accomplished. And now, Sir, if you and your daughter and Mistress Hsia will forgive me, I feel that I should wish to rest before the entertainment which you have promised me for to-night. There will be dancing, you assured me, and I prefer to watch the movements of girls' limbs with less of lassitude in my own. Perhaps a short sleep . . ."

They drank their ceremonial tea and parted. Peony took Wao back to his room.

"Did I talk stupidly enough?" he asked.

"Nearly," she replied, as she arranged his bed.

.   .   .   .

Mistress Hsia looked doubtfully at Jade Star.

"I should go," she said. "Already the sun is low. You will have much to do in preparation for the entertainment of which the honourable Wao spoke to us."

Jade Star answered: "Such arrangements as are to be made are not for me to make. My father never allows me to do that. There are cooks enough in the kitchen, he says, without the interference of the amateur. It is true that I find such an attitude pleasant, for it gives me leisure to enjoy such company as yours. Would it not be possible for you to stay with me until this entertainment, which we shall witness through the screen at the end of the hall?"

They debated through the time taken to eat most of a bowl of melon-seeds, several flat cakes, and some preserved *lichees*, aided by the frequently refilled teapot.

Finally Mistress Hsia agreed: "I will send Tower of Pearl with a message to my nephew, Hsia Nan-p'o, telling him of my intentions. While I am writing this message you will find out from your father whether he wishes to extend his courtesy to my nephew, also. If he does, the two notes can be sent together. It is on my nephew, then, that the duty will devolve of arranging for my escort when I return to the Hsia dwelling. Thus I shall have no need for further organization, no need to consider how to spend the remainder of the day, thanks to your invitation, and a pleasurable feeling of uncertainty as to my nephew's acceptance of your father's possible proposal. And my headache is wholly gone."

They sent for paper, ink-blocks and brushes.

It seemed to Wao, as he lay on his back on the *k'ang*,

staring at the roof, that matters had gone for him better
than he had any right to expect. To-night, at the
earliest, Government troops should come from the City
of Rams, and force of arms would decide where words
were powerless. If not to-night, to-morrow. And it
seemed as if the Prefect, lulled into overconfidence by
Wao's acceptance of his overwhelming hospitality, had
deferred the official enquiry until at least the next day
—a postponement acceptable indeed, for to explain the
events of General Wu's death by an assumption of
stupidity, would be no less difficult than to impress that
stupidity on the Prefect's daughter and, through her,
on the Prefect. Mistress Hsia was, of course, an added
complication, for Wao was under no illusion as to the
keenness of her mind or the penetrating quality of her
judgment. It would never do for Mistress Hsia to
guess that his slowness was an assumed slowness, his
stupidity an assumed stupidity. He hoped that his
attitude had been convincing.

Peony brought tea for him.

"You have said nothing to anyone of what you told
me last night?" he asked.

The girl assured him, and Wao drank some of the
tea. Lying back again, he forced his mind to the problem of what to do when the Government troops arrived
at the *yamen*. Their coming, and their number, could
not fail to warn the Prefect that theirs was no courtesy
visit—it was a short mental step, too, from the arrival
of a body of troops to the presence in the Prefect's
household of a guest who had once held the exalted
rank of Emperor's Messenger and been accustomed to
act with decision and speed in just such matters as the
sudden and ruthless suppression of an incipient rebellion. It would therefore be wise to have a plan to

circumvent surprise. He considered the arrangement of the *yamen*, its strength and its weakness from a military point of view. The weakest characteristic seemed to him to be the fact that the women's quarters were poised on the top of the *yamen* walls, so that the possibility of entry from outside depended mainly on the height of those walls and the difficulty of scaling them. To each side of the block containing the women's rooms, a tower stood, loopholed for archers, but the wide top of the wall, the path whereby rein-forcements could be rushed to a threatened point, stopped short on each side of those rooms and a wide verandah replaced the loopholed battlements which, elsewhere, topped the wall. So, if a determined man held the entrance to these rooms, while a woman lowered a rope of rolled silk for the attackers to climb, the whole position might be turned from within and the defenders assaulted from the unexpected rear. But to hold the entrance to the rooms would leave all the noisy, hostile pack of women between himself, at the entrance, and Peony, at the outer windows, and it was unlikely that the Prefect's daughter, at least, would allow Peony to lower a rope of rolled silk without attempting to stop her. No: his own position would have to be in that last room, where the circle of his sword would guard Peony while she lowered the rope. Or, while the women were present at the entertain-ment. . . . It would all depend on the hour of arrival of the Governor's troops.

He mused on, his eyes shut, occasionally drinking tea, as the sun sank towards the horizon, subconsciously waiting for the shouting from below the wall, and the cry of the defenders. For Wao had no doubt that the Prefect of Sai Kwan would defend himself and his *yamen* (and, incidentally, his daughter), to the uttermost limits of human endurance and human courage. The possibility of capture would not occur to the Prefect, for one who plots against the Emperor can expect no very pleasant fate when once that plotting is unmasked.

It would, Wao imagined, be a hard fight there, in the women's quarters, while Peony lowered the rope to the Government troops below. It was more than possible that Wao would not survive it.

He spared a thought or two for Hibiscus, back at the Kow Loong *yamen*, awaiting his return with her customary confidence, and hoped that her confidence was not misplaced.

Then he slept.

PART THREE

PART THREE

FOR the performance of THE VIRTUOUS CON-
CUBINE, a complete theatre on the Palace model
had been erected in one of the inner courtyards
of the *yamen*, although of the usual two-storeyed stage
here was only the lower half, for in that drama there
are no gods or goddesses to live their lofty lives on a
higher level than their earthly subjects do. The palm-
thatched roof shut out the light from the sky, but great
torches threw flickering shadows over the stage. In the
central box the Prefect entertained Wao Hien To and
young Hsia Nan-p'o: from the boxes above this,
according to the old custom, the women of the *yamen*
and their guests sat segregated from the men.

"To follow the ancient precedent," the Prefect
observed, "I should be sitting under the *Nine Dragon*
entrance, where once the Bright Emperor was accustomed to control the orchestra whenever his favourite
Yang Kuei Fei performed upon the stage. But I, alas,
possess no Yang Kuei Fei, so that I prefer to watch
from the comparative comfort of this box."

Wao said, deprecatingly: "I have often, myself,
experienced the same desire to strike the measured
blow upon the musical block, dictating the tempo of
the rest of the orchestra. It would, I feel, make for a
sense of control, of power, without the harmful effect

185

of power." He looked out of the corner of his eye at the face of Hsia Nan-p'o, wondering if he could read in it that censure for the Prefect's presumption which should be there in the face of any loyal man.

Hsia said: " I have always believed that music should be the affair of musicians, so that I have not, myself, aspired." Then he laughed. " Let us listen more closely to the words of the play. I seem to remember that, in this first scene, the Prime Minister, whose political aspirations seek advancement in the days of a decaying dynasty, is suggesting to the Emperor's nephew, Wu Fu, a man whom he fears, that marriage to a princess of the Southern Yeh would be full both of mature wisdom and youthful desire—if the two may be combined. Of course, Wu Fu is only a concubine's son."

Indeed, on the stage Wu Fu was now declaiming to the Prime Minister:

> *In the South there are soft couches—*
> *I will not climb them.*
> *In the South there are riches easy to acquire—*
> *I do not seek them.*

And, in his turn, the Prime Minister sang:

> *Young men may stay at home*
> *If they have no ambition:*
> *They may forego travel*
> *If they distrust themselves.*

Wao remarked: " Pertinent indeed are their words! Each says what the other may think. Ah, here is the maid with a message to her beloved Wu Fu from the Prime Minister's daughter, Precious Vase. And the girl's note is merely a message of love to Wu Fu. He reads it secretly, and replies with news of the Prime Minister's wishes for his Southern marriage. A poor exchange. So far all is clear to me. I observe that, like most women, she puts her own affairs first. You remember the Master? *The pretty dimples of her artful smile.* It might have been written for this."

The Prefect told him : " It is a company which I have especially hired from the North. Their methods are very modern, improving the old plays by directing upon them the light of fresh minds. This play, THE VIRTUOUS CONCUBINE, particularly amuses me : its atmosphere of intrigue is markedly suggestive of the atmosphere which surrounds us here, in Sai Kwan."

Hsia cried : " Ah ! Wu Fu and the Prime Minister go off, while the Chief Eunuch strides upon the stage. You remember the famous passage ? "

Behind his mask, bright in stripes of red and blue, strangely beardless, the Eunuch was singing to the maid :

> *We have something in common*
> *All men would agree*
> *So let us now consider*
> *How we may serve each other.*

The maid replied :

> *You flatter yourself in speaking so*
> *My mirror answers me more truthfully*
> *What can I yield to you*
> *Against the advice of my mirror?*

Wao said : " She is pert. I admit that she is meant to be pert, in the play, but one might complain that she overdoes it."

The other two agreed.

In the upper boxes Mistress Hsia was praising the players.

"I have not seen a play for some time," she said, "so that maybe I over-rate them for that reason. Yet I feel myself experiencing some of the emotions which they so admirably portray. Is there much more of this scene?"

The Prefect's daughter, Jade Star, answered: "My memory is at fault. And yet I believe that this is the essence of the plot, that the Eunuch hints at a present, so that he may enlist the help of the Emperor's virtuous concubine, who shall obtain the retirement of the Prime Minister. This is in the Prime Minister's house, and soon, I think, Precious Vase, the Prime Minister's daughter, enters the stage and says that she does not desire such a fate to befall her father. So the Eunuch suggests that Precious Vase should wed the Emperor's son and heir, so that she, as ultimate Empress, would be more powerful than her father. But she is true to her love, Wu Fu, and will not contemplate the heir to the throne. He is, if I remember, an uncultivated youth. Ah, here is Precious Vase."

The gong clashed as the entrance curtain parted.

．　　　．　　　．　　　．　　　．　　　．　　　．

It was somewhat later, in the Prison scene. Wu Fu, having crossed the path of Prince Benevolence, the heir to the throne, had suffered the fate of those who even unconsciously obstruct those above them. He was, as might be expected, bemoaning his lot.

Alas, the high, white grasses whisper outside my
*　　prison;*
The clouds pass, unheeded, over the three Peaks;

I cannot, through these dark walls, perceive my
love,
Nor does she know how I suffer.

" Poor fellow ! " Hsia said. " He puts into his voice
the very cadence of woe."

Wao answered : " Yes. How ill-chosen is the name
of Prince Benevolence, who has sent him here. And
all because of a quarrel over a serving-maid, for whom
Wu Fu entertains no unsuitable emotions." Then he
laughed. " Ah, here is the servant of his love, come
with food to ease his discomfort. She has bribed the
guards to let her in, I suppose. You are not to ask the
nature of the bribe."

The maid sang :

Food may assuage sorrow:
The certainty of love may ease your bonds:
She sends this poor food for your comfort.
I must go, before the guards demand another
present.

The Prefect commented : " The girl sings well. They
are very good, these Northerners. But I see that the
Chief Eunuch has come to talk with Wu Fu. Hear
him, hinting at what he could do for the highest
bidder ! "

Money is a key to many desirable things
Have you money to spare?
For one prepared to pay the cost
This key will open all doors.

And then, as they were listening to Wu Fu's un-
compromising reply, a messenger came to the Prefect
and reported to him in a whisper. The others could

not hear the whispered words, but Wao sensed that this was the moment for which he had been waiting, and the hair at the back of his neck stirred. Had the commander of the Governor's troops demanded entry, or had they made of sudden force the lever to pry open the city of Sai Kwan?

Hsia Nan-p'o was saying to them: "This eunuch, here upon the stage, does not conceal his purposes. This play was, I understand, not performed upon the Palace stages, for it was thought that to see a eunuch so openly desirous of bribes would lower the opinion which people held of eunuchs."

The Prefect politely heard him out. Then he said: "I must ask you both to excuse me, for I am confronted suddenly with a business which will brook no delay. The play will continue. If you will permit . . ."

He rose from his seat and they all bowed. Then, as he went out, Wao and Hsia sat down to watch the actors. Wao, moving slightly in his seat, contrived to free his own sword-belt for instant use.

Hsia asked: "What has been troubling you? During the performance you have sat uneasily, moving in your seat, as if some other subject than the play were holding the attention of your mind."

Wao inclined his head.

"You have passed the examinations?" he asked. "Good. Then we may talk freely. It is true that I am uneasy, for it seems probable to me that all this film of courtesy and entertainment will very shortly be torn to fragments, and ideals vie with action to recolour my surroundings very differently. Admittedly, I welcome action when it comes at the expense of words, trusting my sword more fully than my tongue, but even now the advent of danger is not without its effect on me."

"I recognize," Hsia answered, "that there is much here of which I know nothing. Nevertheless, I feel that if a man is firm in his adherence to family and to Emperor, he may face unfamiliar events with a just confidence in himself."

Wao smiled. "You take my meaning," he said. "And possibly you have guessed more than you admit. This is the Emperor's ring. You recognize its authority? Good. Do not publish the fact that you have seen it. If I command, the Emperor commands. You are in my mind?"

"I am no man of war," Hsia replied, "but such hands as I have . . ."

"Much may have to be done without arms," Wao said, "if the doer is resolute and his actions are unexpected. Keep close to me, therefore, if we move from here, and while seeming to expostulate at my attitude, make it impossible for the others to attack me from behind. You hear them?"

And indeed, outside the courtyard, somewhere, rose the sound of men shouting, of men battering at the great door. . . .

"Come with me," Wao told Hsia. "Keep close and mould your actions equally of surprise and determination. We are going to the women's quarters. It is on the *yamen* wall, and offers, I think, the best port of entry to the Governor's troops, who have, my ears inform me, rushed the city gates and are now surrounding the *yamen*. Ask no questions, but obey."

On the stage a new character, the Virtuous Concubine, had appeared in the prison. She sang long and shrilly of the loyalty which, one gathered, she felt to all and sundry.

" Women can be too loyal," Hsia observed as he followed Wao from the covered seats, through a door and into a main passageway. " At least I have found it so."

.   .   .   .

The passage was empty. When Wao and Hsia Nan-p'o reached the room which had been given to Wao the night before, Peony and Pheasant were there, tidying. The noise from outside the *yamen* was more distinct now.

Hsia, seeing Peony, said: " Come with us. It may be that there is a use for you."

She shewed no surprise. The four of them came at last to the high, solid door to the women's quarters. A eunuch stood there, with a sword. Wao walked up to the eunuch and halted in front of him. Hsia, taking his cue, advanced and bowed.

" Your mistress is within? " he asked, for want of anything better.

Then Peony walked past the eunuch and stumbled against him. Wao seized the moment, unsheathed his sword and struck, all in one movement. The eunuch gave a great howl as the blade entered. Then he slid to the floor. Hsia picked up the eunuch's sword. Peony pushed open the door to the women's quarters, and the two men followed her. Pheasant came last.

.   .   .   .

The Prefect's daughter, Jade Star, drank from her tea-cup as she watched the play's sequence.

" I find this performance unworthy of you," she told Mistress Hsia. " These actors, although they are from the North and speak the Northern tongue, lack the conviction which an actor should possess. If you feel as I do, we might await the end of the play in greater comfort, in the women's quarters."

Mistress Hsia agreed: "If you will not consider it a criticism of your hospitality, I will admit that their performance lacks fire. It is as though they knew the words so perfectly that their minds were elsewhere."

"There is less noise, also, in the women's quarters," the other said. "I cannot imagine why my father permits this banging outside! I can only think that he and your honourable nephew and the magistrate Wao are so engrossed in the subject of THE VIRTUOUS CONCUBINE that they do not hear the noise. We need not take any of my women—then we shall be spared their everlasting chatter." She shewed Mistress Hsia the way from the upper storey of the theatre, through a door in the wall and so directly to her own rooms. "It is amusing," the Prefect's daughter said. "My eunuch at the main door does not know whether I am within or without, though he guards my person, and that of my visitors, with no less care because of his ignorance. Let us sit down, behind all this security."

Mistress Hsia said: "You are more than gracious in your treatment of me. You will allow me, an older woman, to tell you how I look forward to having you as a member of my family. I am sure that when your husband carries you over the threshold, you and I may look for long years of mutual pleasure—if my health allows it."

"You have many more years before you," Jade Star replied. "It is always those who feel their hold on life to be uncertain—it is always those who retain that hold most firmly. They do not expose themselves to the damp airs of evening: they do not indulge unduly

N

in that exertion which undermines the stronger constitutions. I watched my own mother, *when she passed to the West*, and reflected, then, on the way in which she had exhausted herself on my behalf, in the confidence of her living. And I thought that if she had considered herself more, had taken less care for me and my welfare, she would have seen many more summers. You will not, I am sure, be thus unwise." She sighed. "Alas, when all the poems have been written and all the epigrams made, what is life but a tendering of our bodies for an end which cannot be foreseen? "

Mistress Hsia agreed: "Indeed, what you say is very true. But it is, you will recall, laid down in the books that our duty lies in thus preserving ourselves from illness, so that our parents or our other relatives may have no call to feel anxiety on our account."

Then the door from the other room opened, and Wao Hien To entered.

"Ladies," he said, "where the Emperor's business is concerned, one need not too clearly explain that business in its pursuit. If I bow to you both, as I do now, I do so merely from the courtesy due to the widow of my old friend, the Governor of the City of Rams, and to the daughter of the Prefect of this city. Their rank entitles them to that courtesy. But, having done so, I must demand obedience, on the business of the Emperor." He called the other three into the room. "You, who are called Pheasant, make yourself useful to your mistress. You, Peony, find for me the box of rolls of silk which every woman of taste keeps in her room, and bring me two of the strongest."

Hsia Nan-p'o, who found his classical education a source of unexpected strength, bowed to his aunt and looked at the girl to whom he had been affianced.

She said, understanding his silence: "It can never be, now." Then she turned to Wao. "It is, I suppose, useless to ask for an explanation of this intrusion of men and swords?"

Wao took no notice of her. Outside the building, from the court, and below, the shouts of men rose towards them as Wao, knotting together the ends of two of the rolls of silk which Peony had found and brought to him, lowered the free end over the balcony and secured the other to a door-post.

"It reaches," he said, leaning far out to see. "And I am pleased to observe that Ssu, the driver of my carriage, is there with the Governor's troops, as well as Su Wai, the Censor. All is working for the best."

And then, suddenly, the unreal tension of the scene relaxed. The hanging curtain over the hidden door swung aside, and the Prefect, with Ou Ling-ma, strode in. The Prefect looked at his daughter and made a sign with his sword towards Wao. His daughter drew a dagger from her sleeve and moved to the balcony. Pheasant, throwing herself in front of her, tried to protect Wao with her body, and as the dagger flashed Wao turned, to see Pheasant take the point in her breast and fall across him. She slid to the floor: Wao stepped over her and with the flat of his sword struck at the Prefect's daughter. Hsia Nan-p'o, the dead eunuch's sword in his hand, tentatively pushed it into Ou's shoulder, as if to attract his attention. The Prefect struck Hsia's sword aside, just as Wao leaped forward to attack. Peony, throwing her arms round the Prefect's daughter as she reeled from Wao's blow, pinned her down on the couch and wrested the dagger from her hand. The four men faced each other across the room, Wao and Hsia with their backs to the light from the balcony, knees bent in the style of the sword-schools, double-handed swords held before them on guard.

" Surrender to the Emperor's authority ! " Wao cried.

The Prefect smiled. His huge bulk moved forward. Their swords met, clashed, slid, withdrew, clashed. Hsia was conscious of his own inadequacy in sword-play, striving to conceal it with a fierceness which certainly held Ou's attention. Through Hsia's mind ran the adage : *If you cannot drive a chariot, do not confess your inability to the horse.* He made little leaps with bent knees, and Ou's eyes followed him as Ou's sword moved in a small arc of defence.

Then Wao called, as if to a man behind the Prefect : " Disarm him ! " In the instant when the Prefect's eye moved from its keen attention, Wao leaped and struck at the elbow of the Prefect's right arm. The blow slid neatly between shoulder and sword, took muscle and half the bone in its stride, to bury the blade deeply in the wood of the floor. The Prefect, his sword still in his left hand, still smiling, stepped forward, menacing : blood spurted rhythmically from the cut artery, to stream down the useless, hanging forearm and drip from the still fingers. And his daughter, twisting herself free of Peony, rushed at Wao, pushing him away from the handle of his own sword, still firmly fixed in the floor.

It was at this stage that Mistress Hsia, who had remained seated, guarding the tray of tea-cups, decided on action. If she, who usually watched the actions of others with a carefully studied calm, had been called upon to analyse her thoughts, she would have advanced her affection for the nephew who now, somewhat foolishly, had stopped his little leaps and was waiting, a comparatively easy victim for a practised swordsman such as Ou Ling-ma, and her instinctive feeling that Wao, whatever else she felt about his tiring energy, represented the authority of the Emperor and the stability of Society. She would have set against these two emotions the reverence due to a Prefect and the solidarity which any aunt must feel for the father of her nephew's affianced. Fortunately, she was not consciously aware of any of these thoughts: she took the tray firmly in both hands, threw the cups and their contents at the Prefect's face, and with equal speed swung the tea-pot at the back of the head of Ou Ling-ma, now pondering where, and in what manner, to strike the young man with the ineffectual sword. She then sat back with a sigh of delight to observe what events would follow in the train of her impulse.

Wao, seizing the respite offered, side-stepped and tripped the wounded Prefect. The floor shook. Hsia Nan-p'o, delighted to see Ou stagger (for his aunt's aim had been excellent) placed his sword's end against Ou's stomach and pushed with all his strength. Then he withdrew the sword. Ou staggered again and fell to the ground, writhing a little.

"*I have hit the middle of the target,*" Hsia cried.

Wao threw the Prefect's daughter from him with a sweep of his arm, wrenched his own sword free from the floor and held it, point down, on the Prefect's throat.

"Bring more silk, and bind him," he told Peony. "Then bind up his elbow. He must not die too soon."

Mistress Hsia drew the Prefect's daughter down beside her as Peony hastened to obey.

"Do not sorrow too greatly," she said. "He has probably been a good father to you, and you will have that to remember him by."

Then a soldier climbed on to the balcony, steadying the hanging silk for the next man. Soon the room was full of the Governor's guard, and then the corridors echoed with the sounds of fighting and the cries of protesting women, as the men of the guard passed out from the women's quarters and slowly, steadily, fought their way against weakening opposition.

.   .   .   .

It was after the seventh scene of THE VIRTUOUS CON-CUBINE that the players noticed the complete absence of any audience. The flute wailed to silence in the middle of a cadenza, and they all stood, foolishly undecided.

.   .   .   .

The Censor, Su Wai, sat with Wao Hien To in the great hall of the *yamen*, issuing orders, hearing news. . . .

A soldier entered.

"There is a driver, one Ssu, who desires to speak with you," he said. "He has with him one of the rebels, and will not hand him over to our charge."

"Let him be brought in," the Censor ordered.

Ssu bowed low to the two men. While he bowed, he kept a tight hold on the collar of the boy Keung. Keung, also, bowed as well as he was able.

Ssu said: "This frightened youth besought me to save him from retribution. It seems that he knows something of what has taken place at the city of Kow Loong, something which you should hear."

Wao observed: "He is so accustomed to dealing with magistrates that he omits the extra ceremony due to a Censor. Yet, Sir, if he may speak, I should be grateful."

"Speak," the Censor said to Ssu.

"I have found this boy, from the household of the

merchant Tung Ho," Ssu told them. "He says that his master sent him to interview the girl Jasmine, at the Convent of Jade Serenity, whither you, Sir, had sent her. He tells me that the girl Jasmine revealed that when you, Sir, came to her room hurriedly on the evening of the death of General Wu, your clothes and your sword were bloody. He told this to his master and was immediately sent here with a letter to the Prefect. That is all that he knows."

"Which means, in its turn," Wao said, "that this merchant has solved the method of the death of General Wu, when that unfortunate came to Kow Loong to tell me of the conspiracy to rebel, and that Tung Ho will probably, in the manner of merchants, strive to revenge himself on my family and my dependants. He may even imagine that, if he obtains the persons of my family and my dependants, he will be able to bargain with them against his punishment for treason. Sir, if you will permit, I will send this driver to my *yamen*, so that he may take action suitable to whatever situation he finds on his arrival. He is a man of discretion and initiative, I have found. If he drives through the night, he should reach the city in daylight to-morrow."

"The idea is sound," the Censor agreed. "It will set your mind somewhat at rest, so that during our Summary Court, which you must attend, your mind will be with us, not with those in Kow Loong whom you have cryptically described as 'family and dependants'. He may take an archer with him—one of the Governor's bodyguard. Such a show of force may make it easier for him to do what you may have in mind for him. Not more than one: speed is the essence of your plan, I see, and a body of men moves slowly. And there should not be much trouble in so small a city." He sighed. "Add this womanish boy to those who shortly must appear before us."

The boy Keung was led away, protesting his innocence.

.　　.　　.　　.　　.　　.

Two days had passed since Jasmine returned to the Convent of Jade Serenity.

Hibiscus had sent the old nurse, Ah Sai, to gather gossip in the market, for behind the *yamen* walls, it seemed, there was little of the ebb and flow of personalties which go to make the life of men. Here only the more respectable emotions were admitted: here the phrase 'of course' had greater power than in the city outside.

Ah Sai shook her head sadly.

"Things are not what they were," she said. "In the market-place there is not the respect for authority which there was in my late master's time. The eyes of the people are discontented; their thoughts do not follow the WAY—any way. It is like the first signs of simmering in a pot over the fire."

Hibiscus said: "You are imagining things. Of course things are not what they were. How could they be so? Just as the successive seasons alter the earth's face, so the thoughts of men change and grow. Spring will return, and Summer—do not fear. What did you hear when you took my small present to Mistress Tung, the rich merchant's wife? Did anyone speak freely in your hearing?"

"The boy Keung has gone to Sai Kwan," Ah Sai told Hibiscus. "I could find out no more than that, for I did not dare to ask directly, and they were for ever speaking of other things, which I had no wish to hear."

Hibiscus sent Ah Sai back to the kitchen and, when she had gone, sat long, thinking what it might be her duty to do, in the absence of Wao.

. . . .

Almost all wisdom, Hibiscus thought, may be adapted to action or to inaction, for wisdom, whether of the ancients or of the present, can serve as a guide. That was the purpose of wisdom, its only justification. In the eleventh chapter of the Tao Te Ching, that collection of the epigrammatic sayings of the Old Master, the subject was emptiness.

> *There are thirty spokes to a wheel,*
> *But the empty hub makes it a wheel.*
> *Clay vessels are moulded:*
> *But the space within the clay is the vessel.*

A wheel, a vessel . . . what lesson here! Were not these very walls the things which made the city, whose emptiness served to house these many people? Were not the straight streets, crossing centrally at the Drum Tower, the spokes of a wheel, the Drum Tower the nave, the hub of that wheel? If this particular piece of wisdom were to be a guide, would not the very emptiness of the Drum Tower prove its worth? She formed a mental picture of the four streets running to the ancient, studded gates: she remembered how, nightly, these four gates were barred and a guard set in the Tower. This guard could stop all cross-passage: their field of fire from the galleries of the Tower ensured that direct attack could only happen at the cost of what death a flight of arrows might deal. Then, with the dawn and the opening of the main gates of the city, the Tower gates, too, were opened, so that once again it was possible to travel freely through. One sentry, above, remained in the Tower from dawn to dusk, in charge of the weapons, the bows and spears, which it would have been folly to carry every dawn from the Tower to the *yamen*—and every dusk from the *yamen* to the Tower. This sentry would be alone during the hours of light: some woman would bring his food. . . . And once in daylight possession of the Tower, it would be possible to resist attack for a much longer time than in the straggling, indefensible rooms and courtyards of the *yamen* itself. And why expect attack? She was unable to give herself an answer to that question: there was only the feeling of suspense, of impending danger, of the unspoken hostility of the people, the discontent (as Ah Sai had said) in their eyes. Tze Hung had lately been reluctant to enforce authority: Hibiscus had complained of the lack of respect in the streets, but Tze Hung had begged to be allowed to leave the disciplining of the populace until the return of Wao. And this in itself was suspicious, for Tze Hung was usually a somewhat officious Captain of the Guard, ready at a moment's notice to enforce respect for the dignity of Authority. That had been until a week or so ago. Yes, about the time of the death of General Wu. And if the populace seemed glum and resentful, if Tze Hung shewed no wish to help in the enforcement of discipline, it would be necessary to prepare for the perils of action instead of waiting, helpless, for that action. Hibiscus realized that the guard, as well as the people, must be counted on the side of the enemy, whom, as yet, she did not know, so that she had only herself to rely on, only her immediate servants as a frail support wherewith to defend things as they were against the impact of things as some unspecified rebels would have them to be.

Rebels! She admitted the thought, at last, to her conscious mind.

But events did not wait long upon deliberation, for on the next day, not long after morning rice, a messenger came from Tung Ho, requesting very formally the presence of Hibiscus at his house.

You may not be aware, the letter read, *that I have bought a property in the immediate vicinity of the Drum Tower, at the junction of North and East Streets, in which I purpose to install the girl Hidden Gold, whose affection for me you will, I trust, remember. It will give me great pleasure if you will drink tea there after the hour of high noon. The girl Hidden Gold and her friend Mountain Stream will be there to receive you, if you will have the graciousness to authorize, in your honourable husband's absence, their release from detention.*

This house of Tung Ho's must stand, Hibiscus knew well, an easy stone's throw from the gallery of the Drum Tower, an even easier bowshot. She welcomed her opportunity. A seeming acceptance, a procession in carrying-chairs, and she might reach the Drum Tower before Tung Ho (who must, she realized, be of her enemies) should find in her actions anything other than a natural and very feminine acceptance of his invitation. Silver Lantern, the two girls and the babies could follow in other chairs: it would be for Hibiscus to cajole or overcome the solitary sentry, and then the others could come in, the doors be shut, and (short of siege engines) they would have a brief space of suspended safety. If only Wao had returned from Sai Kwan. It might be that the Prefect was holding him there. Almost anything might be . . .

She sent one of the guards with authority over her hand for Hidden Gold and Mountain Stream to proceed to the new house, adding that the sentry who had been left to guard them was to accompany them to this house.

Even as she wrote the authority, she found herself blaming herself for a certain neglect of both her social and official duties in thus keeping the girls confined without considering what Wao would have wished her to do, had he been able to advise her.

They were, she remembered, both cultivated and charming girls, and would be almost certain, in their irresponsible way, to confuse the situation.

.   .   .   .

The little procession passed through the hostile streets without any incident, in the comparative quiet of the hour after midday. Tze Hung had not offered escort, and this had saved the need for refusing escort. Silver Lantern's chair moved parallel with but a pace behind that of Hibiscus: the two hired women, Ah Lau and Ah Sam, followed with Silver Lantern's child and Lien Ming Tsu: Hibiscus, turning, saw that this infant daughter of hers seemed supremely interested in all that went on around her. Last came the old nurse, Ah Sai, in another chair, carrying the Lien heir as if he were porcelain. Jasmine might have borne the child, but Hibiscus felt that Ah Sai owned him. Ah Sai's wrinkled face, as she bounced along, expressed pride and disdain. The baby wore a new rabbit's ear hat.

Under the shade of the Drum Tower Hibiscus stopped her chair. She and Silver Lantern descended and the chairmen were sent back to the *yamen*. The hired chairs for the others also stopped: their bearers were paid off. Hibiscus sent Silver Lantern to the first-floor guardroom with a covered basket: she herself followed Silver Lantern, hoping that fortune would favour her where reason and common sense promised little hope.

The sentry was asleep.

. . . .

"But," Hibiscus was saying a little later, when she had seen the ladder safely drawn up and the heavy trap-door lowered, "your duty of which you speak so often without defining it, is towards us, who represent the authority of the magistrate. It is nonsense to claim that because your immediate commander, the Captain of the Guard, might possibly order otherwise, therefore you should not obey me. You should not assume that the Captain of the Guard might possibly order otherwise, and that therefore you should not obey me. You should not assume that the Captain of the Guard would order you to disobey me, for he has not, in the past, so ordered, and therefore is not likely to do so in the future. You study the military arts?"

The sentry replied: "I am a man whose living is orderly, whose actions are the actions of a man who is not compelled to think. If soldiers had to think, there would be no time for fighting. So I do not think."

"So far," Hibiscus agreed, "you are wise. I was going to advise you, that, in the words of the old maxim, you should *Dare not to be a host, to attack, but dare to be a guest, to retreat.* Does it not imply that, when in doubt, you should give way? Does it not mean that, in a situation such as this, you should accept things as they are, that seeing me here as the symbol of the authority of the magistrate and so of the Emperor, whose symbol the magistrate is, you should obey me, by doing nothing, rather than obey the imagined instructions of the Captain of the Guard?"

" Wisdom," the sentry said, " is hard to come by, for a soldier. These matters are too difficult. But since you say that you claim the Emperor's authority—and I have not heard anyone dispute it—I shall do as you say. What is your wish, pray?"

" You may resume your position of contemplation," Hibiscus replied. " There will be time enough to tell you, when I desire other service from you."

The sentry lay down obediently; his eyes closed.

Hibiscus inspected the room in which they were. The floor was of tough beams; the walls, of worked stone, gave a feeling of security. There were four high, narrow windows. A door opened on to the narrow, projecting gallery running round all four faces of the Tower: it was not possible for two men to pass in this gallery. A series of wooden steps led from the room up to the next storey, where the arms were stored and the great drum, hanging in its wooden framework, could serve to declare an alarm or to summon aid. Beside the drum two heavy drum-sticks lay upon a stand.

She descended again to the first floor and stepped out through the door to the narrow gallery, to find herself at the corner nearest to the new house of Tung Ho. A wall ran to the house from the angle of the tower below her: a glance served to assure her that similar walls ran to the nearest houses at the other corners. Thus all traffic in these, the main streets, would have to pass beneath the Tower, and if the doors were shut below, no passage would be possible, whereas if the main doors below were open, there would be no reason for Tung Ho or indeed for any other to suspect the presence, here on the first floor of the Drum Tower, of a number of hostages very useful to a rebel. . . . If, later, it were needful to fight for safety, that necessity could be faced. Until then, Hibiscus decided, secrecy would be a better weapon. She listened for a little while to the querulous voice of Tung Ho, enquiring her whereabouts, and then withdrew to the room behind her.

In a corner, Silver Lantern and the two women tended children. In another, the sentry slept. Hibiscus went to a third corner and made herself comfortable on a pile of padded leather-covered armour. Nothing would happen until sunset, when from the great drum above them should sound the summons to close the city gates for the night. Or slightly before that, when the sentry should be relieved and a small guard take his place. The sun was only half-way down the sky as yet.

.   .   .   .   .   .

Tung Ho regarded with distaste the three men who had come from the City of Rams and who now sat eating his best melon-seeds. He did not blame them for the melon-seeds, for even in rebellions it is wise to comfort the stomach when opportunity affords. He did not blame them for the fact that they so obviously sat together, a solid phalanx of invasion in his new household. That, too, was inevitable, for their necks were indisputably in danger, and men who suffer the same danger tend to sit on adjacent seats. He blamed them solely because they were issuing orders to him, in his own house, and he knew that his vows (his ill-considered vows to the Society of Five) compelled him to obedience. He particularly resented that these orders were being given to him in the presence of Tze Hung, the Captain of the *yamen* guard, whom Tung Ho had often used for his own purposes, and whose actions had been hitherto conditioned by Tung's wishes.

Another source of disquiet was the unpleasant way in which these three men acted as one man, sitting together, eating together, walking together. . . . His imagination saw them, even, sleeping together and snoring in unison. . . .

"The woman," Tze Hung was saying, "is reported to have left the *yamen* at high sun with four women and three children in arms, to have traversed the streets in this direction, and then, set down almost at this door, to have vanished as vanish fox-women in the old tales. The bearers of the chairs say that they set down the women and children and were then dismissed."

Tung Ho said: "It is almost the hour when the city gates are shut and the evening drum-roll heralds the dark."

The three men rose together and looked out of the window. High against the darkening sky they could see the massive outline of the Drum Tower, its overhanging gallery and the curving roofs of each storey making it into a fantastic Thibetan hat. Below the tower six of the *yamen* guards were paraded, awaiting the return of Tze Hung to complete the ceremony of guard-changing. The three heads of the three men at the window turned together to look at Tze Hung, but they did not speak.

Suddenly Tze Hung came to life and understood everything. He pushed his way through the others and called loudly from the window: "Search the drum-tower!"

Now discipline, as the old writers on strategy and tactics have remarked again and again, has its justification in the steadiness with which trained troops, even if ignorant of the larger situation, will resist attack, will even die at their allotted posts, under the assault of those less disciplined, so that their commander can, at a moment's notice, state confidently the disposition of his troops, be they living or dead. And discipline, too, takes some of its strength from custom, from ceremony.

Therefore, in the absence of the expected opening commands for guard-changing, the six men standing neatly in two ranks remained so standing, though their heads, peering hither and thither in the growing and overdue dark, broke the fine symmetry of their formation, as they looked to see to whom this strange, this unwonted order might be addressed. And, in any event, the Captain of the Guard was used to give the orders from a position to the front of the Guard, not, as now, in a voice which held more than mere command, from a window of the adjoining house to their flank. Even if it were the voice of the Captain of the Guard, which they much doubted, for a voice from an open window at a bowshot's range is not quite the same voice as it would be did it come from the expected front.

Therefore these six men stood still, waiting upon events. And Tze Hung, realizing the cords of custom which bound them, turned with an impolite curse from the window and went across the room, down the passage and out at the main door of Tung Ho's house, towards the six waiting men.

As he reached the foot of the tower, he heard above him the voice of Hibiscus.

"It is more than time for the sunset drum," she called from the gallery. "The city gates should have been shut. I shall call upon the sentry, here in the

o

tower, to beat the drum. Tell your men to stand steady."

Tze Hung shrugged his shoulders. After all, the drum-call had to be sounded, so that on whose order and by whom mattered little, provided that the drumming were competent. He recalled that to-day's sentry, a man with the unprepossessing name of Kwong Hui, was an accomplished performer. . . .

The notes were at first faint, like rain on distant roofs. Then the volume grew to the roar of wind through spotted bamboos, to the deep clatter of a falling house, then back through all its sequences to the dim sound of a dry brush and dried paper, finishing with a single immense blow which startled. Tze Hung and the guard stood rigidly for the prescribed ten breaths, then relaxed. Tze Hung walked into the dimness of the lower storey of the tower. And, as he did so, the sound of three children in full throat came from above him and the voices of women calming these children. . . .

He walked out again from under the tower, and when he was at neck-craning distance looked up to see Hibiscus standing in the gallery outside the tower, looking down at him.

"Why did you not accept the invitation of the honourable Tung Ho?" he shouted.

She replied: "I did accept his invitation, but did not follow up my acceptance by my own presence. It seemed that for me to visit him thus would not be the wish of the honourable Wao Hien To, who is magistrate of this city. It would not have been right."

Tze Hung cried: "You have nothing to fear."

She answered: "No—not in this tower."

Tze Hung walked away to Tung Ho's house. Tung Ho and the three silent men joined him.

"She suspects," Tze Hung told them.

"That is not to be wondered at," the merchant replied. "It did not seem to me that your actions were clearly peaceful. Had you gone alone, having dismissed your guard, she might have parleyed with you and seen wisdom. But now . . ." He rose to his feet. "I shall speak with her myself. Prepare a ladder for me. To carry on a conversation at a storey's difference in height makes that conversation difficult. I must persuade her to come down from the tower. Your practical, military methods have brought little fruit: it is now the turn of the business mind."

Tze Hung gave orders for a ladder to be fetched for Tung Ho. Then he said to the others: "For you, I doubt if even the possession of these women hostages will point the road to safety. We may speak freely—the merchant has gone. For those of us who are not of the Five, yes: the Governor's men might bargain with us. They might even keep to their bargain, if they make one. But to you—they will be merciless. No hostages, nothing, will keep your heads firmly on your bodies, once Wao comes to this city. He would, I believe, regret losing the woman Hibiscus, for he is fond of her, but he would not allow her life to interfere with what he conceives to be his duty to the Emperor. That is his nature, and it cannot be altered." He sighed. "For myself, I do not propose to seek safety in distance. That is my nature, also. But you . . . The news is definite. The Prefect's *yamen* is under assault: the rebellion has not ripened to united action, and further fighting is foolish. You would be wise to go. He will be talking to her. Take a supply of

money—Tung Ho's money—and put miles of sea
between us. You will be well advised."

He left them to their thoughts.

Outside, as the big moon rose to finger with silver
the Tower, the walls, the houses and the now empty
streets, Tung Ho advanced to the foot of the Tower.
Behind him a man carried a ladder.

"I wish to speak with the Lady Hibiscus," he cried.
"And to avoid strain to our voices I shall, with your
permission, ascend this ladder. You will observe that
it is too short to constitute a means of entry to your
tower. Is your wish my wish?"

Hibiscus, on the gallery, replied: "To speak is any
man's privilege. But do not go further than speaking."
She turned and went in. To Silver Lantern she said:
"Take one of these brooms and stand on the gallery
on the side remote from the door. If any man sets a
ladder against your side of the Tower, you know what
to do. I am going to allow the merchant to speak with
me. Speech always makes for delay, and delay is the
only weapon which we possess." Then she took a
broom herself and went out on to the gallery where
the city lay in black and white patchwork under the
moon.

.   .   .   .

In the room above, where the great drum stood, the
sentry named Kwong Hui was testing the stacked bows
of mulberry wood and setting the arrows in order.

"I am a man who seizes opportunity," he told the
admiring women and the sleeping children.

The old nurse, Ah Sai, smiled scornfully. The
sentry, watching her, wondered that a smile could so
little help to make a wrinkled face attractive.

"If I obey the Captain of the Guard, two things may

happen." He pursued his theme. "Either the rebellion succeeds, and I remain a soldier in the *yamen* guard, or the rebellion fails, when I lose my head. Whereas if I obey the Lady Hibiscus two things may happen. Either the rebellion succeeds, and I lose my head, or the rebellion fails, when I shall receive rewards quite beyond my imagination to conceive. Now of these four possibilities, the last only attracts me. So I shall strive to help to hold this tower unentered, as long as is possible, until the arrival of help from elsewhere. That is the course of wisdom, as well as the course of courage, and I am deficient in neither wisdom nor courage."

Ah Sai sniffed: "You talk too much, but there is sense." She turned to the two women. "I observe, also, a stove, water, and a number of boiling jars stored here. It would be wise to use the stove to heat the water in the jars, for boiling water is a woman's weapon, and we are women. There is charcoal under that sacking, yonder. Give me the three babies, and boil water. Not oil, yet, although its effects are greater, for we may need to cook with it. Later, perhaps, if the situation becomes difficult."

The women hastened to obey. Kwong Hui opened one of the four windows and looked out.

"I could eat fried bean-curds now, at once," he observed to the moon.

. . . .

The great hall at Sai Kwan was dark now, heavy with the breath of many men, choked with the words which had flowed in never-ending spate, stifled with the emotions which those words had betrayed and with other emotions which men had kept in their hearts. Fear there had been, and pride, greed and gain and lust for power, besides the simpler, sweeter motives which make the common man.

The details of the conspiracy had proved hard to set in order, for the Prefect had maintained a sullen silence, and his daughter, looking at him, had broken into such a storm of sobbing that the Censor, angered, had ordered her removal. Ou Ling-ma, dead from Hsia's deliberate thrust, could throw no light, and the other three of the Five were nowhere to be found. They had, in fact, last been seen by a guard hastening on borrowed horses down the road to the coast and the city of Kow Loong.

The small figure of the Censor, Su Wai, might have seemed insignificant had it not been for the glitter of his ceremonial clothes in the light of fresh torches, and the way in which all attentions were directed on him as he listened to evidence and questioned witnesses. Wao, beside him under the great gilded words which promised justice, had little to do save to agree. He had early given his own story of the meeting with General Wu and the secrecy with which he had surrounded his knowledge of General Wu's message. He had told how he had been invited by the Prefect to explain, at Sai Kwan, points on which the report had deliberately left the Prefect ignorant, how Peony had told him of the ceremony in which the Prefect had assumed the rights of an Emperor, of the last fight in the women's quarters.

The Censor said: " And this girl Pheasant, who herself took the blow of the dagger meant for you? What of her? "

" She died, though she knew it not, in the Emperor's service," Wao said.

The Censor shook his head.

"No," he said. "She died in trying to save you. Her motives were not as noble as you would make out. Nevertheless, she died well. Have her body suitably dealt with. She has no parents?"

"She told me of none," Wao answered, remembering that their conversation had been on a very different subject from that of parents. "If I may be allowed to arrange for her coffin. . . ."

"Do as you will," the Censor replied. "And this other girl, Peony, who seems to have helped you?"

Peony said: "My father was a magistrate. I could do no less."

"Then," the Censor observed, "you are rewarded by your conscience. We thank you." He turned to Wao again. "I shall have the Prefect and his daughter taken to the Capital for examination. Mistress Hsia. . . ."

"Mistress Hsia has gone to her own *yamen*," Wao told him. "She begged to be excused, and was taken away by her nephew. I had only opportunity to thank her for the excellent aim with which she turned the scales, and said that I should, later, hope to give myself the pleasure of discussing matters with her. She said that if I could find my way to her in a maze inhabited by two old women and her nephew, I should be very welcome."

"We declare the court closed," the Censor said. "It has been a tiring day."

The guard took up positions, and the two of them went back towards the living-rooms of the *yamen*.

As they walked, Wao said: "I should take it as a favour if you would permit me, myself, to return to Kow Loong, where certain duties await me."

The Censor smiled.

"Those duties, so far as they are the duties of a magistrate and not of a man, devolve now on another. I have authority to make a number of changes of an official nature. Had young Hsia Nan-p'o been here, I should have presented him with the paper of his appointment in your place. Perhaps, therefore, it would be as well if he and you went together. Then he may prepare for his own formal reception, and you may do such other things as you need. Besides, the two of you will be better able to deal with any eddies and backwaters of the revolt."

"I will do my best to aid him," Wao replied. "But as magistrate of Kow Loong he will, of course, be able to call for my aid as of right." He called Peony, who was waiting near. "Summon the honourable Hsia Nan-p'o to this *yamen*."

Peony asked: "May I take the summons myself?"

The Censor nodded. "Any fool can see that you will make a good messenger," he said. When Peony had gone, he went on: "If you will not ask me your own destiny, I must perforce tell it to you. Such diffidence to rank on your part is alarming in its cor-rectitude."

"To be expected to ask," Wao replied, "is to ask. I therefore ask my destiny."

The Censor produced a scroll.

"The Prefecture of this city," he said. "Again, on my authority, but I do not expect it to be questioned. You have done well. It may be that your new post will fit better with your intended domestic purposes than would the roving commission of an Emperor's mes-senger. You have only to say. . . ."

"It is not for me," Wao answered, "to question your wisdom. And indeed, as you say, I have for some little while felt domesticity creeping upon me and entwining me. It would be good, I think, after this display of worldly ambition and the inevitable evil which it brings in its train, to relax for a while and consider some philosophical viewpoint. You remember how Lao Tze said : *The Sage does not need to go outside the door, in order to know the world. He does not need to look through the window, in order to know the Way of Heaven.* That seems to me to authorize at least a brief space of contemplation."

The Censor shook his head.

" The textual experts," he said, " have often queried whether that is a statement or a question. You should read them. Nowàdays, of course, the saying has been modernized. *Can the new-fledged scholar, from his study chair, know all under the blue heaven?* "

" You have added blue from your own store of wisdom," Wao replied. " What if clouds lower? "

Thus they passed a pleasant and literary hour, until the return of Hsia Nan-p'o from the Hsia mansion, and a little later Wao and Hsia took the road to Kow Loong, riding at the head of the comforting security of half a hundred of the Governor's horsemen.

.   .   .   .   .   .

Ssu, driving fast down the winding road from Lo Fu ferry, sang happily. The archer listened, sitting in comfort on the floor of the carriage.

Ssu sang :

> *The archer aims to hit the gold,*
> *Yet does not strive to pierce the leather;*
> *Each arrow's loosed—it flies—behold,*
> *The archer aims to hit the gold!*
> *But lovers lack control, I'm told;*

Their shafts want point, as well as feather—
The archer aims to hit the gold
Yet does not strive to pierce the leather!

The archer replied, lazily: "I ask nothing better than to sit here, on my ease, not even compelled to look at the probable beauty of the scenery. And my comfort would be even greater, did you spare me your songs about subjects of which you know nothing beyond the technical terms. How if I, from my place here, should sing you a song of chariot-driving?"

"I will spare you the effort," Ssu said. "I have a great collection of these songs, and there is one, also, for chariot-driving. Listen."

> *If driving is an art indeed,*
> *Few men there are that have the knack*
> *Of suiting methods to the breed!*
> *If driving is an art indeed*
> *You should not treat a mettled steed*
> *Like any spavined soldier's hack—*
> *If driving is an art indeed,*
> *Few men there are that have the knack.*

The archer observed: "Two objections. First, who is spavined, the soldier or his horse? Second, there is no mention of women in it."

"To drive women," Ssu returned, "is beyond the wit of man."

The rounded, green slopes of the hills, cut by the terraced rice-fields, swung by.

.   .   .   .   .   .

At the Convent of Jade Serenity, Jasmine struggled against boredom. Of what evil, she felt, was it to spend hours in supposed contemplation, other hours in speaking rituals whose words meant little—and that little foolish? She was young—the green weeds between the flagstones in the courtyards called up the greener grass on wind-swept hill-tops—the song of a misguided bird on the roof recalled the open air and the sun.

Further, she was the mother of a son, of the only son of the dead Lien Kin Wai, and this motherhood entitled her to respect and to consideration, so long as Hibiscus, Lien's wife, had not herself given him a son. And for Hibiscus to follow her daughter with a son was now impossible, for Lien Kin Wai lay in his coffin under the humped grave in the parcel of land which Hibiscus had bought with the money which she had saved. It was not right, Jasmine felt, that the mother of Lien's heir should thus be sequestered in a convent. . . . Not that Hibiscus, she was sure, would neglect to tend or have tended this heir which was Jasmine's son. But still, even mother-love entitled her to something better than the never ending pretence that all virtue came from above, from the inaccessible gods, instead of from the warm, intimate emotions of men and women. . . .

So she was more than pleased when her ordained prayer-time was cut into by the arrival of Ssu, the *yamen* driver.

" I was to enquire after your well-being," Ssu invented hurriedly, "and to ask if anything could be done which has not yet been done to make this stay of yours pleasant to you."

Jasmine said: "I am alone, and that is not right. I have done my duty in presenting my late master with an heir, and I do not think that I should be compelled to stay here, as if I had taken their foolish vows, as if I, a woman, had nothing better to live for than have these half-women around me. The Abbess comes to talk with me. She urges contemplation and thought for the spirits of men. I do not want to contemplate! "

Ssu said, deprecatingly: "It is easy to understand why you should find this life not to your taste. Yet I know that the honourable Wao Hien To, my master, does not intend you to stay here long—he has said as much to me. And then you will, doubtless, return to the *yamen* to enjoy the position to which your motherhood entitles you. Yes. That is so. And is your stay here as barren of incident as you make out? Does nothing happen in this world of women? It there no laughter? "

"There is nothing," Jasmine told him. "And all the days that I have been here, I have had but one visitor—a visitor who hardly counts, for he is only a boy—that Keung who is of the household of Tung Ho, the merchant. He came here, and we spoke for a little while of things which we knew in common, and shortly he left me—I thought—a little hurriedly, as if he had remembered something which previously he had forgotten. That was all." She laughed a little bitterly. "Listen to some of their prayers! They are just starting. Will the gods be more particularly likely to listen to the entreaties of women if those entreaties are many-voiced? If these moanings are multiple? You see, I have been reading words since I last saw you."

Ssu nodded.

"You certainly speak well," he agreed. "The boy Keung—what did you and he find in common to talk of? I seem to remember an earlier occasion on which you and Hidden Gold made the lad blush. But you would hardly speak of that."

" We spoke of little," she answered, " of his family and of ours. Of the events of past days."

" Of the murder of General Wu? " Ssu demanded, suddenly.

She faltered: " A few words. He did not seem interested, for he went away shortly afterwards. He said that he had come to see me about my going into the household of the rich merchant, Tung Ho. That would be a very good thing for me to do, for I do not feel that I am needed now, with you others. It is not the same as when my first master was alive."

Ssu said: " So you told him of the death of General Wu? Then tell me. Now. No—do not attempt to produce an imaginary tale. You have imagined too much already. Tell me what you told the boy Keung."

Jasmine repeated about Wao having come to her room, suddenly, just before the search of the *yamen*, and how his clothes and his sword had both been bloody.

Ssu rose to his feet.

" Come with me, now," he ordered. " It may be that we can undo some of the mischief which you have done—it may be not. Come. And do not forget, this time, that you know nothing of anything, that your mind is filled with wonder, and that, above all, *you do not know*. Remember that, and perhaps you will be able to do something to repair the ill into which your untied tongue has led you."

Jasmine put a few clothes in a bundle and followed Ssu to the waiting carriage. She brushed aside the nun at the gate, when she tried to stop them.

As Jasmine stepped into the carriage, the archer said: " A woman? And a bundle? I thought that you were on government business."

" She is government business," Ssu answered, as he took up the reins.

The archer moved over to give Jasmine room. It was approaching the hour of the cock, when women begin to think of preparing the evening meal.

. . . . . .

The *yamen* at Kow Loong City had proved to be deserted, save for a single sentry at the gate. From the centre of the city rose the sound of men shouting, of a crowd which watches events from a safe distance. As the carriage neared the Drum Tower, there was no need to demand what was happening, for those on the outskirts of the crowd were asking news of those in front, and those in front were passing word back.

Ssu told the other two : " Do nothing, say nothing, of your own invention. Model yourselves on me, however strange my actions may be." Then he edged the carriage through the protesting crowd, towards a roughly built pile of stones near Tung Ho's house. As they approached, it could be seen that these stones came from one of the four dividing walls which had run from the base of the Tower to join the buildings at the four compass points, and that now it was possible to move round the Tower from every angle. Archers had been posted behind the four piles of stone, and every little while the whistle of an arrow and its thud in the woodwork of the gallery shewed that there had seemed to be a movement on the part of those within.

Tze Hung, the Captain of the Guard, was standing in the shelter of the stones as Ssu drove up. A dead man lay beside the wall, an arrow in his throat. Two more lay almost under the gallery.

Ssu threw the reins to the archer, stepped down from the carriage and went to Tze Hung.

"I come," he said, "with orders from the Prefect of Sai Kwan that the women of the late magistrate should be taken into safe custody. It would seem that your men, here, are making that custody unsafe. A woman with an arrow through her will not please the Prefect."

Tze Hung cried: "But news reached us that the Governor's troops had taken the city of Sai Kwan. How then can your news, also, be true?"

Ssu said: "Men in haste are poor judges of fact. But there is no doubt that what I have said is the will of the Prefect, for he told me so himself. As regards the Governor's troops, they have changed sides, as troops will. So, with your permission, I will go and acquaint the women with the Prefect's instructions. Will you take charge of this girl, whose name is Jasmine, while I go to speak with those in the Tower?"

Jasmine said to Tze Hung: "The boy Keung told me that the merchant, Tung Ho, would do me the honour of taking me into his household. Where is he?"

Tze Hung, watching Ssu and his archer stride across the intervening space towards the Tower, told her: "Who am I, to know where Tung Ho has gone? Do not interrupt my thoughts. Stand there. Those two are strangely confident. There has been no danger for them as they walked, unprotected, to the Tower. I wonder . . ."

Below the balcony, Ssu cried loudly: "By the order of the Prefect of Sai Kwan, lower the ladder below the Tower."

Hibiscus answered from above: "What news do you bring?"

Ssu said, in a quieter voice: "For your own ear, the Prefect's name is Wao Hien To. Now lower your

ladder and turn the trapdoor back, for they expect you
to come out, not us to go up. Quickly."

At the top of the ladder, while Ah Lau and Ah Sam
pulled the ladder up and lowered the heavy trap-door,
Silver Lantern greeted her husband with such obeisance
as was right, while Ssu bowed to Hibiscus. The guard
with the name of Kwong Hui had stood with bow-
string taut, the arrow aimed at Ssu's archer.

Ssu said: "You should not keep the bow at tension,
thus. It is bad for the bow. Either loose the arrow,
or relax the bow."

The archer who had come with him agreed: "A
bow should not be treated thus. It is not a sword, to
be held over a man's head without harm to the sword.
My name is Mu, and, unless my memory betrays me,
you and I competed together in the archery contest at
Sai Kwan. How many moons ago?"

"You shot one point better than I," Kwong Hui
admitted, relaxing his bow.

Ssu said: "An end of old comrade's tales. Up to
the next storey, and keep them away. There are plenty
of arrows?"

"There is a store of them above. I will shew you,"
Kwong Hui said. "Come quickly. It may be that
again we may compete. I have killed three persistent
ones." They ascended to the roof.

Silver Lantern was proudly shewing her son to Ssu.
"He has grown, has he not?" she asked.

.   .   .   .

Behind the pile of stones Tze Hung stood, taking
himself very seriously. For, as the old adage says, *if
a soldier does not consider the results of his actions,
why should his wife?* He asked himself whether, indeed, it could be true that the Governor's troops had

sided with the rebellion. Could the three men who had, they said, escaped from the city, anticipated the outcome of a battle which had not yet taken place? Was Ssu telling the truth? He strode over to the Tower, alone.

" When are the women coming out? " he called.

" Do not loose your arrows," Ssu said to the archer and the sentry. "Let me talk with him." He went to the gallery and put his head over, cautiously. Nothing happened.

Tze Hung called up again: " When are the women coming out? You have been a long while, talking to them in there. And the ladder has been drawn up. Were you telling me the truth, when you said that the Governor's troops had revolted? Did you actually receive a message from the Prefect? "

Ssu said: " Let us take your questions in sequence. It is true that I received an order from the Prefect, telling me to safeguard these women. I do not know why he should be solicitous for them."

Tze Hung cried in anger: " Nor I. But we have talked long enough. I order you to bring them down, together with last night's sentry, Kwong Hui, who has to answer for the deaths of these three of his fellows."

Hibiscus joined Ssu on the balcony.

" It would have been better for you," she said, " if you were one of those three who have *ridden the dragon*, for certainly the final end of you will not be as quick, as pleasant, when you are punished."

"Get back into the Tower," Ssu told her in a whisper. "I could have continued talking to him for a long while, and now you have made him suspicious." He called down: "She is distraught. I dare not bring her down now, or she might do herself a damage, and

P

the Prefect would blame me. I do not wish to en-
counter blame. And, while I remember it, it would
be wise to send the carriage back to the *yamen* stables,
for the horse is tired with journeying. He should be
rubbed down before he catches cold."

Doubtfully, Tze Hung walked back to his pile of
stones and gave the needed orders. The horse was led
away.

Then Tung Ho came out of the house, dressed for
travelling.

"When facts are certain, it is better to recognize
them," he said. "You have allowed this man Ssu to
mislead you. It is certain that our rebellion has failed.
It is certain that unpleasant death awaits us if we stay
here. I have had such of my money, as I can immediately lay hands on, taken to a boat, and I shall not publish my destination. Will you come with me?"

"But the man Ssu spoke of the Prefect's orders,"
Tze Hung objected. "How can the Prefect be giving
orders if the rebellion has failed?"

"He did not tell you the Prefect's name," Tung Ho
replied. "It is quite clear to me that the Prefect, in
view of his solicitude for the women, must now be the
man whose women they are. Yes, the rebellion has
failed, and Wao Hien To has been made Prefect. The
other three are coming with me. Make up your mind."

Tze Hung waved him away.

"Go on your boat," he said. "I am a soldier, and I
retreat only before seen enemies. I do not believe those
tales of yours."

Tung Ho shrugged his shoulders and left him.

. . . .

The archer Mu and Kwong Hui, the sentry, stood
side by side on the upper gallery of the Tower. Below

them the wide space was bare of people: only occasion-ally did a figure slip from cover to cover near the houses.

" As a life," Kwong Hui observed, " this has much to recommend it. There are no parades to attend, the brightness of our equipment is our own affair: the women have plenty of food in the store and cook it to perfection. What more could I ask? "

The archer said: " The advantages which you catalogue are certainly advantages. Yet there are others. Look at the space below us: consider the ample supply of arrows which we have here. Are these not the ideal conditions for a resumption of that contest in archery at which, I do not remark how long ago, I had the honour of defeating you? "

Kwong Hui said: " Good. What shall we shoot at? There are no golden orioles here, no gleaming targets for our skill."

The other replied: " You spoke too soon. Look! On the roof-top of that house yonder."

Kwong Hui recognized the brilliant neck and wing-plumage of the *green-beak*. The bird looked down at the adjacent courts: its feathers gleamed as it moved.

" The range is about a hundred paces," he said. " More than my skill would be needed. The bird is yours."

The archer objected: " No. For, if you miss it by a wide enough margin, the bird will not stir, and I may shew you how to draw a bow. Whereas if I shoot first, you will have no chance."

Kwong Hui drew his bow.

" Poor arrows, these," he said as he steadied himself. The shaft ran to the right, and low. The bird stirred, but did not take flight. " I wonder where that shot finished! "

The archer Mu slowly drew back the string of his bow. Standing with his feet correctly apart, his back arched, for a moment he was a figure on one of the old bas-reliefs of an earlier dynasty.. Then the string straightened, the arrow rose gently and fell again on its line of sight, to strike the roof-tree just below the bird.

"Better," Kwong Hui agreed. "Better. Had the arrow been flighted with fairer feathers, you would have scored."

The archer shook his shoulders.

"You are right about the arrows," he agreed. "But look: they are coming."

In fact, men appeared from each point of the compass, bearing bundles of straw not too heavy to carry at a run. With them, two others bore ladders, and the whistle of arrows, thudding into the woodwork of the Tower, shewed that the attack was being covered by hidden archers. Mu loosed another shaft, and one of the straw-bearers fell.

"I prefer cooking to be done in a kitchen," he said. "And there are better foods to cook than men, women and babies. Look to your side."

Kwong Hui called to the women and ran to the other side of the Tower. Hibiscus and Silver Lantern filled small bowls with boiling water, in readiness.

"Not oil, yet," Ssu said. "If they are trying to burn us out, water is better."

.   .   .   .

Mountain Stream looked sideways at Hidden Gold, as they sat in the main room of Tung Ho's new house.

"It would seem," she said, "that rebellion and opportunity have conspired together for our advantage. If merchants seek safety in flight, what matter so long as they leave their houses behind? This is a very pleasant house."

Hidden Gold said: "Yes. We are like the flotsam left behind when water recedes. But I suppose that we shall find little difficulty in convincing men that the house belongs to us. After all, he wrote his intention to the Lady Hibiscus, and it is by her authority that we are here."

They looked round them at those pieces of furniture which Tung Ho had apparently intended for Hidden Gold's delight.

Mountain Stream observed: "He has left behind quite a quantity of goods. I suppose we shall have to ensure that his wife does not send to fetch it away. We had better lock the doors."

The guard who had been left to look after them said: "All the doors are locked, but not for the reason which you have given. There is my point of view to be considered, too. Outside, men are fighting, and I prefer to keep behind good walls when arrows fly. Whichever side wins, I shall have obeyed orders. Nevertheless, I find that a man, however wisely employed, must eat, and there seems to be a deficiency of food here. If you will give me money, I will go out by the back way and buy sufficient for at least to-day. Then you can cook it, and all will be well."

Hidden Gold told him: "Go and do as you have suggested. We shall stay here until one side or the other has triumphed. Here is money."

The guard, well satisfied, left them. Mountain Stream went down to lock the door at the back entrance until the guard's return.

"We can sell our other house in the street of Happiness," she said to Hidden Gold when she had sat down again. " That will bring money for furnishings. And this is a very central house, much better than the other. Of course, I am not sure that I shall like the constant noise of traffic."

Outside, they could hear the voice of Tze Hung giving orders.

.   .   .   .

It was a little later. Three of the four straw-bearers had fallen: the fourth was now in the space below the Tower, with his bundles. Two ladders had been placed in position and then pushed sideways by the brooms of the women, who crept along in the cover of the lower gallery and then, suddenly bobbing up, swept the ladders sideways, so that they and their burdens fell to the ground. One man from the ladder had been shot as he fell: the other had joined the straw-bearer below. Ssu, lying on the bottom floor, listened.

" They have forgotten the flint and steel," he said. " Bring boiling water quickly and stand ready, when I open the trap-door, to direct it properly."

When he swung the door over, they could see a great pile of straw in one corner, but no men. Then the straw stirred.

" Throw it on the bundle," Ssu cried. " More. Again."

Two men ran out from their shelter. One fell, an arrow from above piercing his neck. The other ran on. Then he, too, fell with a shaft between the shoulders.

" It is easier than *green-beaks*," the archer said. " That is one more to you and one more to me. But mine was the more difficult."

.   .   .   .

Wao, at the head of the fifty horsemen, turned to speak to Hsia Nan-p'o, riding just behind him.

"We shall attack at the South Gate," he said. "There is a wood yard not far from the walls, and a long baulk of timber in the hands of ten men will form a better key to the city than any words can do. We shall halt in the shadow, dismount ten men and do as I have said. You will take charge of these ten men. When the gate is open, I and the forty others will ride through : your ten will mount a guard at the gate. My men will bring up the ten riderless horses from the woodyard and leave them with you. After that, you will await my orders. Is that clear to your mind?"

Hsia replied : "Yes."

"This is the place," Wao said.

As they halted, in the darkness, the sound of men dismounting and moving timber was suddenly swamped in the great, deep notes of the drum.

"The Drum Tower," Wao told Hsia. "There is light in the sky, too. We must hasten."

The city gates, heavy wood as they were, yielded to the second rush of the ram. A scared guard challenged Hsia from the shelter of the gate-house, and Wao swept through into the empty street, urging his horse up the slight slope to the intersection of roads where the drum-tower stood. Between the houses on either side, at the top of the rise, he could see the flicker of flames. The great drum, deepening now, was beating out the rhythm of the "call to aid" : figures moved against the background of the flames. As they came nearer, it was possible to see the Tower itself. Fire was bursting from the windows above the lower gallery.

There are times when a man's knowledge of himself, his consciousness of the orderly progress and arrangement of nature, fail suddenly before something outside himself, some cataclysm, leaving him amazed, swallowing at saliva which is not there, his heart sinking. So now Wao, riding into the circle of movement, saw in the licking flames no hope, saw even in imagination the gaunt shape of a burned-out building. What wind there was blew towards him, from the North Gate. But yet the great drum echoed over the now audible crackling of the fire: some at least lived. He knew instinctively that Hibiscus at least must be alive: she could not herself be responsible for the measured, skilled rhythm of the drumming, but only under her will and direction, Wao felt, could so formal and so compelling a sound still proclaim the control of men over nature, of determination over fire, of confidence over disaster. The ring of spectators closed a little as they reformed after the passage of himself and his men: he was reminded of a boar-hunt, when the circle of spearsmen would close for the kill, and the bitterness of rage moved him as he rode without question towards a knot of men whence a girl's voice called: " Here! " Then the voice went out suddenly, like a lamp in the wind. The voice had been Jasmine's voice. He spurred his horse: the figure of Tze Hung, the Captain of his Guard, loomed up through the smoke and the film of anger over Wao's eyes. He struck at this face as he rode, saw the face dissolve, knew nothing of Tze Hung's answering sword-thrust and the cut which now gaped in his right forearm. . . . The horsemen with him rode straight through and over the group. . . .

Wao reined up.

" Ladders! " he cried. The drum-beats ceased.

And then (for they had come to the North, the windward side of the Drum Tower) he saw the rope being lowered from the second gallery. Here the wind blew into the window, and the side of the Tower was dark against the lit sky. At the end of the rope a bundle hung, swaying, bumping gently against the stones, and from the bundle proceeded a mingled babble, a compounded wailing. Wao's men received the bundle, untied the rope, and let the corners fall.

As at a signal, from their seat upon the ground, Hibiscus's daughter, Jasmine's son and the boy of Silver Lantern set up a prodigious howl. Wao laughed with relief, to find that, again, he could not swallow.

Hibiscus came next, on the rope, and then two ladders, tied together, were set against the side of the Tower, and thereafter due precedence was followed. When Ah Sai, the old nurse, came down, she said: "All the food-baskets are burning now. We shall have to buy more, to replace them."

Silver Lantern and Ssu, hastening down the double ladder, joined the group, then the two hired girls, Ah Sam and Ah Lau, then the archer whom Ssu had brought with him, his bow across his shoulders. Last, the sentry Kwong Hui descended.

"I was compelled to come last," he said, "for in a manner of speaking it was my tower. Alas, I have lost some of my own property, up there. And the drum—that will burn, too. It was a good drum."

Hibiscus said, when she had bowed to Wao: "Sir, I am glad that I can give you back all those whom you entrusted to my care—and some others. The children are not harmed?"

Wao answered: "I have seldom been as glad to hear their noises. No: they are dirty, but that is all." He turned to his men. "Tze Hung? He is dead?"

When they told him so, he nodded. "That simplifies matters," he said.

Hibiscus told of the sentry's actions, as she bound up Wao's wounded arm.

"He seems a worthy man," she said, and paused for comment.

"Collect your men," Wao told Kwong Hui, "and place them in the care of these forty. We shall deal with them at dawn. Send to tell the honourable Hsia Nan-p'o, at the South gate, that all is well and that he should come to the *yamen*. Then let all the guards, save those on the city gates, return to the *yamen*. That done, you may sleep until my court at dawn, when justice shall be swift. Go."

"Should men from the Governor's troops replace those at the North, West and East gates?" the sentry asked.

Wao nodded.

"He has a head for detail," he observed to Hibiscus. "Good. Come."

The fire had reached the upper storeys of the tower, and flooring fell with a crash. Wao led the way to the *yamen* on his horse.

Ssu began the task of requisitioning carrying-chairs for all the *yamen* party.

.   .   .   .

Dawn hesitated just below the horizon. Wao's mind ran over the ideas which dawn called up—the courts held in this inclement hour, the poems written to immortalize the moments when first-light coloured the edges of things, the lover's reluctance at cock-crow, the criminal's last, unhappy glance round the things which were familiar and which were soon to be seen no more. He remembered the dawns of the several seasons. . . .

At the Season of the Small Ice.

White moon mazes
Courtyard and steading,
Roof-tree and palm thatch.
Black walls are shadowed.
Slow frost glazes
The open eyes of the dead.

It was Spring, not late Autumn, and they were bringing in the body of Tze Hung for his inspection. The wound in Wao's forearm itched under its bandage: Hisbiscus' hands had been tender as she washed the wound and bound it up.

He rose to his feet and went over to the door on which they had laid the body of Tze Hung, to perform his official identification. There would be much to write in the report which he must render, first to himself and then to the Provincial Governor. . . .

The few torches drew moving shadows on the faces of the motionless guards. He had struck well, when his sword had swung at Tze Hung's face. The man must have died instantly, even while he struck back. The blade had entered just above the left eye, and appeared to have cut through cheek and jawbone until it had been stopped by the bones of the neck. He had bled much. Above the wound the face was unchanged, and this gave Wao illogical satisfaction as he looked at the dead man.

"Take it away," he said.

Then Ah Lau, the hired girl, came in through the guards at the same time as Hsia Nan-p'o.

"They have brought Jasmine," Ah Lau said. "My mistress asked if you would come. She is dying."

Wao turned to Hsia.

"If you could bring yourself to listen to what they have to say, I should be grateful," he told him. "I think that you will have to make a new appointment in the place of Tze Hung: I suggest this man who helped to defend the Tower—Kwong Hui, I think his name was."

"I will do what I can, and await your confirmation of my judgment," Hsia replied.

Wao nodded and went out with Ah Lau.

Jasmine was barely conscious.

Hibiscus said: "The doctor said that she was kicked in the spleen, and that there was no hope for her recovery. So I sent him away. She was asking for you." She sighed. "Do not be angry at my message—it is a small thing to do for the child, and I feel more than a little guilty myself."

"You have nothing to regret," Wao told her. "Is she speaking?"

"She was asking for her son—my son," Hibiscus answered. "I told her that he was well, and she seemed satisfied."

Wao said in Jasmine's ear: "We shall look after the boy. You need not fear on that score."

It seemed that she smiled. Her pulse was slow and regular, her breathing a little noisy. She lay on her back, motionless, her face the unlined, innocent face of a girl who had no troubles. Then her lips moved, and Wao bent close, to hear.

"You called me Dusky Tower," she murmured. "You will stay with me? She will not know. Can you not call me Dusky Tower again?"

Wao breathed the words.

She seemed to try to shake her head. Then she said, quite clearly: "Not you." Again her face became

without expression, and her breathing seemed to catch
a little.

"You can do nothing," Hibiscus told him. "I am
sorry if I fetched you from your duties."

He said: "Do not regret that. Be kind to her—you
can do nothing more."

Then he went back into the great Hall, to see what
Hsia had done. His eyes were wet.

.   .   .   .   .   .

In the cold light filtering through the high windows,
Hsia seemed to have been waiting.

"Subject to your confirmation," he told Wao, "I
have instructed the men of the guard in the art of
obedience to authority and the sometimes wisdom of
withholding that obedience. I have shewn them how
to distinguish between loyalty to a superior and treason
to the Emperor. I have indicated to the man Kwong
Hui that you may be gracious enough to place reliance
on him. . . ."

Wao said: "Kwong Hui will be your Captain of the
Guard, not mine. If he is agreeable to you, as new
magistrate, he will be agreeable to me. You have im-
posed punishments on the men?"

Hsia smiled.

"I have not punished them, as men understand punishment," he said. "I have ordered them to perform
certain guard duties which would not normally have
fallen to their lot, duties which will prove onerous
reminders of their unwisdom in following the dead
Captain, Tze Hung. Thus they will suffer the pangs
of gratitude for my lenience as well as the pangs of
inconvenience as regards their leisure and personal
comfort. My studies of the great authors of the past

have convinced me of the need for both emotions in a
repentant man. You approve? "

Wao nodded agreement.

"The girl Jasmine is dying," he said, "and I, who
have often looked on death, find her death strange and
different. She is wandering in her mind, and imagines
that she is speaking with Lien Kin Wai, who had her
first. I find this distressing. It is like listening to an
intimate conversation which was intended for another
man." He shook his shoulders. "And now yourself?
You have plans? "

Hsia replied : " I desire, first, to arrange for repairs
to the burned Drum Tower. For that, I intend to take
the man Ssu, the driver, since he knows the identity of
the masons and the carpenters who will have to do the
work. That done, with your consent, I propose to
travel to Sai Kwan. There are ceremonies—a marriage.
The girl Peony. I think that you know more than a
little of her. When I have carried her over the threshold of my family house, I shall send her down here
to prepare against my coming. Then I shall return
myself."

"And I," Wao told him, " shall return to Sai Kwan
with you. The Lady Hibiscus will organize the
removal of her household. I have perfect confidence in
her."

They set about the arrangements for the immediate
future.

.   .   .   .

Peony was back again in the household of Mistress
Hsia, in the room of the Hsia mansion which she
well remembered. She sat alone, for Mistress Hsia
had gone to visit the Lady Loong, her sister-in-law,
and the two women must be, even now, indulging

in the delight of recreating the incidents of the last few days.

Peony sat on a porcelain stool, looking across the courtyard. The maid, Tower of Pearl, was making the noises of superfluous work, somewhere near. Peony remembered at her present leisure the delight which she had felt when she had carried the Censor's summons to Hsia Nan-p'o.

" And if," Hsia had replied, " I ask why you, you personally, have brought me this summons, I suppose that you will have an answer, even for that."

She had said : " To bring the summons to you myself was not of my own choice, entirely. I was ordered to summon you : I asked if I should bring the message myself. The Censor smiled and said : ' yes '. So I came. Truly, I do not desire to deny my pleasure in coming. But, for a woman like myself, part of the joy of things is in finding that, at long last, fate is not unkind to me. Often, in the past, I have thought joy within my grasp, but as often it has eluded me."

Hsia had answered : " I shall have much of which to be jealous—in this past of which you speak. It may be that I shall have the time to be thus jealous. Or it may be that I shall find the present world, the world about me, too full of incidents, too insistent of its presence, to afford me that time for jealousy."

Tower of Pearl brought in a pot of fresh tea. Peony noticed how assiduous the girl was in her attentions to herself, who had, a little while back, been one of her fellows. It was curious how self-interest moved a girl, without in the least seeming to make her seem unattractively selfish. It would be necessary to give the girl a present. . . .

Hsia had said : " My mother will be difficult, especially while the late Prefect's daughter yet lives. My mother is very much bound by convention. To her the employment of a go-between in a marriage is all-important: she does not even consider, I think, what are to be the results of the go-between's activities. To us, convention is merely a convenience, a thought-saving. To me, who have been brought up to think, thought-saving is not so vital a necessity. To you, who have always evaded convention, the need is merely another thing to be evaded. Is it not so?"

She had heard him through, for she knew that she would have always to hear him through. Then she had said: "I, too, was brought up with education in the Classics, and I have only avoided convention where convention was straining my life to unnatural shapes. You must not forget that my father was a magistrate."

Hsia had laughed: "I said 'evaded', not 'avoided'. If you aim to come to my household, you must learn to pay due deference to accuracy and exactitude."

"And what is the precise shade of difference," Peony had demanded, "between accuracy and exactitude?"

It was a pleasant prospect, thus to have again stability and affection stretched out before her. She knew, also, that Hsia Nan-p'o had learned enough from his classical studies to rise above their stereotyped restrictions, and spared a moment to remember how her earlier husband had, indeed, possessed learning without distinction, culture without flexibility. It would not be so with Hsia.

Love? What was love? From the adventurous frailties of the adolescent, through the supposedly four-square safety of a formal marriage, to the wider possibilities of comprehending, companionate tolerance.

There was now none of the unbearable possessiveness of her love for Lien Kin Wai, when even to think of sharing him had seemed a futile folly. Maturity had mellowed desire.

And yet, smiling though the future might be, there was still the fact of her inability to bear sons. Was the bearing of sons an essential part of her projected marriage with Hsia Nan-p'o? His was an ancient line —neither he nor his relations would endure the possibility of its ultimate, last extinction in a marriage of minds which skirted the need for children. How far, too, did a man's affection pass with the passing years, if children did not cement the bond? When the alertness of minds passed to the tedium of shared memories, would tolerance yet live?

She thoughtfully poured herself more tea.

.   .   .   .

"Life," the Censor observed, commiseratingly, "is by its nature untidy. There is waste." He found this girl, this Prefect's daughter, immensely disturbing. "I have heard you through. I have not been deaf to your pleas for your father, though I have been unyielding. It is not for me to say how, and in what manner, your father will die, since only the Emperor "—he bowed— "can say what punishment is merited by those who conspire against the Emperor. But since man, as we read, strives to undo the untidiness of nature, the family of your father must pay whatever penalty is meet for treason. Treason is in the blood, and must therefore be purged from the blood. No matter what motives stirred your father—ambition, gain, or even the illusion that he was doing a public good—treason shakes the Empire, and that is all. It is bad to shake the Empire. No—he must go to the Capital to be judged. And

Q

small mercy, at times, is only the attribute of small men. There is the greater mercy."

"But why," Jade Star cried, "cannot the thing be done with now? We do not dispute—we do not defend."

"To dispute would be impossible, to defend impossible," the Censor said. "The throw has gone against you."

Wao observed, dispassionately: "I, too, understand the seeming waste. Regrettably, your father did not consider the possible results of his actions. Or, if he did so, he did not allow due weight to discretion. And, for your possible comfort, your regrettable ends will not greatly discommode the people. For them suns will rise and moons set, unmoved by your small corner of history." Then he laughed. "I myself was not unconcerned with events: had it not been for the naïve way in which the girl, Pheasant, staked the softness of her breast against the temper of your steel, I should not, possibly, be sitting here in common judgment. What have you to say of her?"

Jade Star replied: "She did it for you, not for any Emperor. And, as women do, she paid the penalty of those who love."

"And so she died," the Censor concluded. "She has no parents, and her ghost shall walk forever, if no family tombs receive her. She was of your clan, by purchase?"

"She should rest in our tombs," the girl said. "She has, as you say, a right to that."

Wao nodded.

"I can think of no reason to forbid such a course," he said. "The suggestion is to your credit. And now, Sir, if you do not desire further to talk with this girl, her disquieting presence might be removed."

The Censor agreed, and Jade Star was taken away. She did not weep now.

.   .   .   .

The Lady Loong observed: "If my son has the un-wisdom to wish to wed you, it would at least be wise if we talked together first. This is no matter of an in-experienced girl praised to the husband's parents by a hired go-between."

"By *inexperienced*," Peony replied, "you call to the hearer's mind its opposite, *experienced*. And you are right to do so, for I have no claims, nor any rights. In the past, I have striven to bend events to my own will, but now I accept. Like the wise general, I yield to events. Like water, I take the shape of constraint."

"You are skilled in the use of words," the Lady Loong admitted, "and a girl to whom words afford no matter of deliberate thought can make a wife with wisdom. For if you have to think of the meanings of words, of the just word, there is less time for the con-sideration of your husband's comfort. Sit down by me. Forget that, as many an unwise mother has done, I sent you away from my house, lest you should entangle my son in the net which every mother imagines to be laid for his feet. And yet . . ."

Peony took the porcelain stool and set it facing the Lady Loong.

"You are kind to me," she said as she sat down, "in thus not continuing opposition. Particularly are you kind in thus talking to me without the mediation of go-betweens. As to my family, I have none save a younger brother, in the city of Che Kiang, and at such a distance he will not, I fear, be able to take part in such negotiations as are usual, or in such ceremonies as

Q*

are customary. So I have to submit myself to your care."

"My son will return," the other replied, "when he has done whatever official business is necessary at the city of Kow Loong. It is, I feel, not wise too obviously to flout convention, and so you will continue, I hope, to live with my sister-in-law, Mistress Hsia, with whom you seem to have much in common. Then the business of your leaving one house to come to another as a bride will not be difficult. Did he fight bravely?"

"He fought," Peony said, "as a man of letters should fight in the service of his Emperor. I saw him kill the man Ou Ling-ma, and his thrust was the thrust of a man who has chosen the right word and is confident of his choice. You may feel pride in him."

"I should feel pride whether or no I had cause for pride," the Lady Loong answered. "Such is the prerogative of mothers. Yet it is good to know that my pride is justified."

They drank ceremonial tea, and Peony returned to the room of Mistress Hsia, wondering how, without money, one could obtain a dowry and the other gifts which it was customary for the bride to bring with her to her husband's house.

When she entered the darkened room, she found that Mistress Hsia, indeed, had been considering the same problem.

"Now that you, girl," she said, "are about to become respectable, it is necessary to think of dowries? Is it not?"

Peony said: "Your honourable sister-in-law brought the same question to my mind when I was speaking with her. Indirectly, of course. We must consider."

PART FOUR

PART FOUR

THE city of Sai Kwan shewed no evident traces of the clash of arms, as Wao's eight-bearer chair swept up the main street from the *yamen* to the entrance of the Hsia mansion. The guards whose duty it was to carry the obstructing fans which would enable Wao to avoid meeting acquaintances bore those fans carelessly, for they knew that Wao had no acquaintances here, in the city of which he was so newly Prefect. Those of the Governor's troops who had been left as a stiffening for the local men laughed as they shouldered passers-by to the side of the street.

At the Hsia entrance Wao was set down, and as he stepped from his chair he saw that Hsia Nan-p'o, also, had chosen the morning for going out. Hsia bowed. Wao returned the courtesy in the formal manner.

Wao said: "I had seized upon a moment of leisure from my duties, in order to pay a visit to your aunt, Mistress Hsia, and to thank her for her admirable aim with a tea-pot."

Hsia replied: "She will, I am sure, be delighted to see you and do her best to minimize her service to you. My mother—no. She still feels herself ill-used by circumstance, since events shaped themselves without her whim, so that she found it hard indeed to treat my wife with the courtesy due to my wife."

"That is the way of women," Wao said. "It must have been a relief to you to send your wife to Kow Loong to prepare the *yamen* for you, even though it is unusual to part so soon from a newly-wedded bride. I, too, am set about by women, though in a different way."

"Let us call on my aunt together," Hsia said. As the two men moved off through the bright courtyards, he went on: "Is it permissible to ask in what way you are discommoded by women?"

"It is no secret," Wao answered. "No secret at all. Actually, the blame lies at the door of the late Prefect. Now that he and his daughter have killed themselves —fortunately outside my jurisdiction—I shall be unable to bring it home to him."

Hsia said: "I cannot regret their deaths. I was affianced to the girl. But in what way . . . ?"

"Any man," Wao complained, "even a Prefect, should make sure that he does not leave too many embarrassments behind him. Fortunately the Governor's men killed the eunuchs—there were four besides the one whom I despatched—and similarly disposed of all but five of his girls. The girls, you remember, who had been trained to dance for him. It came out in our enquiry. But those five! They complain most piteously of their lot. My admiration for the late Prefect—and indeed he had many admirable qualities—has grown since I have learned of his prowess from these girls. I am looking forward to the coming of the Lady Hibiscus, for she at all events, will be able to deal with them."

They had come through the last courtyard. It was one of those still, overcast days when Spring might well be Autumn. The leaves hung without motion:

in the stillness the cries of men in the distant streets came clearly to them. Through the moon doorway they could see in the next courtyard washing hanging limply on a line.

"Women," Hsia said as they had come to the reception-room and Tower of Pearl had been sent for Mistress Hsia, "women are by nature cruel and without restraint. The Empress Wu Hou, for example, was one such. You remember how she had the hands and feet cut off her rival, and was then no further troubled with her? That is but one instance of a woman who, possessing power, lost all restraint in achieving her object."

Wao agreed: "They may become thus. But, even if not intoxicated with power, as was the Empress Wu Hou, women recognize in other women the possibility of such actions, and take their own precautions accordingly, to protect the man with whom they happen to have thrown in their lot. Like watch-dogs, they guard. Like armour, they protect."

Tower of Pearl returned.

"My mistress asks you to visit her in her own room," the girl said. "She asks you to excuse her failure to come to you, but is sure that you will pardon it."

"The child has learned her message by heart," Hsia laughed as they followed Tower of Pearl.

Mistress Hsia had prepared for their reception, so far as melon-seeds and tea were concerned. She rose when the two men came in, bowing to them.

Wao, returning her greeting, said: "This is an embassy of gratitude. Your family must have a distinguished military record, judging by the accuracy of your aim with a tea-pot."

"No, no," she objected. "Let us sit down. No—

my family has been tied to the land and to the interests which concern the land. We have not been compelled to resort to arms for any purpose but the defence of this estate from marauders. And that happened long ago. The times now are too peaceful for ordinary people to take up arms."

Hsia said: "My family is undoubtedly proud of this hereditary, feudal land. Once, as you will imagine, we ruled this city. There were even cultivated lands within the walls. Now our farms lie further off."

"Supervised by bailiffs who have, themselves, to be supervised," Mistress Hsia told them. "Now that my nephew here is becoming an official, we shall have no men folk to send round to look after our interests. The prospect is not bright. Of course, it is my sister-in-law's duty: I merely venture to advise her."

"I think," Hsia said, "that she is coming now. She knows everything which happens within these walls, and the attraction of your company, Sir, was more than she could resist."

Tower of Pearl went to the door and ushered in the Lady Loong.

"We were speaking," Mistress Hsia said when they had greeted one another, "of the troubles consequent upon the management of an estate."

Lady Loong replied: "And you, as a Hsia, spoke with a certainty which I, a Loong, could not expect to achieve. I know."

Wao said: "I had come to thank Mistress Hsia, here, for the accuracy of her aim with a tea-pot."

"My son told me," Lady Loong answered. "She was fortunate to have the opportunity to serve you thus."

"Further," Wao went on, "I had hoped that when my wife comes to my *yamen* you would do me the favour of calling on her. Your traditions of culture will help her in her tasks."

"Culture!" Mistress Hsia laughed. "We have culture, it is true, but we have little else. You behold, Sir, two widows who have known better days. What is there for us to do save to remember the past, to praise our ancestors and suffer misgivings as to the future?"

"Yet," Wao replied, "it is the great body of culture which makes probable such a conversation as ours, or such conversations as, I hope, you will have with my wife. And, if you care to, with myself. It is this ready agreement upon the truth of the obvious which makes speech other than halting and tongue-tied. For we each know what the other will say."

Young Hsia objected: "Originality?"

Wao said: "The whole strength of our method of life is to be obvious—in the daytime."

"Not before the girl," the Lady Loong reproved him, shooting a glance at Tower of Pearl. "You will upset her."

Tower of Pearl went out, tittering behind her hand. Lady Loong frowned as she saw this.

"Servants are coming to forget their station," she said.

"I am sorry," Wao apologized. "I have led a life wherein I did not have greatly to consider the effect on girls of what was said in their hearing. I shall learn." He turned to Mistress Hsia. "And how soon is your nephew to leave you both?"

"He has sent his new wife in advance, as you know," she replied, "and follows her after two more days."

"When I," Lady Loong complained, "shall have no one left to submit to my organization. For you know, sister, that you go your own way."

Wao said, tentatively: "If you care to consider it, there are five girls from the late Prefect's store, whose presence in my own *yamen* would be inconvenient. I wonder if you two ladies would accept at least a couple of them as a gift. Then you would have scope for ruling."

"They would be wild things," the Lady Loong said, looking pleased. "But if you are kind enough to give them to us, we shall be able to instruct them in the ways of tradition. You would care for one yourself, sister?"

Wao lifted his tea-cup. On this signal for the end of the visit, Hsia rose to do the courtesies, and the sisters-in-law ranged themselves in readiness. Before he drank Wao said: "Do not make up your minds too soon. Many there are who dash into the irrevocable without due consideration. You will let me know? After all, if the Lady Hibiscus would permit it, you could return them to my household if they proved uncontrollable."

As he drank, the Lady Loong observed: "Uncontrollable? Here, in our households?"

Then Wao went, and Hsia Nan-p'o attended him.

.   .   .   .

In the plot of land outside the walls of Kow Loong City, a second grave had been prepared.

"They buried the girl Pheasant, too, just before I came away," Peony said. "In the graves of the late Prefect's family. You heard that both he and his daughter killed themselves? Fortunately they had been sent under guard to the City of Rams, and it happened on the way. They had poison hidden. The soldiers of the escort were punished for letting it happen, but no blame fell on my husband, nor on the honourable Wao Hien To."

She and Hibiscus were sitting in carrying-chairs at the edge of the field, watching a coffin carried to the grave.

"I felt that it was my duty," Hibiscus told her, "to have Jasmine buried here, in the plot of land which I bought for the grave of my dead husband. It seemed that he called to me—'bury my women near me'—and I could no more disobey him in death than I could thwart him living. But I can go no nearer. It would not seem right."

Peony said: "It is kind of you to do as you think he would have wished."

The priests and the nuns from the Convent of Jade Serenity were making great to do with burning paper prayers and paper money. The sun was high: a slow wind drifted in from the sea. The bearers were chatting and "guessing fingers" over the rise in the land: it was none of their funeral.

"I have done all that I could for the repose of her soul," Hibiscus said. "Her family begged to be excused from attendance: they said that it was my affair. You think these mourning garments are sufficient? I could not bring myself to join the procession, for my assumption of sorrow would have seemed too obvious for courtesy to the dead."

"You are doing all that is your duty," Peony assured her. It was curious thus to be sitting watching the burial of Lien's concubine, feeling no jealousy of the dead girl, feeling no jealousy of his widow, Hibiscus, and yet remembering, even here under the clear light of Heaven, Lien's words, Lien's touch, Lien's presence. She felt empty, as if she had not eaten lately. This tomb, where Lien lay, was not her tomb: this other tomb, where Jasmine's coffin now was, claimed nothing of her care or loyalty. And yet, beside the dead Lien, Jasmine would be nearer to him than Peony could ever come. Yet she, who had so lately been carried over the threshold by her husband Hsia Nan-p'o, sat in a carrying-chair on the short grass, remembering odd words and phrases of Lien Kin Wai, whom she had enjoyed of no right, as had Hibiscus, his wife, and Jasmine, his concubine, but only by the courtesy of circumstances had known for a few brief weeks in the Temple on White Cloud Hill. . . .

"Women ever find themselves compelled to bury a man's errors," she said, and Hibiscus looked at her with a momentary surprise, understanding not at all.

Then her eyes were caught by two other chairs which had just come up. "Those are the two women from the Street of Happiness," she told Peony. "I gave them permission to move to the new house near the Drum Tower, which Tung Ho had intended for one of them."

Peony watched as Hidden Gold and Mountain Stream burned paper money at Jasmine's tomb. The guard stood behind them as they did so.

"I know them," Peony said. "They were kind to me once. It will now be my duty to overlook their future."

"They used to come to dinners, to entertain the guests," Hibiscus said.

The two chairs moved off. Peony remembered the night before Lien had died, when she had received him at the girls' house in the Street of Happiness. . . .

The funeral was over and the great stone stopper had been lowered into the mouth of the tomb. The two tombs, side by side, epitomized unity and completeness. Neither of the two women watching the ceremony had achieved completeness of union with Lien. . . . The bearers picked up the chairs and moved off, back to the *yamen* in Kow Loong. Peony recalled that Hsia would join her in two days, and Hibiscus was going to-morrow. And she, Peony, who had taken his love without question, would remain here, always able to visit his tomb. . . .

She must not become morbid. That would never do, in the wife of the new magistrate.

And yet . . .

" You will share tea with me? " Hibiscus asked, as they moved off.

.   .   .   .

In the market-place the story-teller
Neatly knots the threads of his tale:
So events, in destined order,
Make of men's lives returning patterns.
The lurking two-edged sword is sheathed now,
Unconscious rivals meet on equal terms;
They share their memories: delight is dulled
And custom relegates the unstriving dead.

Hibiscus looked round the familiar room, saw it familiar. Here she had ruled since the day when her husband had brought her here on his first appointment, a young inexperienced bride. It had required fifteen mules to bring all the household goods. Now, re-sorted into mule-loads, it would have required at least twenty-five animals for the move to Sai Kwan. Fortunately, the move was to be made by water, and it would be unnecessary to count mules. . . . She poured out a cup of tea for her guest.

Peony was sitting where Lien Kin Wai had always sat—on a stool between door and high window. She said: "I thank you for all your courtesies. They have made my duties easier; they have enabled me to perform these duties with greater happiness, since I knew that I had not your criticism to face, but your assistance to repay. It has been a strange time, for me."

Hibiscus did not reply at once. She looked at her unbound feet—looked across at Peony's unbound feet.

Then she said: "You, the daughter of a magistrate, must have found the organization easier than I did, a mere hill-girl, when first my husband brought me here. Ruling is in your blood: I was compelled to learn the art."

"There are no evident traces of your schooling," Peony replied. "I am sorry that you have not allowed me to be of greater assistance to you in your own preparations. It would have given me greater pleasure."

Hibiscus said: "I have gratefully accepted what help I have felt able to receive. All my goods are packed for the morrow, save those which you see here, a few necessary odds and ends in the kitchens, and the contents of my late husband's own room. I have left that to the last. Would you wish to see it?"

So Peony, who had lost a lover, followed Hibiscus, who had lost a husband, into the little room which had been his. Hibiscus's quiet voice went on.

"This was his room. That little nest of drawers was his father's, and I have not dared to look inside it. Our son, perhaps. . . . I feel, always, that my husband is still here, that he sits on that stool, writes at that table, turns over the contents of that nest of drawers. To me, he lives as he lived before his death, here in this room. We found him in the morning."

Peony shivered. Lien Kin Wai had come to this room, to die, straight from her own arms; when he had visited her in answer to her invitation. "You represent all that is most impermanent in woman," he had said to her, there in the darkness of the brazier's light, "for you have neither marriage nor children to offer. . . ." And Peony had sung for him the song of the General's Girl. . . .

"It must have been a great shock for you," she said.

Hibiscus replied: "Yes. He had, only shortly before, returned to me from the City of Rams, where he acted after the death of Governor Sung Tsui. I had thought that he was mine again."

"Governor Sung Tsui's wife is in Sai Kwan City, as you must know," Peony said, desperately trying to change the subject. "She is a very gracious lady, whom they call Mistress Hsia. You will meet her when you join your husband, the new Prefect."

"Let us sit down," Hibiscus said. "Always I seem to hear him say 'Sit down', as he used to say it. He would laugh to see me entertaining you."

Peony felt tears near—tears not for her own loss, but for the woman who was now, confidently, talking of her husband to the girl who knew that husband as well as any wife could have known him. She was not jealous at all of this wife to whom a dead husband was still uncomfortably real: she was filled with sorrow that this wife's picture of that husband was incomplete, and that it would ever be impossible to tell her the truth. Peony's own sorrow became thus sublimated into sympathy. Lien was only another, and the greatest, of her own failures, for she had loved him as she knew that she could never love again. He was to Hibiscus as real as if he sat there, in the little room: as real as he had been to Peony on that last night in the house in the Street of Happiness. . . .

"Images," Peony said with difficulty, "may come very close to the heart. I feel for you as if your loss were mine."

Then, before she knew it, she was crying, and Hibiscus, crying a little too, was comforting her.

THE END